# Russian Nonsensical

ALSO BY EDWARD D. WEBSTER

FICTION

The Gentle Bomber's Melody (2013)

Soul of Toledo (2016)

Carlos Crosses the Line, A Tale of Immigration, Temptation and
Betrayal in the Sixties (2020)

American Nonsensical (2022)

NON-FICTION

A Year of Sundays, Taking the Plunge and our Cat to Explore Europe
(2004)

# Russian Nonsensical

Edward D. Webster

Dream House Press

**Russian Nonsensical**

Copyright © 2024 Edward D. Webster

First Edition
Published by Dream House Press
Ojai, CA

www.edwardwebster.com

Author Services by Pedernales Publishing, LLC.
www.pedernalespublishing.com

Cover by Kristin Bryant

Library of Congress Control Number: 2024915573

ISBN:  978-0-9970320-7-9 Paperback Edition
ISBN:  978-0-9970320-9-3 Hardcover Edition
ISBN:  978-0-9970320-8-6 Digital Edition

Printed in the United States of America

*To my Friday morning breakfast gang.*
*Thanks for your support and friendship.*

*It is a tale told by an idiot, full of sound and fury, signifying nothing.*—Macbeth Act Five. Scene 5.

# CHAPTER 1

## CLEM

*LATE AUGUST, 2021*

Clem Dudas learned the hard way that any of God's glorious days can explode into a shit storm.

He wasn't thinking of that, as he drove up California Route 74, a graceful twist of asphalt, sinuous as a diamondback. Ascending from LA sprawl and chaos to oak-studded mountains and sublime rapture. Heaven!

Tonight, he'd dance with his people, not hindered by fancy speech, not challenged by computer logic or financial entanglements. They'd shout the Lord's praise. Clem would hold Maynard in one hand, Dobie in the other—raise them high.

Maynard was one of God's wonders, the biggest rattler anyone had seen. Clem belted out "Mine Eyes Hath Seen the Glory …" as he drew close to the house.

ARLENE'S TRUCK was missing from the driveway. Clem opened the front door and called her anyway—no answer. Both snake boxes were missing from the family room. She likely took the serpents to the meadow as a favor for him. Maybe Arlene was mellowing out. Clem smiled.

No time to shower. No need to shave his fine-looking salt-and-pepper beard. Clem slapped on cologne, put on a denim shirt and a jacket—western cut—fawn brown with turquoise beads on the lapels. No one drank at the holy revivals, but occasionally Clem snuck a nip. He grabbed his flask of whiskey and some breath mints.

Tonight's service would be special. Under the stars on this balmy evening, Billy Daniels was coming to play guitar and harmonica. Arlene knew that, which was probably why she headed over early. Maybe she was out draping the arbor with streamers—something a woman might do.

He drove the quarter mile over, but found only the bare stage and empty lawn where the vehicles parked — *What the heck, Arlene? Where are you?*

The stage had a rose trellis overhead—red blossoms like the Savior's blood. Clem went to the storage pod and rolled the podium out. He set it up center stage and started setting out folding chairs.

Tom and Millie Lovely pulled up in their old blue cab-over camper. Tom got out and called, "Hey Clem. How's it going?" They were in their thirties, a good-looking pair, loyal snake-loving Jesus worshippers. She was a hot one too; a gal who didn't mind him cupping her tight little butt in his hand once in a while.

"You guys hear anything from Arlene?" he shouted.

Millie climbed out of the camper and grinned at him. "Didn't she tell you, Clem? I bet she did, and you forgot. Just like a man." She struck a pose, hand on one hip, and made a face—probably thought that was cute. "Arlene went down to Temecula to pick up a dress she ordered. She asked Tom and me to bring the kids."–A dumb attempt at humor, the kids referring to Clem's snakes.

Millie pulled out a bright blue box with *Melody* painted in white on the side, along with a red image of Satan. Melody was a beauty of a copperhead about three feet long—good sized for a copperhead, not nearly the heft of Clem's rattlers.

Seeing the box cheered Clem up for a second. Snakes represented Satan on earth. When a worshipper took one up, he vanquished the devil, renounced temptation, and demonstrated the victory of the Holy Spirit within his mortal heart.

Clem's brief cheer faded. *Arlene, damn it. Why'd you tell Millie and not me where you went?* Sometimes, when he and Arlene were together, it was all Clem could do to restrain his fists. Hearing the way Arlene had snuck off to town now, he felt that fury rising. *Jesus, hold me back.*

He resisted the urge to hurl a folding chair at Tom's truck as the Lord's calming influence settled him.

"So, you're saying Arlene dropped my snakes at your place?" Clem asked.

Millie set the blue box on the stage. She gave Clem a look of female incredulity. "Honestly, Reverend Dudas, you and your missus gotta talk to one another."

*Yeah.* Clem took off his jacket and wiped his brow with a shirtsleeve. He walked behind his pickup, slipped the flask out of his jacket, and took a slug of whiskey.

Tom fired up his generator. He connected the speakers and spoke into the microphone. "Testing. Testing. It's a lovely night here on the mountain." He grinned.

"Great, Tom," Clem said. "Hey Millie. Thanks for helpin' out."

Millie removed another snake box from the back of her vehicle and handed it to Clem. He brought it to the stage.

All the containers were square with thick screening set in the lids, so you could look in at the serpents. Each box was painted or carved with inscriptions like *Praise the Lord, Alleluia Our Savior, Blessed is He. Never Satan.* Men of the congregation had decorated them with devotion.

Tom and Millie carted Clem's snakes, Dobie and Maynard, over. Clem took in a prideful breath at the sight. The box for his favorite snake had the name Maynard carved on one side; on the back was the image of a mule kicking Satan in the face. This labor of love for Maynard led Arlene to declare that Clem cared for his damned snakes more than he did his wife. Well, snakes never bitched at you.

The meadow sat beside the main road a half mile from their little community. Cars began pulling up on the grass now— pickups, a few sedans—mostly older models, fifteen ... now twenty; about fifty people. Not a bad showing.

Men placed folding tables on stage for the snake boxes. Guys and gals brought out fiddles. A box of tambourines crashed onto the lawn.

Clem ducked behind his truck for a moment. *Lord, I wouldn't be drinking, but for that woman.*

A guy Clem recognized, a regular visitor from down the mountain, sat on one of the folding chairs onstage, with a guitar. He started playing Elvis' "Hound Dog." Lex, the oldest man in the congregation, picked up the tune on his accordion. Another fellow beat kettle drums.

A van marked *Billy Daniels, Music Under the Stars*, pulled onto the grass. The thin, dark-haired musician stepped out, strapped his guitar band around his neck, pulled out his harmonica, and picked up the tune as he strode toward them. Billy was a friend and a man who cherished Christ. Clem wrapped his arms around him—and his guitar—all in one wide embrace. "Thanks for coming, man."

Billy whipped the harmonica from his mouth and kissed Clem on his bearded cheek. He resumed playing as he headed for the stage.

Most of the women were fiddling or beating along with tambourines. Millie hopped onstage, picked up the microphone, and started singing "Bridge over Troubled Water," her voice sultry and fine. She had on a flowered, cream-colored dress that clung to her hips. She moved them slow at first. It was warm still, and some of her blond ringlets stuck to her cheeks. She had a damn-fine body, and she was agreeable for a woman.

The men with no instruments danced, one guy sharing serious eye contact with Millie, who was writhing now, snakelike, at the edge of the stage, gesturing them all to come closer.

Clem stepped up next to her and waited. After the chorus, she passed him the mic. Clem sang out, "A-a-maz-ing Grace, How-ow Swe-eet the Sound." Guitars picked that up. Drums boomed. The people belted out the song. Then, he led them in, "Blessed Our King of Lambs." Two women swirled in circles. A few older men began jumping to the beat. Clem handed off the microphone, not even knowing who had taken it. One hymn ended, and another began. Dancing grew frenzied. Holy zeal ascending.

*Arlene, damn it. Where in the hell?* No one was watching as Clem walked to his truck and took another glug. He popped in a breath mint. Singing loud and strong, he moved among his people, glancing every once in a while, at the snake boxes on the tables by the podium. The reptiles would feel the music, and writhe to the drums' vibrations, first agitated and then hypnotized, taken in by the holy spirit.

On the lawn, near the stage, Zenia, a chubby fifty-year-old, screamed. People gathered around. She bellowed out, "I hear you, Lord." Everyone stopped singing. Drums still beat. Guitars strummed. Someone shouted, "Amen." Zenia shouted syllables that only God could comprehend. "Aya, hyhy, beeeeebub, scranny..." It went on for a few minutes before she collapsed. Two women bent over her to wipe the sweat from her face and comfort her. "I seen the Lord," she crooned.

"Holy, holy," a man shouted. "Praise the Holy One on high."

The singing resumed.

Holy music had pacified the snakes by now, the Lord's essence taking every creature in that meadow on a journey.

Up on the stage, Clem saw Millie open Melody's snake box and reach in. She brought out the copperhead and displayed it in her two hands. The snake swung the top third of its body from side to side, sniffing Millie's mouth. Millie smiled wide and raised the snake over her head, the creature and Millie, each swaying to their sensuous music.

Love for Jesus beat inside Clem's chest. The urge came on strong. He charged up there. His two snake boxes, one for Maynard and one for Dobie, sat on one table. Clem flipped open Maynard's box and glanced in. He stared for maybe half a minute and then bellowed, "No!" The snake inside was not his beloved diamondback, but a smaller—not even full-sized—timber rattler. He jammed the top closed and looked around. Everyone stared. Everyone, except—*fuckin' fuck*. Where the fuck was Arlene? *God damn it; I'm swearing in my head on God's stage, of all places.*

He sprung the catch on Dobie's box. Another timber rattler, not half Dobie's girth. How were his people to respect Clem if he held out these pitiful specimens? Not only that; when a man took up the snake, he had to feel God inside; had to have His protection. All the Jesus-spirit had run out the moment Clem saw that first puny snake. The Jesus-spirit lay in a puddle by his feet.

"Arlene," he shouted. "Arlene," his voice drowned out by the drumming. He jumped off the stage and zigzagged through the crowd, searching, though he knew, didn't he? Arlene was nowhere to be seen. And who else? – Elton Snivel hadn't shown up either. Elton, the parishioner who cared for the roses here at the meadow, who took the collections at these events, the scrawny punk-ass who flirted with Arlene, often taking a snake out of its box and handing it to her, looking soft-eyed and mournful. Wimpy dick. No way Arlene would run off with him!

Clem looked into each of the cars and pickups, just in case they were in one of them, rutting like a couple of high school sweethearts. *Sweethearts*—made him want to puke.

Onstage, a guy from out of town, tall, blond, in denim overalls, was gyrating, holding one of the puny timber rattlers over his head. Clem ran up and held out his hand. "Give me." The guy held back for a second, surprised, and then passed the snake to him. Clem charged off behind the stage and kept going, almost to the oak trees. He heaved the snake toward them. He returned and saw Zenia with the other timber rattler. She held out her snake and let him take it.

He stalked back to the woods. Just as he was about to cast that Satan away, he felt the sting. Damn it. He knew what it was, but he looked down anyway. He'd stepped right up to the first timber and hadn't heard its warning with the music booming. God had commanded the little serpent to bite Clem. Why? Clem had been distracted by the betrayers and hadn't allowed himself to embrace Jesus-love. That's why God commanded the little serpent to bite him. The light was dim, but Clem saw the snake coil up again. He stepped back—too late. Another damned bite.

Clem placed the second rattler in the oak leaves. He watched the two snakes slither away and then sat at the base of a gigantic oak to nurse his wounded spirit.

# CHAPTER 2

## BUD

Returning from his sister Betty's depressing wedding in Poughkeepsie, Bud was five miles from the Newark Airport and pretty pissed off. Sure as shit, they'd be making him mask up on the plane home—Pete Buttigieg and the so-called Department of friggin' Transportation—Bud's face bathed in his sweaty breath all the way to LA.

Masked and sweaty-faced, just like at Betty's wedding. Only chance to take the mask off had been when he was eating the leathery steak and half-baked baked potato.

He'd gotten the crappy vaccine, both doses, and shown Betty his official card. Couldn't she let it go after that? He could still hear her chirpy voice. "Mask up, little brother; it's for your own good too."

Bud looked at his watch—an hour and a half before the plane for LA. Still time to put gas in the rental car and catch his plane. His iPhone showed a gas station at the next exit. He pulled down the offramp, running smack into a mini traffic jam—three long rows of cars backed up from a light, way far ahead. The light turned green and back to red before he even got to edge forward.

It wasn't just the masks. Lots of stuff bugged him, niggled and nagged, as the line crept and halted over the next ten minutes. He loved Betty, but she had a way of looking too goddamned happy about her latest romantic story—hamming up the marital bliss bit, like she had yesterday—and then what? Another divorce next year? Had it been an honor to be an usher at another $50,000 wedding ($100K these days?) with crappy food? Yeah, maybe. She loved Bud. How could he miss her *big day*?

Getting pissed off had its good side; it passed the time. He'd been moving up, just a half dozen cars between him and the light—great—turning red again. Okay, still time to buy gas, drop the car, and catch the plane. A few kids skulked down the rows of cars. One moseyed up to his rented Cherokee, pulling out a spray bottle, and … shot a jet of soapy water on the windshield.

Bud rolled down the window. "Hey, stop it."

"Dirty glass," the kid said. Now that Bud got a better look, the guy was closer to forty, maybe Hispanic, Italian, or …

"I said knock it off. This ain't my car. I'm not gonna tip you."

The maybe-Hispanic guy ran a squeegee across the windshield in a figure-eight swish. He gaped in through the re-arranged smudges. "Now this side's clean." He pointed toward the passenger side. "My brother goin' to wash you up over there."

A scrawny, dirty-faced kid, maybe fifteen, black, grinned at him and shot a jet of soapy water onto that side. He applied his squeegee. The maybe-Latino held out his hand, ready to receive payment.

"I told you, it's a rental car. I'm not tipping."

"Suit you-self, man. You see that white dude, up aheada you? He don' clean windows. He here to improve you paint job." He called out, "We got a cheap Sonna B here, Jamie." He looked back in at Bud. "I hope you bought all the 'surance on this car, 'cause it might be needin' some new paint job."

Bud scrutinized Jamie; ripped blue jeans, a little overweight with slicked-down hair, eighteen or twenty, with his hand in the pocket of his hoodie. There was a bulge. What did he have in there? Would he key the car or something worse? Shoot a couple of holes in the fender—or Bud?

Bud whipped out his wallet and handed five to that scam artist, as traffic cleared to the light. He slowed as he reached Jamie. The light turned yellow. Bud shouted out the window, "Get a job, you creep." The light turned red as he rolled through. In his side-view mirror, he saw the kid grinning.

Fuck. Red and blue lights flashed behind him. A cop pulled him over and sauntered up to the Cherokee. The window was still open from his *conversation* with Jamie.

The cop approached, ticket pad and pen in hand. Bud looked up at him. "You see what those dicks are doing over there? They said they'd key my car if I didn't give up a tip."

The cop had a nicely pressed blue cop uniform, short sleeves. He got ready to write the ticket. "Yeah. Dicks. I can't do a thing about that, and it ticks me off."

The cop looked pretty frustrated by that. Bud took a chance and said, "I hope you're like me, 'cause I really need a break. Gotta catch my plane."

"What do you mean, like you?"

"You like Trump, right?"

"He's still President," the cop said. "I went to the rally, on January sixth"

"You break into the Capitol?"

"Nope. That's why they didn't arrest me, and I'm still writing tickets for mopes like you."

"I probably saw you there," Bud said. "I was the one in the red cap."

The cop laughed and lowered his pen. "I got three of those… Go catch your plane, friend."

He gassed up, returned the Cherokee, caught the shuttle to the airport, and ran like hell for the plane, an obligatory mask strapped on to cover his damned germ-spewing mouth.

He'd reserved an aisle seat in economy plus for extra legroom. That worked fine for Bud's five-foot-seven frame, but the bulky, six-foot-three guy in the center found himself wedged between Bud and the overweight middle-aged woman in a blue pantsuit at the window. The guy planted his arm firmly on their shared arm rest, Bud's half (really a sliver) included.

They took off, and a flight attendant rolled out her drink cart. Hard to tell much with the mask, but she had a good shape and a pretty blue-eyed sparkle. Bud ordered two gin and tonics. She gave him one of those cute disapproving looks that stewardesses specialize in.

"Long flight," he said.

The tall fellow requested a Diet Coke. The woman ordered apple juice. The guy was probably in his sixties, with gray hair, gold-framed glasses, reading a magazine, content as he could be in that tight space.

Bud lowered his tray. The flight attendant set little bottles of gin, cans of tonic and plastic glasses half-full of ice cubes on it. She leaned past him to pass drinks to the others. She had a name badge that said "Joyce," and she smelled like lilacs.

That reminded Bud of Wanda, not the lilacs, but the idea of a sweet-smelling gal. Wanda and he were going out. Bud's business partner and buddy, Stan, called her Bud's girlfriend, but he didn't. She wouldn't call him a boyfriend either. They were *not* going steady and never would. That was the deal. Maybe if he focused on Wanda, he'd stop being pissed about the guy hoarding his armrest.

Bud poured the first gin into the glass and mixed the drink. He eyed the guy's arm, violating their communal territory. "I'm thinking that when we're over Omaha or some god-forsaken place, I should get a turn at that fine armrest. Or maybe we alternate, one hour for you, one for me, and like that."

"I'm John," the guy said, not budging a centimeter. "I need what room I can get in this crate."

"Yeah maybe." Bud held off a second and said, "You pay extra for that luxurious middle seat with arm support, John, like Economy Plus, Plus? I didn't know they had that."

John gave him a crooked smile. "No. I guess …" He retreated his arm, which he had to pin against his side.

Did Bud really want his arm pressed up against the big guy? No. He tilted a bit toward the aisle and said, "Never mind. You can have it. I'm Bud."

The guy's arm returned to borderland. His eyes went back to his magazine.

Bud downed his drink in a couple of minutes, thinking how so many things in life could piss a guy off. Of course, there was the big one: Trump and the STEAL. The way it had fucked up his relationship with Stan, who thought Trump was a lying son of a traitor. Bud had been training himself though; whenever he started cogitating on that topic, he moved on to some other annoying shit.

Bud smiled. Sometimes he surprised himself with the words that came into his head, like *cogitating*. Yowzers!

Masks—always fucking masks, traffic jams, squeegee kids and other hooligans, rioters burning cities down. Even running to catch a plane, car rental agencies that tried to sell you extra insurance, the Department of Transportation, and every other damned Department ... plus his sister's delighted smile as she looked into her lover's eyes. That shouldn't tick him off, should it? Unless he was some kind of controlling dick.

Why give a shit about any of it? For five crappy bucks to those kids? Because a fellow usurped his arm rest. Because the squeegee man was too shiftless to find a job? Jealous of his sister's few precious moments of euphoria before she returned to reality? –Bingo.

John nudged his elbow. "This is a super arm rest. Thanks."

He laughed. "Sure."

"When the stew' comes by again, I'll order a drink for you. Payment for that extra Plus in my Economy Plus, Plus."

"You order me one, and I'll order me another. You know, John, you're not such a friggin' bad guy."

After he'd drunk his fourth gin and tonic, including the one John paid for, Bud tried to fall asleep. Maybe he fell off.

Joyce caught his attention with a nudge to his arm. She pulled her mask down for just a second—not as pretty as he'd imagined—and then replaced it. "Cover up," she said. How could he resist that smile?

About an hour out of LA, John offered the magazine he'd been reading. "Another payment."

"Thanks." Bud glanced at it: some international business rag. He shoved it into the seat pocket. Before leaving the plane, he slid it into his carry on.

Bud took a taxi home from the airport, tossed his bag onto the ratty sofa, popped open a beer, and left it full on the counter, as he went to bed.

In the night, he kept seeing his sister smiling, *joyful*. –Not a word he'd normally use, but he was half asleep, brain numbing up. Betty was only happy when she was in love—no *infatuated*. Bud had felt nothing like it in one hell of a long time. Even a little infatuation could have picked him up right then.

# CHAPTER 3

## STAN

Stan proposed, and Melanie accepted three months ago. Engaged ... Engaged! Too pretty and too smart for him by a mile. She slept with him four nights a week now. The other three, she stayed in her apartment, upstairs in her mother's house. The lovely, devoted daughter with an ailing mom. Stan hadn't seen her this Saturday night or all-day Sunday. He went into the office early on Monday to grab a moment together before Bud arrived.

Was Stan a starry-eyed lover? Sure.

He balanced the two Starbucks cappuccinos he'd bought, one on top of the other, as he opened the office door to S. Stein Investigations. He held the door back with his foot, split the coffees, one in each hand, and stepped inside.

Melanie got up from her desk and headed for him, beaming. She wore blue jeans with a red short-sleeved blouse, woven beige sandals with a bit of a heel that made her a touch taller than him. "I missed you so much this weekend." She eyed his hands. "What, no Danish pastry?"

He laughed and wrapped his arms around her, holding the coffees behind her back. She held him tight. They kissed deeply and sweetly. He loved all of this; from the way she called him "dear," to the feel of her body against his, to the comfort of sitting at their desks, working only a few feet apart.

Stan sat and began scrolling through his emails. "You filing those Worker's Comp cases today?" he asked.

She nodded and made a show of looking around the room. "One heck of a fine office I found for us; don't you think?" She'd said that every day for the past week since they'd moved in.

"You did great, Melanie."

They'd solved a few missing person cases in the last couple of months and used the income to buy new furniture and move the business, S. Stein Investigations, into this place. It was on the second floor of a building in Santa Monica—a super upgrade from the old spot in an industrial park, next to an auto body repair place. Stan was feeling proud, worried too. Higher rent; more pressure. They needed to keep fresh cases coming, or they'd be out.

"Those corner windows are fantastic," she said. "And Bud's happy to have his own desk."

"To the extent that Bud's happy these days." Stan saw worry appear in Melanie's eyes.

"I don't think it's about the election anymore," she said. "He didn't exactly get over Trump losing, but it's better now that we can mention it."

"Other stuff's eating him, too. He just won't open up about it."

"Bud thinks he's the strong, silent type. He'll only tell you if it's killing him."

"You have to admit I tried, Melanie. I leased that snazzy company car for him."

She chuckled. "Like buying a pet rabbit for a mopey kid?"

"Something like that." Stan hadn't mentioned to her the short-term loan he'd taken out to cover the first and last months' rent on the office and acquisition fee for the Prius. "He would have preferred a noisy, smoky, gas guzzler."

Melanie laughed. "You kidding? He's over the moon with the Prius, in his strong, silent way. He loves you, Stan; you know that."

# CHAPTER 4

## MELANIE

You don't know me yet, and I'm going to marry Stan, so I'd like to fill you in. Stan said to confide in you like I would with a friend. I hope that's okay.

Just saying the word *marriage* sends a flutter through my chest. Yes, I'm totally in love. It's not about how beautiful he is—Stan *is* a great-looking fella. It's more about the way he looks at me. He thinks I'm gorgeous, which I don't believe. No way.

We fit together perfectly when we hold each other. I shouldn't say this, but I adore him partly because of the sex. Science says that when a woman falls for a guy, oxytocin plays a big role. (But knowing that doesn't spoil the thrill.) Stan knows how to tickle my hormones. Unlike most guys, he wants to please way more than to be pleased. Oh, God, I shouldn't be saying this.

Moving on, then: My love has nothing to do with the fact that Stan owns the business. He's not a killer entrepreneur, and marrying him will no-way make me rich. Some other woman might pressure him to earn more, but I want Stan just as he is.

Stan's the kindest man I know. He makes me feel beautiful and loved, respected … and so very happy.

He and I met working together in the fraud department at SimiBank. I was employed there days and taking night classes in Criminal Justice at USC. We didn't know each other really well, but I missed Stan when he left the bank to open S. Stein Investigations. He was a bright spot in my day and a sympathetic ear. When he asked me to come work at his agency, I had my doubts. For one thing, Stan was the kind of guy I could like … a lot—too much for a boss-employee relationship.

I totally had no idea about Bud, and I worried about working for such a small company, where things could be uncomfortable if you didn't get along with all (two) of your fellow employees. What if Bud was a misogynist? As a black woman, what if he was a bigot or just a plain ass, for that matter? (I've encountered my share.) To tell the truth, my first meeting with Bud, after I'd taken the job didn't reassure me all that much.

Now that I know Bud and I know Stan so very well, I have to tell you; I love working with these guys.

Stan says I'm the heart of our little company. Bud says I'm the *brains*, except, really, he thinks he's due that title. If I'm honest, and suspend my modesty, I may truly be the brains.

Stan's the heart, by a mile.

# CHAPTER 5

## CLEM

Clem leaned against the oak. How long since the snake bites? Half an hour … an hour? His ankle throbbed. Fire blazed from his calf to his thigh and scrotum after a while settling to a slow burn. He'd had snake bites before. This one felt like a doozy—a double doozy. No self-respecting worshipper would seek medical attention. It was up to God's mercy now. God's mercy, and Clem's faith. "I'm sorry, Holy Father. I should've worshipped You better."

He sought comfort in the music and the lights over by the stage, fifty yards away. It stopped for a while, and he heard a man preaching. He didn't recognize the voice. Taking Clem's part! What would his people think of him? What rumors would pass about Arlene and him? Had they noticed Elton Snivel missing? Had Millie told them how Arlene cut out and how clueless Clem had been about it? "Damn it, God; is this what You want?"

He smelled the distinct odors of beef casseroles, meatballs, and sausages, chicken enchiladas maybe, drifting on the breezes. The women always made plenty for these events. Arlene would have brought her *burn-the-devil-at-his-own-game* chili, but Arlene was somewhere with Elton, burning something else (marriage vows being just the half of it). Everyone would be hungry after dancing and worshipping. They'd praise God for the food and devour it like wolves. His brethren, his wolves. Would they forget all about him if he died back here? He bent sideways and puked in the dirt.

He raised the flask to his lips but found it empty.

As he drifted to merciful sleep, Clem saw Arlene dancing in a field of wildflowers, the way she had when they first met. He watched her for a while, her flowered skirt fanning out as she twirled. He would join her, holding her close, slowing the pulse to an intimate tango. Swaying together, laughing for the sheer joy of it, her body would seduce him to a lust that no minister of the gospel could entertain outside of marriage.

He yearned to get up and dance with Arlene now, but his body refused. Arlene disappeared, along with everything else in his world.


HE WOKE THE NEXT MORNING, sprawled beside the oak, his leg swollen and excruciating, the crotch and legs of his pants soaked. Crap! His head pounded. He looked around and saw no snakes, so he propped himself back against the tree—each little move killing him.

He ran a hand across the side of his face, down to his mouth. Blood on his fingers. He used his other hand to feel under his eyes, clear. Along his lips, okay. So, only his nose was bleeding. Snake bites could have that effect. Lucky if it was only his nose.

Feeling woozy, he looked up to the oak branches and blue sky, God's heaven. He heard a kind male voice. "Peace be with you."

He talked to Jesus from time to time, as any Christian might, seeking guidance. "I know I've strayed," he said. "Not that often, and I repent every time. I've tried to hold my temper with her."

He didn't see Jesus, just Arlene sitting on a branch up there, with Maynard and Dobie lolling across her lap. He wasn't far enough gone to believe she was truly there.

He closed his eyes, banished Arlene, and spoke to the Lord. "I preach for you, Lord. I share your word with the people. We fight Satan every day." He shifted. Pain stabbed his ankle. "Ohhh, Lord. I know you'll command me to forgive her desertion, as you forgive our trespasses, but this is different. Lord, ain't a thing more damnable she could do than steal Satan from your faithful preacher."

Asleep again. He woke to the sound of voices. Agony in his leg. "Clem, what ya doing here?" Millie said.

Tom came over and touched his face. "You're boiling, Clemson. Snake got you last night?"

"Yeah, one of them crappy timber rattlers. Bit me twice." He nodded toward his ankle.

Millie stood over him, looking kind of stricken. "Oh, God; I'm sorry, Clem. We assumed you wanted to be alone after Arlene and Maynard … and all. Didn't start worrying about you 'til you didn't answer your phone."

Clem gritted his teeth as Tom eased his pant leg up and pulled down his sock. "Sure got you," Tom said. "Not your first. Probably not your last."

Clem tried to smile. "That your way of saying I'll live?"

"You will. We'll get you home now, brother."

They helped Clem to his pickup and got him into the passenger seat. Tom drove, and Millie followed in their camper. Back at Clem's house, Tom took out a knife and worked to slit the side of Clem's shoe so they could take it off. They stripped him to his underpants and helped him into bed. Clem, in his pain, didn't even have the presence of mind to be embarrassed by the way Millie glanced at his flabby belly and his droopy pecker in the wet jockeys. She pressed a towel against his privates to dry his pissy unders as best she could.

"You got soup in the kitchen?" she asked.

Clem nodded. Millie and Tom headed that way. Tom brought back a glass of water, and Clem gulped from it.

"Easy," Tom said.

Millie brought him a warm bowl of chicken noodle and a spoon.

Clem sipped a little and handed the bowl back to her. "Leave it on the side table, will you?"

Millie set the bowl down. "You got the herbs?" She meant snake bite herbs, of course.

"Under the bathroom sink," he told her. Clem didn't remember what plants were in the mix, but he'd bought a big batch of the mixed herbs from a shop in LA's Chinatown and distributed them to members of his congregation a couple of years back.

Tom and Millie came back with the hot, mean-tasting herbal brew and stood by while he drank. Millie wiped his forehead with a damp towel. "We'll come back later," she said. "Drink that soup when you feel up to it."

As he lay back, he wondered if the towel she ran across his forehead was the same one she used to dab his balls.

# CHAPTER 6

## BUD

When Bud entered the office, Stan and Mel were busy on their computers, so he sat at his new desk with its high-class leather chair. He had a view out the window, to a playground surrounded by trees, and a school across the street. He spent a couple of minutes taking in the scene. A little black bird swooped close to his window, giving him the eye. A little creepy, but it reminded Bud of something cool he was following on the internet.

He spun his chair once around a full 360 plus another 90, ending aimed toward Stan and Mel. The spin made him laugh. Happy; was he happy to be here with them? He was. Happiness came short-lived these days—a glance out the window, a quick spin of the chair, a smile from his friends—nice.

Stan and Mel had stopped wearing masks after they had Covid and took the vaccine. Bud had pretended to be anti-vax for a couple of weeks, just for laughs. Then he confessed to getting a shot too. Fun to tease them, but they worried about him, damn it.

Mel gave him a brilliant smile. "You look cheerful, Bud. Have a good time at your sister's wedding?" She got up and walked toward him, but stopped by Stan's chair. She laid her hand on his shoulder. Stan smiled up at her—casual, comfortable, affectionate.

Obviously, Stan was amazed that Mel had fallen for him. He was a handsome guy, but he'd never figured that out, and Mel was one of the most attractive women Bud had ever met, tall and graceful. They were both lucky, a great couple. Bud was happy for them. He was, but … Stan rarely went out for beers with him after work anymore. (Really, that custom had disappeared during the election last year, when jovial banter at their favorite bar turned to arguments about Trump. The cops had hauled one guy out after he'd shattered his beer bottle and threatened to gut the bartender, which happened the night of the Trump-Biden debate. That was the past now. Things were getting better.)

Mel and Stan were upbeat, as usual. And Bud had a nugget that would give them a lift still further up the levity ladder.

"You didn't mention taking Wanda to New York for the wedding?" Mel asked.

Bud shook his head. "Wouldn't be interested." He stood up and stretched. "There's something I think you two might like."

Mel chuckled. "From the internet?"

"Right."

Stan reached for Mel's hand. "Here we go," he said.

"Actually," Bud said. This story has been out for some time. Vital information for us detectives.

"Go for it." Stan and Mel said that simultaneously.

"About birds. You see the way they watch you from up in the trees and zoom down close? You heard about this?"

Stan was nodding, like maybe he had heard. Before he could interrupt, Bud hit them with, "Like that creepy black bird outside.

You know they're all little drones spying for Central Intelligence? Actual birds went the way of the dinos."

Stan and Mel laughed then, which felt super. Bud told them lots of little factoids like this, not because they were true—some of them maybe weren't—but to get them thinking about alternative facts, and because he treasured the feel of their glee. *Treasured*, and *glee*, two un-Bud-like words.

Bud put on a serious face and said, "The CIA killed off the birds and replaced them with drones. There was this informer CIA guy on YouTube—Facebook, too. Real Deep State. They blurred up his face and disguised his voice to protect him, because, well, you know … the CIA."

Mel and Stan exchanged skeptical looks, which they did sometimes when Bud was imparting his wisdom. All part of the fun.

"The Agency had good intentions. They wanted to do away with bird poop for the good of humanity and spy the shit out of their fellow citizens. Two for one. Millions believe this. They give it thumbs up on Facebook."

"I love it." Mel said, warming Bud with her laughter.

"Fantastic. Thanks for informing us," Stan added. "You planning to work today?"

"Yeah." Bud reached around and grabbed the file off his desk. "Finchsmith case."

"That bird story's a load of pigeon crap, right Bud?" That was Stan.

Bud didn't believe the story … did he? Funny, but Stan's comment pissed him off a little. Stan went all know-it-all on him, not only about these theories, but sometimes about serious stuff too. Bud's resentment could come from out of the blue. But he played it cool. "How do you think they found Bin Laden?" he asked. "Mechanical pigeon, that's how."

"That's what I heard too." Stan's grin dissolved Bud's annoyance.

Stan came over and hugged him, and it felt pretty damned good. Bud let himself breathe. "I love you, man," Bud said, as he held Stan tight.

BUD'S CASE—Barbara Finchsmith—was not one of those scary missing person's assignments. Mrs. Finchsmith was only missing to the extent that she wasn't where she claimed to be. She was supposed to be on a fun holiday in Costa Rica with a girlfriend, Francine.

Her husband, Ned, was enjoying the bachelor life, until he ran into Francine's spouse, Bob, at the racket ball court. Bob couldn't stop raving about the chicken fricassee Francine was cooking for him that night.

Ned felt like a rotten chicken carcass had landed in his gut.

Ned related all of this to Bud over the phone. Most people would have wanted to meet in person, but Ned insisted that was unnecessary. Made Bud wonder about the guy.

Mel checked the internet and placed some calls. There was no sign of Barbara Finchsmith at the supposed hotel in Costa Rica or any other lodging nearby; missing, too, any charges to Ned and Barbara's credit cards. Which made sense if some dude was keeping her comfortable in an as-yet-unknown nookie den— Bud's theory. He had a sixth sense about these things.

Mel tapped into Barbara's Facebook pages, both the public and the for-friends-only private sections. (Mel had a magic touch in cyber-land.) She found shots of Barbara snuggling with a gray-haired dude by a swimming pool. Both looked over-the-top happy.

With facial recognition, Mel ID-ed the guy in the picture—a realtor named Adolphson. She tracked down addresses for Adolphson's realty office and home, both in Redondo Beach.

Bud tailed Adolphson to an open house at one pricy property, $3 Mil—not a great place to hide a mistress, with people coming and going. Later, the realtor visited a couple of other houses for sale. One was vacant, 225 Front St.

After the guy left, Bud searched but found no signs of life. He returned in the evening and observed. No lights. No one visible inside. He went around back and peeked in the windows. The oval pool invited him. Bud shucked his duds and dove in. Just the right temperature. California; gotta love it.

# CHAPTER 7

## SVETA

*YERUNDA RUSSIA, TWO HOURS EAST OF MOSCOW.*

E very Wednesday evening, Svetlana Ivanovna Mikhailov attended the Orthodox service in her hometown of Yerunda. She loved and took comfort in that old church; its spirit, its intricate woodwork steeple and two marvelous onion domes. Inside, priests swung censors, spewing fragrant smoke. Gold-adorned icons and gilded candelabras gleamed. She breathed in the heavy air and felt the Holy Spirit, but she attended only the Wednesday evening services.

Sunday morning, while the rest of the faithful worshipped, Sveta hustled through the cemetery, past graves marked with simple crosses, slabs of wood or stone. Heading straight to the special chapel on the east side, she genuflected at the threshold. With all the parishioners in church, Sveta found solitude here with her ancestors.

This Sunday morning, the first in September, she approached the solid silver coffin, set on a limestone pedestal at the far end. A two-meter-high stained-glass window above the tomb—Mary touching a kneeling woman on the head—cast blue and red light fragments over her.

The silver coffin bore a glass viewing portal, revealing the holy face of Alyona. The white lace collar of her gown and sapphire pendant gilded her aura.

Sveta gently touched the coffin's crown. "Великая бабушка, я приветствую тебя." (Great grandmother, I greet you.)

She took a deep breath and gazed at her ancestor. Despite the church women cleaning it often, the glass over that blessed face had discolored edges where the glass met the silver framing. Still, Sveta noticed the parchment skin and the bare patch on one side of the forehead where the skull peeked through. Sparse gray hair still clung to the scalp.

"I revere your memory. I pray for you, great grandmother. I keep my promises to the Church and honor its teachings. Please bless me and help me hold my promises true. Help me be a good woman and accept my life."

Even as she said this, she yearned for a different life; not the one chosen by circumstance, but one she could find if she was clever enough and strong enough, even while holding true to her beliefs.

The local Orthodox congregation built the little chapel in reverence to Sveta's great grandmother, Alyona, who was considered as much of a saint as the local population had ever produced.

Alyona served as a humble handmaiden in the home of the last Tsar, Nicolas, while he was confined in Tobolsk during the Russian Revolution. She had been companion and helper to the Tsar's youngest child, seventeen-year-old Anastasia.

When the Tsar's family was evacuated from Tobolsk, Alyona accompanied them to Yekaterinburg, where the Red Guards assassinated the Tsar and his family. The Guards imprisoned Alyona under suspicion of "traitorous inclinations." After months of privation, they marched her into town and demanded she declare allegiance to the Bolsheviks. As a soldier leveled his rifle at her, Alyona refused. After a terrifying minute, the man lowered his weapon. Another soldier shoved her to the ground and kicked her in the head.

Alyona's punishment was to be sent deep into Siberia. She married a man there —Sveta's great grandfather, who died two years later.

At one time, it was thought that Alyona helped Anastasia to escape; perhaps to America. A false rumor, but the people back in Yerunda took note.

Years after these events, witnesses reported meeting Alyona in the hinterlands, where she lived a humble life, always proclaiming her loyalty to the royal family. She died in 1940 at age 41. They buried her in the permafrost of frozen Siberia, the grave abandoned but not forgotten. Stories circulated in the area, stories of the healing power of her gentle embrace.

Her daughter, Sveta's grandmother, Polina, found a good marriage and enough money to exhume her mother's body and move it to Yerunda.

In 2000, nine years after the collapse of the Soviet Union, the Orthodox Church regained its revered position. The martyred Tsar's reputation flourished. Nicolas was being considered for sainthood by the Church. The townspeople of Yerunda knew of Alyona's brave and steadfast loyalty to his majesty. The church again exhumed her, planning to give her a proper, marked and honored, grave.

What they found in her tomb shocked and amazed. Her body remained in a fine state of mummification. The locals speculated and argued. Scholars theorized about all those years, frozen and desiccated in icy Siberia. More providentially minded churchmen pontificated about divine intervention.

Articles appeared in newspapers about "the saint of Siberia," who, during her time in the distant lands, had served the destitute and the infirm. She raised her patients up with heroic efforts, fatally undermining her own health, while rescuing the lowliest of the peasants from death by starvation or disease.

The Yerunda elders petitioned the Patriarch in Moscow to recognize the miracle of her physical preservation and the holiness of her sacred work. At great expense, they produced the fabulous silver coffin. They paraded it through the streets in a horse-drawn hearse and displayed it in the church vestibule. Donations poured in to build the small chapel where Sveta now stood. At her grandmother's insistence, the chapel became a family crypt. There could be a space here for Sveta someday.

Behind Sveta lay the white stone vaults where her mother, Ksenia, her grandmother, Polina, and Polina's brother lay.

Sveta withdrew to the back of the chapel.

She whispered, not wanting her great grandmother to overhear. "Mother, Grandmother, I live a proper life, with little sin on my conscience. I heal the sick, like great grandmother did. I honor my ancestors, as you did, grandmother Polina. I share my sister's burdens, as you would have me, mother. Yet my life is unfulfilled. I do not find joy in…"

She poured her heart out to those two women who raised and nurtured her. She tried to disguise her hopelessness about ever finding love and omitted how vulnerable she felt living now in her sister's home with her brother-in-law, who assaulted her senses and wounded her spirit with his drunken outbursts. To speak of it would only anger her mother and sadden her babushka.

Sveta didn't hear their voices as clearly now, but she still perceived their spirits. She knew how each would advise.

Mama—*Don't be so damned particular, daughter. Find a man with a decent job. You are far too old to be choosy—and stop moaning into our old dead ears.*

Babushka—*Dear, beautiful girl, you were always so bright and so special. Your mother is too serious and dull. You're not too old. Find a dream, dear. Do something different with your life. Create. Live. Enjoy.*

Sveta was, in fact, thirty-five. Years ago, she'd followed a man and married him—her imagined dream come true. That dream had turned to dreck. Divorced after ten years of false hope; her father, her ex-husband, and now her brother-in-law; all heavy drinkers.

She was too late for some dreams, but maybe not all.

She rose, crossed herself and walked outside, pausing for a moment to breathe deeply of God's fresh air.

# CHAPTER 8

## BUD

Bud had been back from the east coast wedding a few days and hadn't seen Wanda. After that delicious swim in the pool at the vacant house, he headed to Jake's, the bar where she worked. He figured she'd serve him a pickled egg, and some microwaved chicken nuggets. He'd have a couple of beers, wink at her and say, "So what do you think?" If she thought *yes*, she'd pass her apartment key across the bar. He'd go to her place, take a shower, and fall asleep in her bed. She'd pop in around 2:30 AM.

Which really didn't sound that inspiring right then. Maybe the jet lag was still kicking his butt. Maybe seeing Wanda would kindle a flame.

Bud entered Jake's and headed to the bar. Wanda poured his first draft as he settled on the stool. She wore a short sleeve black tee with sequins spelling, *Jimi Hendrix,* and a picture of the rockstar. Bud thought it went nicely with the bluebird tattoo on her forearm. Black jeans too. The jeans and shirt fit just right.

She passed him a bowl of chips, set her hand on her hip, and shot him a look. "How was the wedding, hon? Your sister go through with it?"

"She did, and she looked incredibly happy."

"Really?"

"Yeah, her new husband did too; no kidding."

Wanda wasn't looking all excited to see him, and Bud wasn't feeling that way either. He nursed his brew, watching her pull the handles on the beer spigots and stroll to the tables with a tray of drinks—sexy. She glanced back and added a little strut to her stroll just for him.

Watching her, the only thing Bud felt was a desire to go outside and walk home in the chilly night air. By the time she returned, he'd gulped the rest of the beer and set a twenty on the bar. "Going home."

She didn't look hurt or surprised, maybe a little pissed, but not much of that either. "See ya."

BACK HOME, Bud drank a beer, sitting on his worn-out sofa, watching *Law and Order* reruns on the fifty-inch flatscreen. The guy who cast that show—had to be a guy—did a nice job. The Assistant DAs were all great looking gals, one a gorgeous blonde, the next one with black hair—beautiful eyes, all of them.

Which brought Bud back to those romantic looks Stan and Melanie flashed at each other. *Companionably intimate* was a good way to describe it. *Companionably intimate*—something a man could crave.

Betty's lustful gazes with her new husband at the wedding— Bud could get into that too, with the right woman. Even if they might fade over time? Maybe even then.

How long since a woman smiled into Bud's eyes like Melanie did with Stan? What sort of woman—attractive, of course— would see anything that smile-worthy in him? Not Wanda; her smiles could be seductive or wicked, not loving.

Wasn't that how he'd always wanted it?

Bud noticed the magazine then, still on the coffee table, the international business rag from John on the plane. Might as well just toss it out … but … on the cover he saw a woman he recognized from somewhere—the head of the European Union? Serious-looking gal.

He took the last sip of beer and leaned back, resisting the urge for another bottle. He thumbed through the pages and saw articles about Luxembourg's plans for something-or-other, the latest on Brexit's challenges, a piece claiming to offer the best places on earth to retire. Sure. Next month, another list.

There were ads too—hair loss treatments, hearing aids, a bathtub with a door in the side. This rag knew its readers, and they were even older than Bud felt. Maybe he was closing in on that demographic.

Next came a half-page ad with a stunning brunette smiling right out at him. She wore a tank top that showed off her shoulders—sexy collar bones.

Beneath her image were the words, *BEAUTIFUL RUSSIAN WOMEN WANT TO MEET YOU.* There was more writing, but Bud didn't bother. He went to the fridge and opened another beer, while *Law and Order* played in the background. Muting the TV, he walked back to the coffee table and gazed at the woman in the magazine. He thought to himself, *Stan gave me a $3000 bonus a couple of months ago, more than sufficient for a flight to Russia.*

He left the half-full bottle on the table beside its empty brother and went to bed. In the middle of the night, he pictured Betty and her new man … then Stan and Mel, so happy together … the Russian honey who wanted to meet him.

At 5:00 AM, Bud made himself coffee on the Keurig and read the rest of her ad:

*Meet Anna from St. Petersburg.*

*Anna yearns to meet a bloke like you.*
*Not spoiled by Western affluence, Anna would be grateful to*
    *marry and share your comfortable home.*
*The man who chooses Anna will be her king.*
*She will worship and support him.*
*His fondest wish will become her command.*

*Yeah*, he thought. *Submissive and sexy as hell. I could live with that.* Then he asked himself, *Does a guy need to command a woman, or should there be a little give and take? Compromise? Mutual respect?* Not questions any of Bud's old buddies would expect from him, but there they were. Surprised the hell out of him, too.

He'd observed Mel with Stan the past couple of months …. A beautiful woman, funny too; a woman who would let you know damned well if she disagreed and who could be passionate about issues and causes. (Passionate in other ways, Bud imagined from the way she and Stan acted.) Was Mel spoiled by western affluence? —no. Grateful to share Stan's home? Probably, but not because of his wealth (such as it was).

But here was the thing: so many American women—even Mel a little—were *woke.* That's the dopey expression they called it lately. Women who thought, like Biden, that blacks should be compensated because their great-great grannies were slaves. That big bucks should be spent for extra bathrooms everywhere, so guys could become girls and feel comfy and *self-actualized. Get over it already, and move on. Use a friggin' men's room like the rest of us.*

A Russian babe would be grateful to come to America, would want to pay *him* reparations for the privilege.

It was probably afternoon in Russia by then. Bud dialed the number in the ad and heard the message, *"Russian Brides*

*Unlimited*—" an authentic-sounding accent "—Please call back during business hours, nine AM to six PM Eastern Daylight Time."

An hour later he called, and a guy, clearly trying for some accent, informed him: The five-day *Voyage to Rapture* package, to a town outside St. Petersburg cost $10,000. The recommended ten-day *Adventure in Paradise* ran fifteen grand. Each package would guarantee that he spent time with at least three gorgeous new gals each day. Women like Anna.

"That's a lot of cabbage," Bud said.

"Airfare, accommodations, and meals included. We help you obtain a Russian visa and match you to women who share your interests. Very professional. This is our premier service."

Intriguing, but too damned expensive. Bud asked himself, *Why not just go back online for more internet dating?* He answered back, *Because you hated it; because it embarrassed you; because it felt pathetic to ask a computer to match you up with someone you'd probably already met at a bar.*

Better to spend big bucks that he didn't have to share vodka with a gorgeous Russian chick-nik?

"You got a less premier?" Bud asked. "Like economy plus?"

"Glad you asked."

He tried to ignore the fake Russian accent.

"Three hundred dollars. You send us information about yourself—what you do for a living, what you like and don't like, what kind of girl you want to meet. We match you with ten sweet, pretty honeys—submissive, very nice. We send their information. You can write them emails and get to know them like that. Later, maybe you decide to plunge with a package plan."

"Yeah, maybe."

"Full disclosure; there's a small additional charge for each email."

"Small?"

"Twenty-five dollars. Then, if you come to Russia later, you can meet the ones you like or take the full package and meet a gang of *amazing* women."

"Twenty-five each one?" The guy didn't answer, so Bud said, "You're in New York, right? Born in Jersey, work in the City?"

"I'm Russian in my heart, bud."

He didn't remember telling the guy his name, but a guy from Jersey might call anyone *bud*.

Like any horny cheapskate, Bud plunked down the $300 and started writing his profile. He shot a few more bucks on a couple of books about Ukrainian and Russian brides.

He felt tempted to bring this up with his great friend, Stan. But how deep into humiliation did he want to dive, now that Stan was riding the crest of euphoric romanticality? (Good new word, eh?) Stan was cool, but he was a guy. A guy would naturally mock him. A woman might lend a sympathetic ear.

# CHAPTER 9

## BUD

Mel identified more friends from the photos on Barbara Finchsmith's social media. Bud interviewed a few and followed some guys. Not exciting work, but when he found Barbara holed up with a fella whose house was in the backyard of his art gallery, it made his day. Bud snuck in and placed a bug in their kitchen while she was out, and the guy was selling lithographs in the gallery.

It turned out there was no romantic talk between Barbara and this dude—more news than schmooze at dinner time. Bud snuck into the bushes in the yard one night and watched them in the pool. Bathing suits in place. No snuggly, kissy stuff. They retired to separate rooms. Bud used a heat sensor thing to find that out—just like they did on *FBI Most Wanted*.

Bud surprised Ned Finchsmith by delivering the news in person. The guy, a touch shorter than Bud and pudgy, was still wearing his red plaid pajamas. He acted antsy, eyes darting side to side. Didn't want to open the door—Bud could tell. Bud gave him a solid stare and Ned gave in.

They sat on a sofa in the snazzy den; all chrome, and white leather. Bud filled him in and handed him photos. Ned looked them over and dropped them to the floor. He sighed and slumped forward, resting his face in his hands. His bald patch glistened from the overhead spotlights as he mumbled something about being glad Barbara was alive.

Giving Bud the brave act, he figured. Pretty clear their marriage was circling the drain.

Bud waited Ned out for several minutes. Then Ned mumbled something to himself, raised his head, looking calm and determined. "My wife's *friend*, you say he has an art gallery?" He waited for Bud to nod and declared, "I'll pay you to burn it down. You private detectives do that kind of thing, right?"

Bud lost his breath for a moment. Then it annoyed him; what did the guy think he was, some low-life schmuck? Then he smiled. Right here was one of those rare, absurd moments he lived for. Ned the ass-wipe deserved a little torture. "I could get off on that, Ned. How much you offering?"

Ned hesitated. "...Don't know. I'm not wealthy, but ..." He sighed.

Bud slid closer on the sofa, touching Ned's shoulder for a second. "This isn't one of our normal services, you understand?"

"But you could ...?"

"I won't torch the gallery myself. I'll have to find someone."

Ned nodded like he understood, but the fury was draining out of him.

"A bottom-level mafia type, some kind of real moron," Bud said. "Naturally there'd be a finder's fee."

Ned was back to looking plain miserable. A tear ran down his cheek, a guy who'd suffered a shock. Maybe a fool but probably not a horrible guy. Pitiful, not malignant.

"A thousand dollars for you? And then I could pay the … arsonist." Ned swallowed hard, like the word *arsonist* was choking him.

Ned, gagging that way, made Bud feel guilty. The guy was in pain. Bud took a breath and pointed a finger, almost touching the guy's nose. "This is nonsense, Ned. I will not find you a dick-head with a can of gasoline. You gotta deal with Barbara, not the innocent turd who's giving her a roof to sleep under."

Ned looked at him, wide eyed, like Bud had provided a holy revelation. "You're right." He sighed again. "Of course. I'm just so … I don't know. It's such a …"

Bud stood, looking down at him. "Here's what else I won't do; tell you where she's staying. I don't want you doing something stupid. Tell you what, I'll have her phone you."

Ned slouched back on the sofa. "Okay, thanks."

"We'll email a bill for the rest of our fee." Bud walked to the door. He turned back and saw Ned still sitting there. "If she doesn't call in the next few days, let me know. If the guy's art gallery burns down, I'll call the cops on you."

Satisfying as that encounter had been, none of this encouraged Bud to look for a long-term relationship, let alone at the price of a Russian *Adventure in Paradise*. Still, five days a week he saw Stan with Mel, snuggly, lovey … lucky.

Bud finished typing his Finchsmith report at the office. Stan was out on a case, so he gathered his courage and rolled his chair over by Mel.

"Hey, Mel, could you help me with a project?"

She gave him a warm smile. "New case?"

"It's personal. Could you snap a few pictures of me?"

"Not for a job application?" She frowned.

43

He chuckled. "I would *never* leave you, dear ... or my buddy, Stanley."

She wiped imaginary sweat off her forehead. "Your obituary then?"

He swore Mel to secrecy and confessed what he was up to.

She didn't smirk at the idea of him going to Russia for a date. She didn't hesitate, either. "Ludmila," she said.

"What?"

"*Ludmila*; I like that name. Find one of those and bring her home to meet us."

"Thanks. I'll look for one." He gestured at his face. "You think I have a chance? These Russian gals are all hot, and I'm ... "

"You're a good-looking guy, Bud."

"Yeah, sure."

"If you can be dependable ... dependable and kind ... to one of these women, she'll think you're the best-looking guy on the planet."

"Can you take a pic that makes me look dependable?"

Mel looked at him straight-on. "Damned right I can."

They drove down to the Santa Monica Pier where Mel talked a guy into loaning them a surfboard. Bud posed with it, standing on the sand by the ocean. Next, they did one of Bud sitting behind the wheel of his company car, the red Prius Stan leased for him.

At Jake's that night, Wanda took close-ups of Bud sitting at the bar with a beer. After she finished, he said, "I'm signing up for a dating site." No mention of Russia. He watched to see if she'd flinch.

"I'll shoot a few more," she cheerfully suggested. "Put a gleam in your eye, if you want to lure a hot one."

She looked fine with the idea. What else did he expect?

She poured him a second beer. "Does this mean you're not coming to my place after?"

"Tempting, Wanda, but I'm going home to snooze the night away."

# CHAPTER 10

## THE MAN IN THE TRUNK

He felt himself breathing. Waking up ... Where? He exhaled and heard his breath in the stillness. In a cramped space, he was lying on his side. He tried to straighten his legs, but something blocked them.

So tired! His eyes wouldn't open. He slept some more. Waking. Wondering. He opened his eyes. *Really dark.* Closed in, breathing stale air. There was a downy material, like a comforter or sleeping bag, beneath him. He reached up, blocked again. He was about to shift his weight when he felt something press against his thigh—something living. Outside of this little world, a click, a clunk. A door opened and slammed shut. His enclosure vibrated.

Then he knew where he was, and that she'd drugged him and what was moving against his legs. If he kept still, maybe the snake—snakes?—would be still too. Maybe they wouldn't punch their fangs into his leg and inject their poison.

The car started; the radio came on. Music ... familiar, a song he liked ...... "Wastin' away again in Margaritaville ..." Jimmy Buffet ... The driver kicked up the volume, singing loud with the radio.

The man in the trunk didn't feel like singing.

Jimmy sang, "Some people claim that there's a woman to blame, but I know it's my own damned fault."

*Right, Jimmy, rub it in; no one to blame but myself.*

Jimmy— "How it got here I haven't a clue."

That tracked. *Clueless … Pissed of …. Really damn scared.* Hyperventilating. The snakes would sense it.

He considered yelling, but pretending to be unconscious seemed wiser. Escape before she realized. He reached up, trying to find an emergency release. Didn't all cars have one in the trunk?

The car rolled forward, picking up speed. Gravel grated under the tires, clacked against the underside of the car, detonating shards of regret and humiliation in his frantic brain. Bumps. His body bounced a little. *No!* The snake—snakes? — writhed against him. *God, no!*

One—please let it be only one snake—slithered up onto his leg. He located a knob above and pulled it. There was no pop, no trunk lid rising, no rush of fresh air. He wanted to pull harder, but the snake was progressing toward his armpit. Any movement could invite a fatal strike.

The snake held still. The man held his arm motionless. Once again, the car—and the man—bounced. The snake rode him up and down. *Okay. Okay then. Steady.*

He sensed another creature now. Something not touching him, in that space behind his legs.

*How it got here I haven't a clue.*

He heard the rattle and knew; the second serpent was about to strike.

# CHAPTER 11

## BUD

Bud researched Russian visa requirements and prepared a profile as honest as he could make himself. He was a thirty-seven-year-old man (Okay; he shaved a year or three off) divorced fifteen years, looking for a permanent, serious relationship. (!!!) Hoping for a woman under thirty-five, his ideal match would become a life partner who would also bear his children. (Bud hadn't known he wanted that until he wrote it. But he left it in.) *I would be kind and devoted*, he wrote. *I'm not wealthy, but I'd protect and encourage my wife. I do not smoke, and I drink only in moderation* (more of an aspiration there).

Was he writing this about himself or Stan? ... or the Bud he'd be if he had a good woman?

He emailed the profile and pictures to *Russian Brides Unlimited* and received ten profiles in return.

Several sounded interesting. A few of the pictures took his breath away. Real or doctored?

Bud had enough money to go to Russia. He could pay *Russian Brides Unlimited*, RBU to support his visa application, but not for their premier service. He sent emails to eight of the women (cha-ching $200 in email fees). Eight replies, all charming. None of them made it sound like money was an issue. (Still, cha-cha ching, another $200 to pay for their email responses).

Intrigued, he sent messages back, extolling the joys of life in California. Seven of them replied, oozing enthusiasm for meeting him. An eighth message came from *Russian Brides Unlimited*: *We are sorry to inform you that the lovely woman you desired, Alexandra, has found her perfect man. RBU can bring you happiness, but only if you act fast.*

That irritated the piss out of him, worried him too. A car salesman one time gave him the BS, "This deal won't come back in your lifetime!" (Something that might work with a guy like Stan.) He told the sales jerk to piss off.

He checked his credit card bill online the next day. RBU had charged him for all eight of his emails and eight replies, including their kiss-off about Alexandra. Fuck them.

He took a long walk by the ocean, trying to fight the notion that this whole crazy scheme was just a plan to bleed him dry, at $25 a pop.

A WEEK LATER; amazing development. The phone rang; caller ID from Moscow—Moscow, Idaho. Bud answered with his usual, "Yeah."

"Andrew Randolph?" – A young woman's voice.

No one used his given name, except the occasional telemarketer. "I'm going to hang up now."

"Your uncle was Jeremiah Randolph?"

That stopped him. His father's brother Jerry? "Maybe."

"I'm sorry to inform you—"

"You're going to tell me my dear uncle is in trouble and needs me to send money, right?"

"No, I'm—"

"He's in jail in Butte and needs to be bailed out—or down in Mexico?"

"—Sorry to inform you your uncle died, leaving you $200,000."

That stopped Bud in his tracks. He tried to remember what Uncle Jerry looked like.

"He passed a few weeks ago, but we had difficulty finding you."

"You should hire a private detective. I know a good one." Bud glanced at the magazine, still on his coffee table.

"Thanks for the helpful suggestion, Mr. Randolph."

"You'll send me a cashier's check?"

"We could transfer the money directly to your account once you've verified your identity."

"No thanks. A check will be fine." No way Bud Randolph was giving his account information over the phone.

Bud asked a notary to certify a couple of forms and went down to FedEx to overnight them, along with his birth certificate and copies of a few bills that were sent to his home address. A week later, he deposited the $200K.

Bud signed up for the one-week package at *Russian Brides Unlimited*. Then he sent emails to five of the Russian women—the three hottest looking and two who sounded most sincere. (Was he growing old and dull or what?) *I'm coming to Russia next month. Can you meet me?*

# CHAPTER 12

## THE MAN OUT OF THE TRUNK

The man woke, lying on his back under a huge tree, some leaves dark green, some turning yellow. He remembered being stuck in a fetal position, in that car trunk, with a snake lying on top of him, the other snake rattling in the space behind his legs. After failing to unlatch the trunk lid, he'd carefully lowered his arm. The one snake remained docile. Behind him, the other rattled. The sound echoed in the tight space like hopped-up popcorn in the microwave, sending chills through him.

*Slow your breath,* he told himself. *Be calm, and the rattler might hold back.* His heart hammered. He was breathing in gusts. His gut turned over. The snake struck his thigh, fast in and out, like the jab of a dart. Rattled and struck again. How many times? Four … five. He decided the creature must have run out of venom … maybe… It attacked again.

Before discovering the snakes, he'd planned his escape; when his captor opened the trunk, he'd spring out … hammer her with his fists, take the keys and drive away.

Discovering the first snake changed the plan; he'd lie still, pretending to be unconscious and hope the snake bit her instead of him. Or maybe he'd fling the Satan at her.

The second snake crushed that idea, as it struck, again and again. He grew woozy. The new plan was to beg for mercy and a trip to the hospital.

Blacking out and regaining consciousness, he found himself under the tree with the car and the woman nowhere to be seen. He lay on what looked like a sleeping bag. He wasn't a small man. How had she moved him out of the trunk and laid him here? All by herself?

Sunlight touched his legs. Soon it would light him up from toes to ears, hot, like bacon in a pan. How long could he live with venom coursing in his veins and the sun blistering his face? How long?

# CHAPTER 13

## STAN

Stan waited until Bud left the office. He gave Melanie a tender kiss and headed out to follow up on one of their workers' comp cases. In the parking lot, he found Bud leaning against his Ford Escape. Bud wore one of his dopey grins. "I got something to tell you, partner."

Stan pointed to their office. "We were together in there five minutes ago."

"Private stuff, Stan. Mel will stay with her mom tonight, right?"

"Yep." Stan clicked his fob to unlock the car door.

Bud stepped close and clasped Stan's forearm. "Clancy's at six. What d'ya say?"

Stan had always loved their bar nights, but they'd been few since arguments about Trump screwed things up. Somehow, they hadn't renewed the habit since he and Melanie fell for each other. He smiled. "Yeah, we should go there more. You've got big news?"

Bud gave him a thumbs up. "This is juicy. Life-changing, something that will take more than one drink, to tell."

"*Life-changing, wow!* Give me a hint?"

"My clamshell is shut tight until six."

CLANCY'S WAS a friendly place with hokey bouquets of paper shamrocks stuck on the mirror back of the bar, a dozen bottles of different Irish whiskeys on the counter. Stan's drink was Scotch (blasphemy in this place), while Bud would drink either beer or gin (British gin, even worse).

At the bar, Stan ordered his Scotch and water, light on water. Bud looked Aaron, the bartender, in the eye, and said, "Beer, my friend, but none of that Guinness swill." Aaron growled at Bud and poured his Corona (neutral territory, Mexico).

They chose a spot in the back room, away from the idle pool tables.

"What's going on, pal?" Stan asked.

"You happy with Mel? I mean, you look over the moon."

"You've got that right."

"I like the look of that," Bud said. "I been watching you two, like a teenager with the hots for his buddy's girl."

Quite an admission. "Really, Bud? You and Melanie?"

"I don't mean Mel. I mean, the idea of …"

Betty's wedding must have really affected Bud. Stan chuckled and poked his shoulder. "Midlife crisis, then. You're driving around in that shiny, new Prius, feeling sporty and—"

"I'm going to do something," Bud blurted. "Don't you damn-well laugh at me."

"You getting serious about Wanda?" Stan asked.

Bud shook his head, not looking at him.

Come to think of it, Bud had changed his look recently, from tropical prints to polo shirts, like the powder blue satiny one he had on now. Classy, like one of the golfers might wear on the PGA tour. It was a good look for his friend whose physique wasn't bad for a fella who never hit the gym. Stan smiled. If Bud was out buying new duds, he must be feeling better. "A new girlfriend, then. You have a picture of her? … or *him*?"

Bud snorted. "My balls are still hanging right side up."

"That'd be okay," Stan said. "If you got something like that to tell me."

Bud pulled a paper out of his back pocket, a page from a magazine, and unfolded it partway—a picture of a great-looking woman.

Stan stared. "This model; you're going out with her?"

Bud flashed a sheepish grin. He spread it out, revealing the words: *BEAUTIFUL RUSSIAN WOMEN WANT TO MEET YOU.* So obviously—

"You got your inheritance and now you're going to Russia! … Bud?"

"You got it. I need ten days off. This company, *Russian Brides Unlimited*, is getting me a visa to Russia pronto."

Stan looked down at his glass for a moment, a little sad for Bud, thinking how desperate he was for love. He couldn't let Bud sense his pity. This could actually be a good move; an adventure to break Bud out of his funk. Stan caught the bartender's eye, lifted his glass and gestured to Bud's. He waited for Aaron to bring the drinks, and said, "Hey Aaron, you have a girlfriend?"

"Yeah, a real honey."

"Is she home grown in America?"

Aaron looked confused, and Stan said, "Bud here, he's looking for an exotic woman, the kind you can't find in LA."

"Exotic sounds pretty fuckin' great," Aaron said.

"Yeah, it does, Bud," Stan said. "If that's what you want to do, I think it's a fine idea."

# CHAPTER 14

## STAN

*OCTOBER 2021*

Stan pulled up at the Bradley International Terminal of LAX. Bud jumped out, even before Stan had shut off the engine. Stan popped the hatch and helped Bud unload his two full-sized suitcases. "Lot of luggage here."

Bud smirked. "I vant impress those Russ-ee-on vo-men." His version of a Russian accent.

Probably lots of those spiffy new shirts in there. "Good luck, Comrade," Stan said. "Come home with a gorgeous babushka."

Bud scowled for a second, so maybe he knew that a *babushka* was an old grandmother type.

Stan watched Bud, rolling his cases, one on either side of him, into the horde of travelers bound for far-off lands.

NEXT DAY AT THE OFFICE, Melanie was at her desk, stroking the computer keys.

A call came in, and Stan picked up.

The woman on the other end introduced herself as Emilia Clark and said she needed surveillance on someone. She had a bit of an accent that Stan couldn't place.

"We don't do marital disputes," Stan told her. (Though, obviously, a missing person could turn into one pretty fast.)

"No problem. This is different. This woman skipped out on her debts from a loan in Spain."

Spain. Probably one of those overseas scams. "You don't sound Spanish."

"I work in the fraud department for KatzBank here in the US. We have an affiliated bank in Spain where the fraud occurred."

"I used to work in the fraud department at SimiBank," Stan said.

"I know. I've seen your website. All you'd need to do is photograph the people coming and leaving a house on Raleigh Drive, Manhattan Beach. I'll give you the address and tell you the hours to record. For now, it's eight AM until noon."

Stan quoted her an hourly rate and told her how to provide a deposit. Something was bothering him, so he asked, "Are you in the area?"

"I am."

"I'd like to meet you. KatzBank's offices are on Wilshire, right?"

"… We can meet outside. Mr. Stein, I must emphasize that this is a highly confidential matter. You cannot come to my office or call me using the bank's published phone number."

Hmmm.

He checked Emelia Clark on KatzBank's website and looked up her Facebook page. He met her around the corner from the bank's office. She looked right, but why would she insist that he never call her at work?

Questions swirled in his head, like; if you know where the woman lives, and she stole money, why not just seek a court order? Why surveil only those hours? Why take pictures of everyone coming and going?

On the other hand, why pass up an easy paycheck? *Not yours to reason why*, he told himself. *Accept the cash and take the photos.*

He found the house in Manhattan Beach, which was set above the street—a suitable spot to snap pictures. Stan parked a little way down the block, within view of the front of the house. With the tinted windows in the Escape, he wasn't likely to be noticed. He snapped pictures of the two people who came to the house for a brief visit, a couple in their twenties. Another shot of a blond woman looking out the window.

If this turned into a long-term project, it could burn lots of his time. Back at the office, he asked Melanie to get in touch with one of his old friends, who might like a few shifts watching the house and its visitors.

# CHAPTER 15

## CLEM

A month now, since that little Satan chomped Clem's leg. That viper may have been pint-sized, but it had really put him down! He was getting back a little energy, but he still felt his heartbeat pounding in his right foot as he tried to sleep at night. The toes itched, the heel of his foot too tender for much walking ... and those shooting pains—damn.

He wanted to get after the bitch, Arlene, and the sneaky, snaky, slimy Elton Snivel. He needed Maynard back!

But, as the Good Lord would prefer, one must commit to business before pleasure.

Days before the snakebites, Clem had secured a contract for his expanded business; he was going to make some juicy movies. He'd borrowed $50,000 against his house, rented space in an old movie studio in Riverside and hired a contractor. Pretty damned fast work, which was just what the contract required. The delay from his *infirmity* had put him behind the eight ball.

The contractor, a guy named Harry Duberry, swore over the phone that everything was looking good.

Maybe.

Clem drove to the studio, took a minute to gather himself, eased out of the Four-by-Four and ran his hand over his light blue shirt and down his chinos—business attire, nice and neat. He grabbed the pole he'd been using as a cane. No, damn it. He had to walk in like the boss. No cane. No excuses. No rural preacher twang. No bullshit. He drew in a breath, telling his leg to get with the program.

Taking the five steps to the studio door, sent pain shooting up from his ankle. He ignored it, flung the door open, and made his way through the empty hallway, to his new set, a 1,000 square foot simulated classroom.

As promised, Duberry was waiting, sitting in the teacher's chair behind a metal desk, a computer, boxes of pencils and crayons, pads of drawing paper and lined sheets there on top—fine.

Duberry stood, extending his hand. Clem took in his yellow polo shirt—*yellow!* —with the little kangaroo-y thing on the chest, the guy's scraggly goatee and phony smile, as he shook hands.

Over Duberry's shoulder, Clem saw the greenboard, with a few three-letter words printed in yellow chalk—nice touch. Above, as expected, stretched the foot-high panel with the printed alphabet. Good; a perfect elementary school, lower grades. The bulletin board was bare, but they could dress it up with a little computer conjuring.

Turning toward the opposite wall. *Shit.* The metal framing for three eight-foot-wide *windows* was in place, but behind them, only naked dry wall, dangling wires, power sockets.

Clem jabbed a finger toward the vacant framing. "What gives, Duberry?"

The contractor shrugged and made a face. "Screens got held up."

"You told me they'd be in *four days ago. Four, damn it.* The computer guy can't start work till he's got his props." The computer geek's name was Dusty. Running behind schedule had a cost. Clem was paying Dusty 100 bucks a day, just to be available.

Another shrug, this time with Duberry's hands off to his sides, palms up. "I got no control over them. You're the dude who ordered those screens."

Clem had put a rush on those and paid the price—high-definition equipment, like they use for sets on the evening news. When they were filming, the screens would become *windows*, revealing a playground with kids racing around, maybe a school bus waiting for classes to end—anything Clem asked the computer guy to put up on them.

"You should have let me know," Clem said, suppressing the urge to take the Lord's name in vain. "Find out what's going on, get the numbskulls moving, and *call* me. *Today*."

"Maybe better if you—"

Clem glared at the contractor. "I'm trying to stay professional, Duberry, but you're pushing me past my limits." Then he noticed the chairs—thirty of them. *Damn it.* He walked over, picked one up, and turned on DuBerry. "Too big. I told you we need seats that fit seven-year-old butts."

Duberry twisted his mouth like he was screwing up his courage, and said, "We were lucky to get these. Every school in America is ordering them."

"But, what—" Clem dropped the chair, and it crash landed. He'd been too damned easy on this guy. "Get the flippin' screens in. Get them hooked up and call me." He turned and charged outside, ankle killing him all the way.

Back in the truck, Clem tossed down a couple of ibuprofen and gulped half a bottle of water. He sat for five minutes, willing his leg to stop throbbing. Then he drove to San Bernardino to meet a guy about a snake.

He'd found the ad on the dark web—one huge mother of a diamondback. Not a replacement for Maynard—never could be—but a stand-in. He found the address, got out of the truck, and removed the snake box from the back—Dobie's box, carved with a portrait of the Lord preaching on one side and the words, *Blessed is He* painted on the other.

He paid a sleezy-looking woman with a missing front tooth and a fake diamond on her finger, $500. She introduced him to the new snake. A good-looking specimen, it struck its cage a couple of times, trying to get at Clem. He hummed to the snake and swayed his head back and forth. The snake calmed down. Clem reached in, brought the serpent up to eye level to give it a good look, and slipped it into Dobie's box.

On the way up the mountain, he decided to call the new rattler *Herbert*, like Herbert Hoover, not a great president, but a fine moniker for a serpent. Back home, he slept for a whole day. There was no word from Harry Duberry, so Clem began his internet search. He found no trace of Arlene or Slimy Elton Snivel—not that he'd expected to. He typed in *California Detective Agencies*. Flipping from one agency to another on the Web, he came across an article from a magazine called *Bizarro for Real* about a sleuth who'd tracked down a missing preaching team. Clem's wife, Arlene, had been part of a preaching team, if you gave her more credit than due. The unconventional pair of preachers, located by this detective, had been gone for twenty years, so Arlene couldn't be much of a problem.

*God damn it, Arlene; you have interfered with our divine work. "Retribution is mine, sayeth the Lord." But retribution shall be had, on earth as it is in heaven.*

"Sorry for that thought, Lord." Clem needed to pray more and forgive her trespasses, but Arlene had twisted his thoughts in a horrible tangle.

Next step—hire that detective to find his precious ones.

# CHAPTER 16

## SVETA

One of Sveta's friends at the clinic where she worked, a younger woman named Nadia, often confided about her sorrows. Maybe she saw Sveta as an older, more experienced woman, or just another single woman in a job that didn't pay enough in a country where people drowned their hopelessness in vodka and perfumed it in cigarette smoke. Nadia had done something about her loneliness. She'd contacted a company called *Russian Brides Unlimited*. Next week, she was going to a conference center outside St Petersburg to meet American and British bachelors.

"Here, I have pictures," Nadia said. She slipped her cell phone out of her back pocket and displayed a few good-looking guys. At first Sveta thought it was silly ... something for a younger woman ... immature ...

Then Sveta thought about her own unhappy life and remembered her Babushka's message: *You've always been a creative girl. Do something special to change your life.*

That evening Sveta looked up *Russian Brides Unlimited—RBU*—on the internet. The standard net that all the Russians used was silent, so Sveta activated her Virtual Private Network. The

Russian authorities warned against using a VPN, but it was the only place to find genuine news from the outside world. – A tool she'd discovered while engaged in "subversive activities," as the government deemed them.

She found the American website for *RBU*. Dozens of beautiful young women smiled at her from the screen in evocative photos, designed to lure red-blooded men to Russia for dates! All so very young. So immodest!

"They'd never take me," Sveta told her friend. "They want babies. They want you."

The next day, Nadia fell, stepping off a bus and broke her left arm. She called *RBU* and told them about her beautiful friend, Sveta. "More mature and more lovely than any of the others," she swore. After some convincing, Sveta emailed *RBU* a picture of herself. To her amazement, they approved.

# CHAPTER 17

## BUD

Of course, Stan thought he was nuts. He didn't say so, but he was Stan, conventional and cheap as Scrooge. No matter, it was Bud's money, and he damned well needed a fling. Needed so much more than that.

He flew into St. Petersburg on a Sunday afternoon—masked all the way! A tough-looking blond guy waited by the luggage carousel with a sign for *Russian Brides Unlimited*. The dude wore a blue blazer and white turtleneck, thick gold chains around his neck. He shook Bud's hand and said, "I yam Boris." His accent reminded Bud of an old horror movie. "Wait with these men," he said. Some other middle-aged guys lingered off to the side. Once Boris gathered a few more, he led them to the parking lot. They re-applied their Covid masks and climbed into two modern passenger vans.

A half hour later, they came into a puny town. Boris got on the PA and announced some crazy Russian name for the place. There were a few larger buildings—one with white pillars in front; a shabbier one, gray stucco with a dozen people lined up outside. Other buildings, blue or white with stone foundations, peeling paint and loose boards. They passed an obelisk and an old army tank and sped up as they left town. Bud spotted a dozen bare wood houses set back in the forest before they slowed to pass through a gate.

"Here," Boris said. "Conference center." As they climbed out, Bud spotted three gray block buildings, like an old, abandoned factory complex, surrounded by lawns and forest.

Dark clouds scudded overhead. Boris gathered them on the lawn and grinned, which is when Bud spotted his gold tooth. With his accent, the looming storm and the shabby industrial buildings, Bud could picture Herr Frankenstein ambling out to inquire if Bud wouldn't mind giving up a leg for science or Boris ogling his neck and saying, "I vant to drink your blood." Their host gestured to the buildings. "Two dormitories. Big building has fancy rooms, where you meet pretty girls. To-mor-row. You must wait until then. Ha. Ha."

Another bus full of *studs* unloaded later, Americans and a few Brits.

Boris announced, "You virile men are lucky. You live luxurious way, each with own room. Women, stacked like dead fish in closet."

He gave the men a quick tour through the three "conference rooms," each like a high school cafeteria back in the States, with a dozen white plastic tables spread around. Not the romantic fantasy Bud had conjured. (Cozy, dark suites, with sofas, champagne, hors d'oeuvres. Mood music playing; a choice of women who smelled like lilacs and looked like Anna from the ad.)

Boris shouted. "You meet first girls tomorrow. Each of you handsome men have date with some girls. You like them, wonderful! You meet many chicks, all beautiful, like we promise. Many. Beautiful. Women. You, lucky fellas." He looked from man to man. "These women may like you. Might love you, but they do not belong you. They belong Boris." He jabbed a thumb toward his chest.

Boris laughed like that was really damned funny. "Each girl promise to meet other men too. Your weekend next will be free. Your nights after dinner free—the girls too. Maybe you go to town for a party, yes?" Another guffaw. "You have plenty time with each beautiful woman. You share a breakfast, a lunch, a dinner … more time after that if you like. We have nice lawn and benches outside, bar for to drink—not too expensive. Music in evening."

Boris sat Bud down after that. He shook his head, regretful. "You choose five women that we send you information for dates, Mr. Randolph."

Bud nodded. What was Boris up to?

"First three women here now." The blond man shook his head.

"Yeah, so—"

Boris held up his hand. "One of your women not call back. Maybe she found man to shack up. Maybe she sent Siberia. Ha. Ha." He flashed a smile, showing off that gold tooth. "We give you four out of five. Number four she say will come Thursday. We will see. You not worry, Mr. Randolph; *Russian Brides Unlimited* find you other amazing girls to dine you with every day."

He'd get to meet three of his picks, maybe four. Bud glared. Was Boris pulling a fast one? Were two of his five choices fake?

"You have three tomorrow, Monday, that we promise. I give you other girls, most special. Tuesday, you have breakfast, lunch, dinner with them. You like them very much."

What choice did he have? Bud told himself that things would work out. Boris would find great women for him.

The Russian took a breath, looking like he might spit. "That girl who not come; she loser. Not woman for you. Not beautiful. I find you better."

"Bud wanted to spit too, but he held back. "All right. I'm trusting you."

He lay in bed that night trying to remember the Russian words he'd learned: *Spasiba*—was that *goodbye*? No *thanks*. *Das vidanya*—*goodbye*. *Skolko eto stoit*—that sounded dirty, but he knew it meant *how much does it cost*, because the *eto* in the middle sounded almost like *it*. How the hell did you say, "You have pretty eyes?" So many of the words had flown out of Bud's thick head after he thought he knew them.

Fuck it. What was he doing there, anyway?

# CHAPTER 18

## BUD

Monday morning the *girls*—most in low-cut dresses and wrapped tight in shimmery leggings—strolled past them, offering sexy leers and hip wiggles. Lots of good-looking babes. Blatant girly factory!

He had breakfast that day with Mila, lunch with Lila, dinner with Milina. How the hell would he keep those three straight? All three were made up and dressed in their finest, looking almost as good as the pictures they'd sent. But …

Mila (or had it been Lila?), the blonde, asked about his life in America over ham and thin little pancakes with orange jam. They strolled outside after breakfast and settled on a bench. She offered to show him St. Petersburg—all the wonderful stores they had there! She snuggled against him and said it would freeze soon. Maybe Bud could help her decide on a new winter coat. "That be very much fun," she said.

The books about Russian brides warned about women who'd spend your dough and then run home to Moscow or wherever, leaving a fella with the credit card bills.

Lila (Mila?), his lunch date, brunette, barely spoke English. She served him salad with smoked salmon. They struggled through lunch and went their separate ways.

In their profiles, the women sounded like wholesome, English-speaking beauties, not greedy for money, interested in a relationship. What a load of crap! Every time Bud spotted Boris, the Russian wore his shit-eating, golden grin and nodded vigorously.

His *dinner date*, Milina—a third-grade teacher—offered him a pretty obvious chance to screw. After dessert, she reached across the table to remove his plate, revealing a tantalizing panorama of cleavage, packaged in red lacy underwear. She leaned forward again, stroking Bud's wrist, lingering, as she mentioned a place in town they could go for a drink. Young and attractive, but not so interesting. Maybe it was Bud. He was annoyed and disappointed after the other two, and put off by Boris's fake machismo—feeling totally off his game.

Why not go with Milina, damn it? What was wrong with him? He kissed her on the cheek and made excuses and then bought a few mini gins—like the ones on airplanes—and a can of tonic water ($80 US) at the bar and sat outside on a bench in the dusk, sipping until he mellowed out.

That night in bed, his brain pacified by gin, he regretted not taking Milina up on her offer. By Tuesday morning, he was glad. After sex, Milina might want to hang out for the rest of his week, hoping to reel him—and his American money—in. Wasn't this the purpose for them? Either spend his money here in Russia or seduce him for a free pass to a better life in America.

In a way, he wanted that too. In another way, he wanted to tell Boris to shove this BS up his ass.

He'd paid good money to come here, not for an easy lay, not to take a pretty woman home when he didn't like her that much. All of a sudden, after years of thoughtless, absurd bachelor recklessness, he wanted what Stan had found; not just boobs and someone to pick up his plate after dinner. He wanted Character with a capital C. (*Character! Him?*)

Stan was his business partner, his best friend and sometimes confidante. They'd fallen out over Trump, their great ex—and still rightful—president. Stan hated Trump and thought his claim to the presidency was bull shit. To keep the peace, Stan and Bud had mostly avoided the subject for that year. Mostly.

Before Trump came along, Stan had given Bud advice about all sorts of stuff. Over beers at Clancy's, he'd claim that if Bud just went after sex, he'd have nothing in the end. Bud laughed that off with the old "Look who's talking," line, until Mel came along, and Stan proposed to her.

Bud's six-month stint in the matrimonial world with Alice had been no advertisement for marital bliss. She bled his bank account on drinking binges and shopping sprees with her girlfriends. That was the past. There had to be someone better out there.

When Bud confided in Stan, his good buddy asked, "Did you marry her because you had lots in common or because you couldn't keep your hands off her?" Stan could sure piss a guy off.

Bud never got the point until he lived to almost forty and thought about … stuff. (And until he saw the way Stan and Mel *sparkled* together. Another surprising word that would never have come out of Bud's mouth.)

# CHAPTER 19

## BUD

Tuesday, his second *dating day*, another breakfast, this time with a woman selected by Boris. He sat at his assigned table, number 5, near the side entrance, not expecting much.

He didn't see her until she swooped in from behind with a carafe and sloshed coffee into his cup. She spilled a little and laughed. "A *boo boo*; is that what you say?"

He looked up and had to grin. This woman had a terrific smile, not like she wanted to seduce him; like she was a little embarrassed and wanted him to like her. (Again, what was going on with him?)

She slipped into the chair opposite. She wore a button-down white blouse with something embroidered on the breast—a little green-and-yellow turtle. Her name tag said "Sveta." He'd noticed her the first day, older than most. Not all made up and low cut. The brochures had promised that all the women were at least eighteen, some twenty-five, a couple *more mature*. Sveta was probably the oldest—north of thirty, no doubt.

They sipped coffee at the table. Her brown hair flowed down to her shoulders, glistening. She smiled shyly. "I am Sveta."

"I see." He pointed at her name tag. "I'm Bud from California."

"You hungry, Bud from California?"

She was good to look at; he didn't want to give her up so soon. "Not yet. Boris didn't tell me about you."

"I not much to tell. What you like know — like *to* know — Mr. Bud?"

He chuckled. "Where you live; what you do for a living ..."

"I live train trip east from Moscow in small town, Yerunda. Physician assistant. I do what doctor not want do. Take blood pressure, run X-ray machine, ultra-sound ... clean up. You need someone weigh you; that is me. Take twenty milliliters your blood and send to laboratory—also me."

They talked for a few minutes. She told him about one of the bossy doctors at her clinic. Bud tried to make *private detective* sound important.

She frowned at him. "Spy on people; you mean like KGB?"

He laughed. "More like Eddie Murphy." He could see she didn't get that. "My friend and I; we mostly find stray dogs and cats."

She gave him another sweet smile. "Meow. I stray cat. I bring you food, Cal-ee-for-nee-a man."

Bud had let Mila or Lila (whichever?) serve him breakfast the day before, but now that didn't seem like the right thing. "I'll go with you."

Sveta inclined her head toward the buffet. "We women, they tell us; we serve you."

"Baloney," Bud said and pushed back his chair.

She shook her head, frowning. "I do it. We don't want *piss off* Boris. That expression, no? *Piss off*? I study English."

"A damn good expression, Sveta." Bud glanced at the buffet line. Only Russian women there. All the guys were at their tables, smug with their cups of coffee. "Okay, fill my plate with every kind of meat and eggs you find."

"No bread?"

"Potatoes if you insist."

She brought back a large plate with scrambled eggs, three kinds of sausage, ham, and lots of bacon. (What, no eggs Benedict?)

A minute later, she was back with yogurt, cheese, rye bread, and fruit for herself.

Sveta and Bud were allotted breakfast, which gave them until noon. They'd each have another partner for lunch. Boris had laid out the rules; some dates lasted only through the meal. But, if couples wanted, they could linger until the next mealtime, maybe go outside and find benches on the grounds. Roaming waiters out there would serve coffee, iced tea and lemonade.

Sveta cut her fruit into small pieces, speared each gracefully. She watched him as she chewed. Her face wasn't perfect, not like Anna in the ad. Her eyes were just a touch wider, chin a bit narrow, lower lip pouty– Slavic influence, maybe. Her skin was pale with a little pink blush dusted on. She had high cheekbones, which he liked. She smiled into his eyes in a way that was a little seductive, but mostly friendly. Not over the top, like Milina. Modest; collar bones covered.

Her eyes were hazel. That light brown hair, *Miss Clairol-insky*, he thought.

Her English was a little slow sometimes, with a flourish of accent, but good. "My mother Russian. My father from Ukraine," she said.

Bud liked the way she pronounced the names of the countries. He knew, but asked anyway; "Where's that?"

"South." She gestured off to one side. She lowered her voice and leaned closer across the table. "Not part of Russia (*Roo see ya*). We were together during U S S R. Not no more. *Not anymore, is it?*"

"*Not anymore*, right."

She gave a sly smile. "So, Mr. Bud, from California (*Cal ee for nya*), you tell me; you do drive a big convertible automobile?"

He laughed. This gal had spunk. "I'll drive one if you come visit me." No problem, Bud had 200K minus the 10K spent for the five days here.

Sveta. That was the first bold question his soon-to-be girlfriend asked him that day.

*Girlfriend*—also not a phrase he thought he'd use any time soon.

The question made him wonder if she was another one of those money-grabbing women, but her teasing eyes said otherwise.

"A Cadillac?" (Cad-ee-lac) she asked.

"Mercedes, okay?"

Bud thought back to that Ukrainian connection; Trump's first impeachment had been around something in Ukraine. Trump supposedly withholding defense money from them—Democratic bullshit. Witch Hunt!

Russia had taken territory from Ukraine a few years back … There was fighting in the east part of the country.

Politicians on Fox News, one of the anchors too, talked about how the US had no business arming Ukraine. Ukraine wasn't a real country, so Russia taking part of it back in 2014—that was the year—no big deal. America shouldn't be protecting the whole friggin' world! That was Trump's take on it, too. MAGA *uber alles*.

Bud made himself calm down, pay attention to her. Not sure what Sveta had just said, he asked, "You ever visit your father's homeland?"

"Yes. Very nice there."

He reached over and touched her hand. "What's a nice girl with a Ukrainian father doing here in Russia?"

She gave a little chuckle. "Looking for you, Mr. Bud. Of course."

He smiled back at her. "What's nice about Ukraine?"

"We go outside now," Sveta said. "Okay?"

"Sure."

"Wait here, one minute." She got up and took their plates to the counter.

They walked out. She linked her arm in Bud's, as they followed a sidewalk toward the forest and stopped to sit on a bench.

She looked around like she was making sure they were alone. "Ukraine much more freedom than here. More Western. Not worry so much what you say."

"You have men here in Russia and men in Ukraine. Why come for this nonsense?"

She blew out a breath. "You have women in Amerika. Why then you here?" She gave him a shy smile. "Russian men, they not drive Cadillacs, Mr. Bud." A breeze tousled her hair. Sveta whisked it off her face. "Men here smoke like burning tire. Drink very much. I know this; I live with my sister and her husband."

Interesting; he'd read about Russians; semi-professional people, like Sveta, even teachers, who didn't make enough to get their own apartments, and here she was, a living example.

"Russian men not appreciate their women. Russian men not take me to Amerika. You have freedom there, no?"

Obvious, wasn't she? Which meant: not devious. He liked her, and the wide set of her eyes was growing on him. He didn't say a word about American women being spoiled—*woke*, as he soaked in her mix of serious and playful.

Bud told her more about Stan and their private detective agency—what they really did, looking for worker's comp scammers. He filled her in on their most fascinating caper. Back during the 2020 election, they'd worked a missing person's case. Bud had followed the missing guy to New Mexico, getting drugged and dumped down an old mineshaft. "And the amazing thing—" he told Sveta— "down in that pit, the guy had stashed his mother." Sveta's eyes went wide, as she watched Bud. "And she ... that's enough I think I'm boring you."

"No, no, Mr. Bud. You must tell everything."

So, he told Sveta more about that amazing case, about the elusive faith-healers, Sarah and Jeff Lamb, mother and son. Being doped and waking up down in that mine pit with Sarah, deciding that she was a crazy fanatic Christian, but she also shared his admiration for Donald Trump. Sarah and Jeff had been so famous that the case was featured in a tabloid magazine called *Bizarro for Real*.

Sveta covered her mouth with her hand, laughing as Bud embellished the story. "You are on magazine. You famous fellow."

Her simple pleasure charmed him. She made him feel ... comfortable.

They walked the grounds of the center and a little way along the road. Coming back, he nodded toward the building. "I guess you'll meet another guy for lunch."

"I think yes."

"Another date for dinner?"

"That is way it works, Mr. Bud."

"If you and I asked them, could we do dinner and maybe have drinks?"

Her eyes narrowed. Little wrinkles fanned out beside them as she smiled really wide—made him want to hug her. "Yes. You ask Mr. Boris. I ask too."

Boris rearranged a few things so they could share dinner. Maybe he wasn't such a prick.

As he sat down to dinner with her, Bud said, "I'm having fun, Sveta. How do you feel about another breakfast?"

"Breakfast good meal to have." She eyed him. "With you?"

"No, with Vladimir Putin."

She grimaced. "Better you; okay?"

So, she didn't like Putin. Maybe she didn't understand how he and Trump had the same aims; to strengthen their countries. America First. Russia First. No politically correct crud. No catering to the so-called *disadvantaged* or sexually deviant and *misunderstood*. *Diversity* was a sham. Putin and Trump called it out.

# CHAPTER 20

## STAN

Melanie was taking a bite of the French cruller with chocolate frosting Stan had brought her for breakfast. The office phone rang. She held up her sticky fingers and shook her head. Stan answered.

"Hey S. Stein, I'm Reverend Clem Dudas from the Free Spirit of our Lord Sanctuary." The guy had a booming male voice, with a southern accent. "I have a need, and I suspect you have the abilities I require."

"Yes, well—"

"Bud Randolph, he works there?"

"Sure, and—"

"You and your partner, is it? —this Bud fella—I learned about you two on the internet. You went huntin' Reverend Jeff Lamb and his mama, Reverend Sarah, last year and you found them in New Mexico, correct?"

"We did."

"So, you're good at finding people and things. Might be the right fellas for my job."

"Good," Stan said. "And what—"

"Ol' Jeff and Sarah, they had a different worship," Dudas said. "I respect that. Like Jeff and his mama, I'm not your ordinary preacher-man." The guy guffawed and Stan pulled the phone a few inches away to save his hearing. "I figured, you deal with Jeff Lamb, you might help me with my issue."

Stan wasn't getting a word in edge-wise. Frustrated, he picked up a pen and tossed it back onto his desk. Outside the window, he saw a crow on a tree limb, observing with beady eyes. "Are you saying someone is missing from your ... Sanctuary?"

"We have missing persons, but that's not the whole thing, not even the bulkiest bulk of it."

Stan waited, figuring the *Reverend* would keep going.

"We're up here near Hemet, and you're down in Santa Monica, right? You need ta come up here, you and your Bud Randolph."

"Bud's out of the country. If you can visit the office, and explain—"

"I want Bud Randolph, the famous preacher hunter. You come too. You're the head of that detective domicile, right? You know; two heads better'n one."

Stan took a breath, putting two and two together. Bud, Melanie and Stan had solved a case back in November 2020. Jeff Lamb and his mother, Sarah, had been faith healers back in the '90s. Jeff had disappeared and come back under an alias. He disappeared again in 2020. The team tracked him to New Mexico. Bud had gone to find him, and Jeff had captured Bud and stowed him and Jeff's mother down an old mineshaft.

The case became sort of famous. Bud and Sarah Lamb appeared on a magazine cover. So now Reverend Dudas wanted Bud, the famous crazy preacher hunter. Bud would go ballistic for a case like this.

"When he gonna be back?" Dudas asked.

"Next Tuesday. Can you tell me about your situation?"

"You ain't going to believe it, Mr. Stein. Better you and your partner, you come here to me. I'll pay you for the time and gasoline. If I like what you say, I'll pay the going rate plus ten percent for your work."

Yes!

Stan took down the phone number and location. He gave the Rev the bank numbers to transfer the fees for their first day of work. Stan hung up just as Melanie walked in.

"What was that about?" she asked.

"Not sure. The guy didn't give me much to go on, but he's ready to pay up."

He Googled *Free Spirit of our Lord Sanctuary* and his eyes went wide. Stan almost never swore, but he turned to Melanie, his assistant, and fiancé, and he said, "Holy shit."

# CHAPTER 21

## BUD

Sveta and Bud held hands as they approached Boris. He watched them come and offered seats at a table, listened to their request, and gave Bud a sarcastic frown. "I tell you rules, first day. These women come to meet men. Sveta has appointment tomorrow to meet new guy. You have woman come see you Thursday. They expect you. You must share Sveta. She is as a queen, no?"

Boris turned to Sveta, who looked embarrassed. "Ты красивая женщина. Вы должны дать шанс другим мужчинам." (You pretty woman. Other men want chance.)

"Hey, man," Bud blurted. "We're liking each other. Maybe we'll want to get hitched. That's the purpose here, right?" (Bud shocking himself.)

Sveta gave Bud a wide-eyed head shake, which made him realize he might be pushing Boris too hard.

Boris cleared his throat. "Rules, Mr. Randolph. I have rules to be with."

Bud's blood was steaming, but Sveta's nervous eyes held him back. He took a breath, thinking, *This is Russia, not California. Don't get her in trouble.* He lowered his voice. "Good publicity for your program, Boris. Sveta and I could pose for a picture, all dressed up like a wedding. Show people back in the USA that even an ugly guy like me can find a beautiful woman."

Sveta laid her hand on Bud's wrist. "Yes, good," she said. "I tell friends in my town, come work for Boris, find good man."

Boris shook his head, patient but annoyed. "Here's what. I try to please all you pushy Americans, even you, Mr. Randolph. I give you one meal together every day. Maybe two, but don't expect."

Bud gritted his teeth. Sveta squeezed his arm, looking happy with the deal.

Boris held up his hand. "Maybe she get tired of you, she not like you tomorrow, if see you too much." He grinned to show it was a joke. "You know what they say in America, 'Absence make heart like you better.' If you eat lunch with different someone, Sveta miss you by dinner."

"Weekend," Sveta said.

They both looked at her.

"Weekend, no bride making." She glanced at Bud and then Boris.

"Weekend, women stay in dormitory, get ready for next week, more men. These men, like Bud, leave. You let my Bud stay two extra day then?"

*My Bud.* That took his breath away.

He'd paid for five nights at the center. Then he had three days before his flight home, thinking he'd get a hotel in St. Petersburg.

"Men's building empty," she said. "You give Mr. Bud room?" She looked hopefully at Bud. "If you still want see me."

Bud offered a small bribe in dollars, and Boris agreed.

They spent those days sharing one or two blah meals a day in the conference center, but that was okay. It was great. In between she "dated" other men. Bud ate with the woman he'd arranged before the trip on Thursday, and a few others.

He and Sveta walked into town Wednesday night and went to a movie—all in Russian—snuggling close together. He had lunch with her on Thursday but didn't see her at dinner, which meant she was eating with some dude in another "conference room."

Afterwards she walked with Bud to a bar in town. Sipping vodka, sitting out on the porch, she said, "Man I eat dinner with, he ask party with me tonight."

Bud sipped, a little nervous at the idea, but staying cool. Straight vodka wasn't bad in small dribbles. "I'm glad you're here with me."

"I tell him have date with you." She took Bud's hand under the table. "He want eat with me again tomorrow. He will ask Boris."

Bud's gut clenched. "You want to see him again? Which one is he?"

She shook her head, watching Bud. "Tall man, blue shirt, belly like this." She puffed out her cheeks and arced a hand in front of her tummy. "Name Douglas. I not want to, but Boris have rules. Maybe he …"

Bud downed the shot, which scorched enough to please him. "I'll set Boris straight."

"No, Bud dear. If Boris want, I have lunch with him. Tell him, thank you for nice time. Now go away."

Bud had to defer to Sveta's judgement in dealing with Boris. She knew Russia, and understood the rules. He wouldn't get her in trouble.

But there was no reason he couldn't have a heart-to-heart with blue-shirted Douglas.

After another double shot of vodka, he walked Sveti back to her dorm. The night attendant told him where to find *Dougie*. A damned big guy, tall and fifty pounds overweight, answered Bud's knock. He loomed in the doorway, wearing only jockey shorts. Not a pretty sight. "Yeah."

Big didn't worry Bud, not with a few shots under his belt and a future with Sveti at stake. (Future!?)

Bud glared, "You had dinner with Svetlana tonight?"

Douglas snorted. "Was that her name?" He slurred a little, drunk as a skunk.

"You told her you wanted to see her again," Bud said.

"I say that to all of them. What's your line? I got laid three times this week. Four if you count what's going to happen after you fuck off."

Bud calmed a little. Dougie wasn't sounding like a prime challenger for Sveti's affections.

"I didn't need that icy bitch, whatever her name is." The big guy swung the door wide and Bud saw one of the Russian women lying in the guy's bed. She offered a cute little wave.

Bud registered the woman and the word *bitch* at the same moment. "What did you call her?"

The guy held up his hands. "Don't go all Rambo on me. Take that cold bitch and welcome to her." He backed up a step, watching Bud, suddenly wary.

As his fist clenched, Bud flashed on the time he'd punched a guy in the jaw; bruised his knuckles pretty bad. Instead, he jabbed hard into Dougie's flabby gut.

The dude pitched forward like one of those drinking-bird toys. "Shit," Dougie screamed, keeping his balance and hobbling to his bathroom. Gratifying retching noises issued forth.

The woman in the bed smirked at Bud, as he made his exit, wishing he could remember the Russian for "Have a pleasant evening."

He thought it over later. After knowing Sveti for only three days, he was acting possessive, jealous. Vulnerable. How could this happen so fast? But hadn't he traveled this far to find a woman who could make him care?

He'd fought for his girlfriend's honor, right? (Lancelot of the gut punch.) But now he worried. Sveti would be upset if she found out. She might have second thoughts about him.

FRIDAY, SVETA AND BUD ate all three meals together. (No mention of Douglas.) That evening, they sat in the local church—dim, smoky with incense, decorated with gold-haloed portraits.

On their walk back to the conference center each night, they consumed chocolates they'd bought in town and kissed, every night more exciting.

Sweet. Bud didn't think he'd ever met a woman so sweet. She charmed him with stories about her mother and sisters, her grandmother and great-grandmother, "the saint of our little town." She talked about going back to her regular job in two weeks, working with the doctors, taking blood pressure and temperature, filling out medical forms, all for little pay. Going back to living at her sister's apartment with her repulsive brother-in-law.

Bud baffled her with tales of his detective work (some true, some almost true). He talked about working with some great friends at that GM factory in Georgia until it closed down. Then about growing up with his big sister Betty, who was so damned good in school that Bud had no choice but to become a class cut-up. (Also, more fun.)

Betty had flipped back then; from straight A high school student to junior year college dropout. She ran off to India with a psychology teaching assistant and slinked home pregnant. Bud's mom hounded him into cutting back his junior college classes to care for the baby. That allowed Betty (the daughter with so much potential) to finish her BA. (Hard to explain the way Bud had caved to his mother back then, especially when it involved changing shitty diapers.)

Bud finished his AA degree and joined the Army. Betty became a manager at a mutual fund company. Smart, wealthy, but without a crumb of sense.

Sveta told him about the hardships of growing up on a farm in rural Russia and about her devotion to the Russian Orthodox Church. He refrained from arguing on behalf of the divine, unknowable enigma.

On Saturday they got a ride into St. Petersburg—thank you, Boris. Bud paid for a private city tour. A couple of hours at the Hermitage was enough time staring at paintings, glittery chandeliers, and mirrors. They strolled the fancy Nevsky Prospekt, admiring the clothing and Russian ornaments in the store windows, but she never suggested they go inside. (Made Bud trust her more.)

They even attended church that Sunday—all smoky incense and spooky foreign chanting—fascinating for a guy like Bud who got off on weird culty-things. After church, their new friend Boris provided a picnic lunch for them. Sveta and Bud caught a bus to a park by the Neva River. They wandered far along the path and settled on a blanket.

After lunch, they lay, holding hands, looking up at the clouds drifting. "Beautiful day," she said.

"Beautiful, being with you."

Little birds flitted from tree to tree, reminding Bud of that internet theory about bird drones, spying for the government. Maybe that wasn't so far-fetched here in Russia. He gave one the finger but didn't mention the idea to Sveta.

"Are you a traditional woman?" he asked.

"What woman?"

"Traditional—they say that in the ads for Russian brides. You know, women who cook for their man, do what their man asks, don't complain."

She rolled onto her side and scrutinized him. "What you want, Mr. Bud? Robot woman. That word, *robot*?"

"You don't seem very traditional," he said.

"Russian man want servant wife; pour him vodka ... light cigarette. Like my sister, my mother. Put up with bull sheet. If you want servant, you not man I want to know."

Her intensity surprised him. "Easy, Sveta. I didn't say that." He reached over and stroked her hair.

She took a breath, still scrutinizing him. "Some tradition and some modern woman; that what I am." She pressed in close, her chest against his arm, her thigh to his thigh, Bud's excitement kicking up. She kissed his cheek and propped herself on an elbow to look at him, ran her hand across his chest. "You want cook maid, or you want me?"

"I'll take you, Sveta, just the way you are."

After another minute she said, "I like you, Mr. Bud. I hope you like me."

He kissed her hand. "Definitely."

She looked him over. "You have something in your pants. One of the birds; it fly in there?"

He laughed. "*Holy cow*—that's an expression for you."

"*Holy cow?*" Still eying his body, she said. "Or big roll of American money, yes?"

Laughing again— "You think I'm too old to get one of these?"

She still stroked his chest. "You not old, Mr. Bud. You strong, good shape. You lift barbell, I think."

"Never."

She leaned over him, her face inches away. "I lie beside you, and you like, yes?" Bud nodded, and she said, "I want you like me, but not want you think I like those other girls. Not be … what is word?"

He shook his head.

"Not want you think I am whore."

Was she offering herself to him or telling him she didn't intend to? "I think you're delightful." (Didn't sound like him speaking.) "You are good and modest."

"*Modest*, what that?"

"Not showing too much of yourself."

She chuckled. "For you, could be I show a little." She saw his reaction and said, "But you not go crazy nuts, right?"

In the old days, people thought Bud was wild. His buddies then, the guys at the GM factory, would have been surprised that he hadn't visited a hooker now and then. He never had. Now, in these new days, he wouldn't want anyone to think that about him. The new days had kicked in pretty damned recently, which had a lot to do with Mel and Stan and their sweet romance.

Sveta stood and stretched. "I take blanket?" she asked.

"Sure." At that point, she could have borrowed anything Bud owned. (It was Boris's blanket, anyway.)

She walked back into the forest, and he heard her call, "My man, Bud. Come to me."

When he walked back among the trees, he found her lying on the blanket. She'd taken off her bra and replaced her pink blouse. She beckoned with a finger. "More private back here. You like make out a little? That word, yes; *make out?*"

Bud took a moment to admire her, before lying down and wrapping his arms around her.

"Not go crazy," she said. She cupped his cheek in her hand and added. "I want go crazy, but I not whore. We not go crazy. Okay?"

"Anything you ask is okay, darling Sveti." It was true; anything. *Darling.* He was savoring this moment, her lovely face, even the breeze flowing through the trees overhead. What was happening to him?

Bud ran his hands over her back and down to her butt, pressing against her.

She pulled back a few inches, gazed into his eyes. "You control the man crazy in you, yes? Even if he make your pants big bump like roll of thousand dollar money."

She slid his hand onto her breast, kissed him deep and long. "We stay dressed today. You touch me on top. You enjoy?"

"Hell yes."

She patted his cheek. "You go home. In U S, you remember; then come back Russia, see me again."

He was about to say yes when she sat up, wide-eyed. "Wait! How long your visa to Russia?"

"The visa has another week. My plane leaves tomorrow."

She gave him a mischievous grin. "You can change plane?"

He liked where she was heading. "Absolutely." Bud's heart hammered. He sat up and kissed her. "Haven't you promised Boris another week?"

"Pook Boris. Boris not my father. Boris just dumb guy. I lose money; that all he can do to me."

Bud figured she was trying to say *fuck*, but missed the mark.

She gave him an uncertain glance. "Swearing okay? They tell us not swear with you men."

He kissed her again, longer this time. "Swearing is great."

"I have place I want you see," she said.

"Where?"

"We take train. You come, meet my mother and grandmother."

Funny. Bud was sure she'd told him her mom died.

# CHAPTER 22

## STAN

S tan and Melanie were at their computers on Monday morning when the call came in. Caller ID: ANDREW RANDOLPH.

Both picked up at the same time.

"Hey, pal," Stan said. "You back in the US?"

"Nope. Russia. I'm hanging here another week."

Stan looked at the office door in case Bud was spoofing them and calling from just outside. "Really?"

"Hey, Bud, I'm here too," Melanie said. "Had any good dates?"

"Damned right. My new girlfriend asked me to linger awhile in Stalin's playground."

Stan felt a little miffed that Bud wouldn't be around to share the work. He shook that off and whistled. "Great, Bud. Stay and have a ball, but not forever. We have a new case that you're going to love—another crazy preacher. And Bud, he asked for you by name."

"Tell the nut job he has to wait, if he wants the genius of Bud Randolph."

"Enough of that," Melanie said. "Tell me about your lady friend. Tell me everything—blonde, redhead, tall, short? Is she there with you? Can we speak to her? Speak English? Will you email pictures?"

"I will," Bud said. "She is. But right now, I gotta jump on a train. Bye." He hung up.

A few minutes later, Stan picked up a call from Emilia Clark, the woman from KatzBank.

"You remember the blond woman at the house you're watching?" she asked.

Stan's reports had included pictures of people visiting the house in Manhattan Beach and the blonde peeking out the window.

"Sure. The one who lives there."

"Follow her tomorrow, wherever she goes. Snap photos of anyone she meets and find out who they are."

"Are you going to tell me her name?" he asked.

Melanie had tried to identify the blonde through facial recognition, with no luck. The property records for that house came up as an offshore corporation. Intriguing, but not informative.

"Not your worry, Mr. Stein. Your work is important. That's all I have to say. I'll transfer another five hundred to your account."

The next morning, he trailed the blonde, in her blue Audi, to a parking lot at the Griffith Observatory. He left the Escape between parked vehicles and edged up the hill. Crouching by a white minivan, he snapped pictures. The woman approached two guys in dark suits—one tall and blond, the other shorter, African American. They didn't head inside but held an intense conversation at the base of the Observatory. Strange place for a business meeting. Finally, the suits seemed to relax. The blonde nodded. They'd reached some agreement.

The woman flashed a tense smile and headed to her Audi. The men gabbed at each other as they walked toward a black SUV with tinted windows. Stan took more shots of the men. As the SUV rolled out of the lot, he zoomed in on the license plate—blue on white—federal government vehicle!

Back in the car, he tried Emilia Clark's cell, not to report but to ask what the heck was going on. No answer. He sat for a few minutes, contemplating. He lifted his hand off the steering wheel and watched it tremble.

No response again at Emilia's number, thinking, *Maybe I should call her at KatzBank.* No—she'd been clear about that.

Heading for his office, he spotted a black SUV behind him. He pulled into a parking space and watched it pass by—California plates. Fine.

He was making too big a deal about this federal thing. They hadn't seen him, so no need to worry.

There was another black SUV parked across from his office. He didn't have a chance to check the plates, as he turned into the parking garage.

He entered the office and headed to the window by Bud's desk. The SUV was still parked with nobody nearby. *Don't be a jerk, Stan*, he told himself. *No one's looking into you.* And then, *Bud wouldn't be so darned skittish.*

Melanie came over and wrapped her arms around him. "What's going on, Stan?"

The hug felt good. He told her about the government men meeting the blond woman.

"It's all right, Stan. Ask Ms. Clark what's up. If she doesn't give you a straight answer, drop the case and move on."

He reached Emilia Clark that evening, and led off with, "Ms. Clark, you need to tell me why two federal agents were talking with our target."

"Oh," she said. "Well, thanks. You've answered my question. That's all I need."

"Emilia, I need an explanation. What is this about?"

"I told you, about a theft in Spain. Look, Mr. Stein, we've done nothing illegal. We're the good guys here. Oh, and don't send a bill. Everything confidential, you know. Give me a price and I'll deposit the funds."

"If you've already deposited the $500, *I* owe *you* money, but—"

"Fine. I'll have no further need of your services. Please don't contact me." She hung up.

He heard no more from Emilia Clark, except for another deposit—$1000 that she didn't owe—to his bank account.

No FBI agents knocked on his door. After a couple of days, he more-or-less let it go.

# CHAPTER 23

## BUD

B ud sent a text to Stan: *Taking the train from St. Petersburg to Moscow and then on to Sveti's hometown. Here's a picture of Sveti to share with Mel. Give her a hug for me.* He attached a nice shot of Sveti outside that little church they'd visited.

Stan wrote back: *If you've got a minute, stop by the Kremlin and ask Putin how he rigged the 2016 election for Trump.*

*Not funny, Stan. The secret police must monitor these texts.* Bud erased the message and shut down his phone.

THEY TOOK THE OVERNIGHT train from St. Petersburg to Moscow, doing their best to sleep in upper and lower bunks. Bud had offered to pay for first class, but Sveti balked. Instead, the Russian version of economy plus.

They grabbed raisin buns at the Moscow station, and jumped on another train, no bunks this time. The faded interior had a fifties vibe.

Smoking was banned these days. Still, a few men lit up. Sveti said, "It's their disease, the men; that and liters of vodka."

Bud walked the aisle, eyeing the smokers. The first two gave him sideway glances, decided he was a harmless foreigner (not the smoking cops) and ignored him. The third took a drag and exhaled in Bud's direction. He was a skinny guy, maybe fifty, in a stained denim shirt, his face etched like the Grand Canyon. He grinned, his teeth yellow-stained, and growled something in Russian. Bud made a choking motion with his hands wrapped around his neck. He kept his *fuck you* to himself and headed back to sit with Sveti.

"Hey, honey," he said. "Another plus for America; our smokers gave up their self-righteous defiance years ago."

She rested her head against his shoulder and napped.

The Yerunda station was small but quaint, freshly painted dark green with wine-red window frames. They walked along the main street, a boardwalk on one side and a roof overhead, like old towns in the US.

"Now I think you hungry," she said.

"Sure."

"In here, good place." Sveti opened the door to a little restaurant with wooden rakes and scythes on the wall. "You get draniki."

Bud gave her a look.

"Potato pancake. And you, meat eating man. Ham very good here."

He had them throw a fried egg on top. Delicious.

She got up from the table. "Now we go see my mother, grandmother too. Great grandmother three."

She recognized his confusion and said, "We go cemetery."

Yeah, confused.

# CHAPTER 24

## BUD

From the end of the boardwalk, Bud saw a striking wooden church with a pointy-topped tower and two onion domes covered in small shingles, old wood, bleached silver over the years. Impressive to a guy who'd only left the US once to serve in Iraq.

"Three hundred fifty old years," Sveti said. "We go around church and fast through cemetery. Don't want become friends with *spirit*—that the word? *Spirit?*"

*Oops. Weird.*

She eyed him. "I not crazy, like you think. Dead person have soul. Float sometimes. Keep us *company*—that right word?"

*Yes, weird.* But was this any different from lots of religious spook-junkies back home?

She marched Bud between white gravestones, some worn and unreadable; other graves with splintering wooden markers, to a stone chapel with a steep roof and a cross above. There were three benches inside. At the far end, a red and blue stained-glass scene. Bud barely glanced at that; his eyes riveted on a coffin of solid silver!

An old couple sat on one of the benches. The man wore a brown tweed jacket. She had on a gray shawl.

Sveti walked forward and placed her hand on the coffin.

The couple got up. Sveti turned toward them. The gray-haired man smiled and nodded to her. The woman curtsied. They passed Bud on their way out, the man giving him a quick sideways glance. Interesting.

Bud came up beside her and saw a raised window over the top third of the coffin. He spotted a form inside! Yikes!

"Beautiful, is she not?" Sveti said.

Not a word that occurred to Bud. He looked closer. Definitely a body in there, skull shrink-wrapped in its own skin, a patch of bone the size of a dime showing at the temple, scraggly gray hair, a silver amulet with a blue stone lying on the yellowing blouse.

"She my *great grandmother*. This how you say it?"

"What's she doing in the fancy box?"

"She saint ... she almost saint. People make her silver coffin, make her this chapel. My grandmother and her brother ... mother here too." She pointed at three vaults by the sides of the chapel.

"I'll be damned. What did she do to make her an almost-saint?"

"You see her, how beautiful? She dead since nineteen and forty, still lovely, yes?"

Bud stared at the body, trying to see *lovely*, with *creepy* screaming at him. The old horror movies came back, instead of Frankenstein, a mummy wrapped in rotting rags, choking people. *Must be in the eye of the beholder.*

"Now you meet my mother and grandmother—you say *grandma*, yes?"

"Yes."

Over at the side of the chapel, she stood by one of the white three-foot-high stone tombs, her eyes welling with tears. "This is Polena, grandma. You help me now, please."

She gripped either side of the slab on top of the tomb. "We move this, so I look in."

He stared at her, wondering if he should cut and run. But lurking here among the dead had its appeal.

"Not worry. You not have to see body."

Bud went to the chapel entrance and scanned the cemetery. The coast was clear. He came back.

She chuckled. "She not bite you."

He helped her slide the stone plate a few inches, giving them a peek at a simple wooden box inside.

Sveti spoke to her grandma for a minute, and then nodded. "We put back." So, they did.

Her mother's tomb was on the other side. Sveti said something in Russian. Then to Bud, "I tell mother, have nice day."

They walked out.

BUD AND SVETI sat on opposite sides of a picnic table in a small park. Between the pine trees, Bud could see the church tower and one dome. Back on the train Sveti had changed into a pink-and-blue plaid blouse, which looked especially pretty on her, even if she might be nuts. She brushed hair from one side of her face, looking nervous. "I want you come here to chapel, because … because I want you to know …"

She frowned, and Bud reached across to take her hand. The move surprised him, because he was kind of stressed out and disappointed. What had seemed like maybe a path to something good was now strewn with—should he think it? — Bodies.

"Want you to know *me*. You nice man. I like you. I tell you what I have to say. If you decide and if I decide … Maybe this foolish. Maybe too soon. Maybe you not want to…"

Bud moved to her side of the table and wrapped his arm around her shoulders. She trembled a little. He wanted to reassure her. Wanted to kiss the side of her head but didn't. He wasn't ready to commit to anything, not after a week, not after visiting the holy ghosts of her past. Maybe it would take only one passionate kiss to convince him. He wasn't going for that right then either. "If you're saying what I think about seeing more of each other, I *might* want to… What do you need to tell me, Sveti?"

She gazed into the pine forest. "You will think I crazy, but I must say it out. I say now; no surprise later. Then you fly away from Sveta maybe." She took a deep breath and looked him in the eye. "If I live in America, my grandma come with me." Her hazel eyes and her cheeks were moist with tears.

*Holy Yikes! Grandma, not great granny or mama?* "You mean her body?"

"Her body, her spirit, her whole … being. Is that how you say?"

Weird, but was this a deal breaker? Hell, there was no deal to break.

"I see look on your face. You want to run away me."

"No, Sveti. This is … strange." What *did* he want? What did he need to say? "I don't want to run. I really don't. It's just hard to understand." *Fucked up might be the word.*

She stopped shaking. Bud was sure because he had his hand pressed onto her thigh.

They got up. She faced him, holding both his hands. "I go my apartment now. You go hotel. Tonight, if you not fly away, you take me good restaurant. We see movie. You not understand one word. We sit in back, kiss like eighteen-year-old mad in love. You like?"

It turned out to be a great date.

In bed that night, Bud wondered if he should get the hell out before dawn, before he really fell for her. *Really fell*, eh?

Close to sleep, random thoughts crept in. *If we move a box of bones to the US, will she want to jack up our bed and shove the putrid thing under it? Our bed—nice.*

# CHAPTER 25

## BUD

They spent those days having picnics, taking a rowboat out on a lake, swimming in a public pool. Sveti looked terrific in her lime-green two-piece suit, and she felt great with his arms wrapped around her wet body, touching the bare skin of her shoulders and back. They made out, lying on their towels in the forest.

Bud's visa was nearly done. Sveti had to get back to work. They shared breakfast sitting across from one another at that same restaurant, woven baskets, and wooden farm tools on the walls.

She answered some of his questions: First, about her grandmother. During Sveti's childhood, her mother, Ksenia, worked six days a week. Grandmother Polina lived with them. Mother tried to raise her as a dull housewife, subservient, putting up with a drunken man like her father, who'd died young, his body buried in his family plot in Ukraine.

Grandma saw to Sveti's needs, granted many of her wishes, encouraged her to be herself. In subtle ways, she mocked Sveti's father, but never to his face. She told Sveti to be patient; to find a better life.

Sveti looked nervous. "You see, I talk with my mother, grandma, great grandma in chapel?"

Bud nodded.

"Great grandmother have divine soul, but she not know me. Grandma know all my secret."

"Not your mother?"

She grimaced. "I talk. Mother not listen."

"I see." But did he?

"Great grandma belong to Russian people. She saint for them. Grandma not belong here. Too cold. Cruel. Too not free." She shook her head, watching his reaction. "I can no have life without my guide woman."

*Still weird, but Sveti's one intriguing woman.*

He tuned her out for a moment, wondering, *How the hell do you take a body out of Russia? Could you book a seat on the airplane, economy minus? Jam the carcass into a carry-on? And when she got to the US? No place for her in Bud's apartment. Stan's house had a big backyard. A little shrine would go great out there.*

All idle thoughts, way too early. "You'd like me to come back and see you?" He asked.

She nodded enthusiastically. "Yes. Yes. You *better* come—that American expression—*better come*—yes?"

"Will your government let me?"

She leaned closer across the table. "You lucky, Mr. Bud. Putin, that son of a bitch, not like America one bit. *One bit*, that expression, yes?"

"Yes, *one bit*."

"But Putin like America money. You spend fifty rubles here, he take home twenty."

The US was getting along better with Russia when Trump ran things. He and Putin admired each other—two tough hombres.

No more with Biden screwing things up. Weak-ass old dude. Bud didn't mention that to Sveti. He forced himself to ignore the anger that bubbled inside whenever he thought of the STEAL.

"You could come to America for a visit; I mean, without your grandma, for a few weeks?"

She beamed at him. "I don't know if they allow this. Of course. Grandma only come if we decide ... You know what I say here?"

Bud pictured Stan and Melanie, him and Sveti, eating Dodger dogs and cheering for Mookie and Kershaw at Chavez Ravine, Otani and Trout at Angel Stadium, riding one of those whale watching boats by the Channel Islands. Getting to know each other for a month or two.

"Sure. I get it." Grandma would only come if they decided to get hitched.

"This is, what you call it?" she asked. "Baba and me."

"A *package deal*."

"Yes, American-ski boyfriend, *package deal*."

*American-ski boyfriend*, so that's what he was.

# CHAPTER 26

## BUD

On his flights home, Moscow to New York, NY to LA, Bud pictured Sveti with a sexy smile, inviting him into the bushes. Braless in that pink blouse shooting him a naughty smirk as she asked about his convertible car … showing him into the spooky family crypt.

He'd confided that he'd probably never have extra cash for a fancy car. She was okay with it.

She'd said, and he'd agreed; America was a great place. Land of opportunity. She'd heard American men were nice to their wives. "Wife" was mentioned just that once during all their conversations. It got him to wondering what kind of husband he'd be, now that he wasn't the argumentative, thoughtless jerk he'd been the last time. (Aspirational or true?)

She wanted America. She yearned for a good man. Bud could be that guy.

Once again, he sat on the aisle in Economy Plus, NY to LA. The guy behind him was in Economy Plus too. An hour in the air, Bud was nursing his second gin and tonic. Something rubbed against his leg. Something brown and furry. He jumped.

A friggin' poodle. Bud unstrapped his seat belt and stood to look at the guy behind him. Mid-forties and half bald, his noggin lolled at an angle against the headrest, eyes closed, blue mask hanging under his unshaven chin. Bud spotted tattoos on his arms. One said *Alice*, Bud's ex-wife's name. Crap!

"What the hell?" Bud said.

The dog barked, and bared its teeth.

The guy jerked in his seat. He glanced at Bud and then at the dog. "Easy girl."

"What the hell?" Bud repeated. "What is *that* doing on the plane?"

The guy puffed up his cheek with a dopey grin. "Support animal."

Politically correct bullshit. Bud snorted. "You ain't blind."

The guy spread his palms. "PTSD."

"Sure," Bud said. "Good way to bring Fido for a vacay on the west coast."

The man's smile turned sour. "What are you, the doggy police? Want to see my doctor's note?"

"Stupid-ass doctors sign anything."

The guy blinked, looking a little hurt. "I earned this dog with a few tours; one Iraq, two Afghanistan. This little plate, where they shot out parta my skull, paid my dues." He pointed two fingers at his temple. "Some-a my brain flew out, too. Fucked me up. You mind?"

That caught Bud in the chest. He took a breath and leaned in close. The guy tensed. Bud smiled, and he relaxed. "Glad to meet you," Bud said. "I'm Bud. One tour in Iraq was enough for me. Buy you a drink?"

"Charlie," he said. "I hear they got whiskey in this dumb-ass crate. If you're feeling rich, make it a double."

# CHAPTER 27

## MELANIE

I'd never seen our friend so happy. Bud zipped into the office, cell phone in hand, with a picture of Sveti on the screen. "Here she is, guys."

It made my heart sing.

He stuck it in Stan's face, really close. Stan pushed it back to a reasonable viewing distance. "She looks great. An absolute beauty."

I came over and waited my turn, so excited to see Bud and Stan sharing this moment. Bud snatched the phone from Stan and showed me a shot of a joyful woman with a river or lake behind her. She was good looking, probably thirty-five with brown wavy hair to her shoulders, a pale blue blouse.

"What's she see in you, pal?" Stan asked.

Bud, holding the phone up to me, flicked to another picture, and gazed over his shoulder at Stan. "I got hidden charms, *pal*." Back to me, he said, "Now look at this one."

In the picture, Sveti and Bud stared into each other's eyes. I saw in the picture and felt in my heart, the joy of his smile. "Bud's beautiful," I said. "When he's happy like this."

After he'd shown us a dozen more, shuttling back and forth between us, we settled around the table. He told us about his adventure, ending with, "… And here's the amazing part. Sveti thinks I can get another visa and go back soon."

I frowned. "You're not quitting work?"

"Can't afford that, even with that dandy inheritance."

"I'm delighted for you, Bud." I hugged him and whispered in his ear, "A little love could be just what you need."

Stan hugged him too, whacking him on the back with both hands. "When you come down to earth, we've got that new case I mentioned on the phone. It's going to be a doozy."

That night I grabbed a bottle of bubbly on the way to Stan's place. The two of us celebrated Bud's newfound joy in the tub.

# CHAPTER 28

## BUD

Bud printed an application from an online Russian visa service. Last time had been easy; he'd sent his passport and a couple of photos to *Russian Brides Unlimited* in New York. They'd done the rest. So, this was no big deal. He filled it out. Purpose: *personal visit*. In the area for the sponsor, he put Sveti's name.

There was an entire list of stuff they wanted, but he skipped most of it. He'd already received a visa, so they had all that. Along with the application, he added a copy of the previous visa, a shot of his passport, and a note, *Previously provided. All information is on file.*

He sent it overnight mail to the Russian consulate in Houston and moved on to the US State Department website, thinking of how much he wanted to have Sveti visit him in the US, even at his not-very-interesting apartment. She was a good woman, not a gold-digger; he was sure of it.

Online info: A Russian citizen could get a visa to enter the US as a tourist, to work, or as a fiancé of an American. Sveti spoke great English, so she could probably find work here if she stayed longer, but it turned out—damn it—that visa could take years, if they even agreed to issue it.

The fiancé idea? (Premature … presumptuous … foolish … so far ahead of himself … needy?)

The tourist visa looked like the way to go. The list of acceptable reasons for travel included visiting a friend in the US. Bud emailed the US State Department asking for details.

In the meantime, he worried. Sveti had met other guys at the Conference Center, like that tall SOB. Maybe she'd gotten in touch with one. Maybe they'd gone out by the river, made out … made love.

*Pissing me off.*

He checked the time zones—9 or 10 PM over there; he wasn't sure which.

She picked up.

"Hi Sveti, it's Bud. Can you talk?"

"Bud! … I very happy you call."

Bud heard a voice in the background—TV? "You doing okay?"

"I home in my sister house. Wait. I go outside." A minute later, "Yes. Good." More quietly, "Think of you, Bud. Think of you every minute."

Bud suddenly understood the meaning of a heart going pitter patter. "I've been thinking, Sveti, would you still like to come to the US to visit me?"

"That sound wonderful … but …"

"You have a passport, right?"

"I have, yes, from when I visit Ukraine."

"I've been checking. You could get a tourist visa. Can you get to the US Embassy in Moscow and apply?"

"I will, darling Bud, just as soon I can."

He loved the way she stretched out the word *darling*.

"I thought you come back see me here," she said.

"I will. I'm working on it. You could come to the States too. You'd like that."

He heard a touch of fear in her voice. Surprising when she'd seemed so bold with him sometimes. "Of course. Oh, Bud, you make me happy."

"Wonderful, honey. Wonderful." They talked for an hour, and Bud ended up wearing a big smile. Later, he wondered if he should have mentioned that he put her name on the visa application. No matter.

THE NEXT DAY, Stan, Mel, and Bud embarked on one incredible case.

# CHAPTER 29

## BUD

Bud was in the passenger seat, Stan behind the wheel of his blue Escape, zipping down I-15, Stan telling Bud about Reverend Dudas and his Free Spirit of our Lord Sanctuary. "This case is right up your alley," Stan said. "They hold rattlesnakes as they dance to hymns."

No way Bud believed that. "Holy serpents, Batman. Snake handling freaking Christians? In California! If you'd said Alabama or Kentucky, maybe. You made this whole thing up to get me excited, and I appreciate that." Stan was such a great friend. "What's the actual case?"

"Snakes, my friend. Reptilia, snake-is, poisonous-is."

It took well over an hour, with traffic, to drive from their office in Santa Monica, out to the boonies in the hills near Hemet. Picturesque, wooded, idyllic. All Bud could think, as he looked out the car window, was *Yeah, tons of snakes slithering in these rocks.* Creeped him out big-time.

Dudas met them on the porch of his white two-story, surrounded by California oaks. About fifty, mid-height with a salty beard and blue eyes.

The house was salty too, with peeling white paint, weathered rocking chairs and two-person swing on the porch.

"Pleasured to meet you," he said, shaking their hands.

Dudas was ruddy-skinned and already a bit jowly, hiding it with the well-trimmed beard, but Bud could tell. He wore a worn red plaid short sleeve and blue jeans. His meaty arms were well-tanned with a coat of fine blond hair.

They moved into the kitchen. Stan and Bud sat at a scuffed wooden table. Dudas made coffee in a blue enameled pot. Looking into the next room Bud saw mounted animal heads, a mountain goat and a buck deer, on the wood-paneled living room wall. He took a quick glance around the kitchen, too. No obvious slithering going on.

Piled in the white enamel sink was a mound of steel pots and pans, along with dirty green Melmac plates and bowls.

Every one of the cream-colored cabinet doors boasted a six-inch American flag sticker. *A trust-worthy American*, Bud thought.

Under the hanging cabinet, on one corner of the brown-tile counter, sat a glass terrarium with two little green turtles. Nearby a 1950s toaster, the kind where the two sides flipped out when the toast was done.

The Rev eyed Bud. "You like turtles?"

"Sure." Why not?

Stan piped up with, "I take it this is a missing person's case?"

The Rev fished three blue enameled metal mugs out of the sink, rinsed them with his grubby fingers and set them, still wet, on the table. He poured coffee and sat down. "I sent you the money to come here and a nice retainer, too. I get to tell this my way. The customer is right, always, ain't it?"

Dudas scratched his chin. "You good with turtles; gotta like snakes, then, eh?" He looked straight at Bud's partner.

Stan glanced at the turtles. "As long as they're behind glass."

Dudas, still watching Stan, said, "See, like I told you on the phone, I learnt about how you, S. Stein Investigations, found that missing preacher, Jeff Lamb, down in New Mexico. That's why I call-t ya. Jeff Lamb and his momma, Sarah, they was a pretty big preachin' deal, and we got somethin' like that here."

*Okay, might as well ask.* "And snakes? What's with that?" Bud said.

Dudas got up and pressed his hands against his lower back, as he straightened. He reached for a framed photo that had been face-down on the counter and held it out to them—a shot of Reverend Dudas, sweat running down his face, fists raised high, holding a big, squirmy snake in each hand. "These here are my pride and joy." *Yikes.*

"Nice shot," Stan said.

"Best serpents ever, Maynard and Dobie."

"Cool. How come you're not back in the Ozarks or somewhere?" Bud asked.

"Appalachians is where we come from. Got a little hot for us there, if you get my meaning." Dudas admired the picture for a bit. He looked from Bud to Stan and back. "See, here's what we got. My alderman, Elton, he took off with the church secretary." Dudas choked up at that.

"Not sure that's a crime," Stan said. "Unless ..."

"The secretary, that's my wife, Arlene."

Stan drank some coffee and grimaced. Not used to so many grounds mixed in with the brew. "We don't involve ourselves in marital disputes, Mister ... Reverend Dudas."

Dudas took a gulp of coffee, let out a mini-burp and said, "Like I tolt you on the phone, the missing persons ain't half of it all. I ain't happy that Elton and Arlene skipped off, but the wicked prick, she stole my two favorite snakes. This is all about thievery."

*Praise the Lord*, Bud thought. *Snakes might be scary as crap, but snake preachers, like any other weirdo fanatics, there's the making of a swell case.* He watched Stan for a reaction.

"As long as we stick to the snakes," Stan said. "We can take the case."

*Yes!*

"Hey Rev, would we be able to attend one of your … what do you call them, revivals?" Bud asked.

"*Services*, Bud. We call 'em *services*, just like your everyday Prez-bee-terians and all. 'Course you kin come. You might fancy a particular snake and want to pick it up and jig a bit." Dudas headed toward the door. "I got a new diamondback in the other room. Be happy to show ya."

Stan stood. "No thanks, Reverend. We need to stay focused. Would you make us a list of Arlene's friends, Elton's too? Phone numbers, if you have them."

Dudas looked a little crestfallen. "You don't want to see my purdy new reptile?"

"Some other time," Bud said.

Stan gave Bud a sideways grin. "We'll need info on Arlene's family, where she grew up and went to school, recent photos."

"I'll email y'all lists tonight. Two lists—one with people to call and check on her and another with folks to avoid, no matter what. You don't need talkin' to no lyin' sinners."

"You have a picture of this Elton guy," Bud asked.

"Yeah. I think." Dudas walked into the living room and came back with a Church roster. He opened it, flipped a page, and showed them. "Kinda small picture," he said. "It's all I got."

"Your wife and this guy, do they have any distinguishing features? You know; tall, short, scars, birthmarks …?" Stan asked.

"And the snakes," Bud grinned at Dudas. "Any tattoos, long sideburns, big ears?"

Dudas looked Bud over, like he was deciding something. He cackled and soft-punched Bud's arm. "Diamonds," he said. "Beautiful diamonds on their backs. Maynard, he's the biggest rattler you'll ever see. Seven foot long. Twenty-five pounds of coiled muscle."

"No tattoo, then?"

"Naw, but I got a chip implanted in him at the veterinarian, like they do with dogs and cats."

"What?" Bud said. "If your snake slithers into someone's backyard, you think they'll take him to the Humane Society for a chip scan?"

The Rev guffawed. "Pulling your leg, Bud."

This Dudas was one strange hombre. Might be fun to see him with his new snake. Snakes, like weird religions, were scary, but also captivating. Bud nodded at Dudas. "Your serpent's confined?"

"In a cage, keep you from hurting him."

"Okay. Show me."

Dudas's face lit up.

Stan stayed in the kitchen while the Rev took Bud to the den, a dark, paneled room with a couple of armchairs and a TV. Dudas flicked on a dim overhead light, which did little good. He swung an arm around Bud's shoulder—a little weird, Bud thought. But not a bad thing if Dudas was starting to like him.

On a side table sat a wire mesh cage, three-foot square with a board at the bottom, a few rocks in there, a little cactus in a pot. Dudas released Bud, bent and tapped on one side. Bud saw movement in there … a pattern of brown and black diamonds, shiny skin rippling and coiling. Rattling. Dudas tapped again, holding his hand near the side of the cage. There was a flash of movement. An open pink mouth. Fangs struck the wire mesh and recoiled so fast Bud barely had a chance to jump.

"You ain't liking my little Herbert so much, is you?"

"Herbert's the snake's name?"

Dudas nodded. "Yup."

Thinking of Maynard and Dobie, Bud said, "You have a knack for naming snakes." Clem smiled at that, and Bud asked: "About those flags on your cabinets, are you …?"

"A patriot?" Dudas asked. "One hundred and ten percent. I love the USA."

"Trump man, then?"

"You bet I am, son. Trump and MAGA one step behind the Lord."

"Trump's my guy too," Bud said. *But I don't bow down and pray to his ass.*

Dudas stood a little straighter and stared into Bud's eyes. "What have you done for Donald Trump lately?"

Bud shook his head. He'd loved Trump, but lost some of his enthusiasm when Trump didn't go to the Capitol that day, like he said. Then Trump didn't pardon the folks who went. Still, Dudas's question made him queasy.

Still eyeing Bud, Dudas said. "I cherish my snakes and my congregation, but I have a business too. Really professional. I work with lawyers and computer nerds. We support the cause."

That sounded funny, coming from the Appalachian preacher. "So, you think I should take you seriously?" Bud asked.

The question hung in the air. Dudas turned, and they headed back in to join Stan.

Dudas sent them out the door with, "Have a blessed day."

THAT NIGHT AT HIS APARTMENT Bud read up on snake worshipers. Really damned interesting. Next morning, he called his new friend with a few questions: "You ever drink strychnine, Clem?"

Dudas laughed. "Well, sure, some of us do that. But only to moderation."

"You been bitten by your little buddies?" Bud had read that a bunch of snake worshippers had died from bites.

"Yeah. I had a quite a nip the night that Arlene went missing. Put me right out of co-mmission."

"You go to the hospital?"

"No way! If you believe in the Lord, you trust in Him. If He wants to call you home to heaven, you gotta go. Ride them snake bites to the pearly gates, if that's what the Man wants."

Bud had read about that too; none of these snake healers sought medical help. It occurred to him then that something (more than the obvious) was off about Clem Dudas. That Ozark twangy thing didn't quite convince him. And what about Clem's serious computer business? Something to keep in mind, while playing *his* part as *Bud Randolph, private detective.*

"Okay, if I come by to see you later today, Rev?"

"Sure. As long as you better ain't be charging me some kind of double time money."

# CHAPTER 30

## BUD

When Bud arrived at the office that morning, Mel hopped up from her desk, grabbed a box from the walnut table, and flipped the lid open. "Celebratory donuts. Take one, Bud."

Mel was a few inches taller than him, even in her white Keds. She could flash the brightest smile in the universe, and she beamed it full force right then.

There were pink, white, and chocolate icings, powdered sugar too. Bud took a custard filled; chocolate frosted. "Celebratory?"

Stan came over and put an arm around her. He was grinning too. "We've set a date."

"May fifth. A spring wedding," she said.

Bud gave her a quick hug and then wrapped his arms around Stan. "I'm happy for you," he said, but all he could think about right then was Sveti.

After some small-talk Stan brought his laptop over to the table, giving them his *I'm the boss* look. Mel brought her computer too, and they settled in.

Stan looked from Mel to Bud. "We need to be careful with this case," he said. "I told Reverend Dudas; we don't get involved in marital disputes. He agreed that we'd treat this as a theft."

"Theft of damned snakes," Bud added, helpfully.

"We can't assume that Dudas is the wronged party here. Sure, his snakes are gone, but when we find the serpents, we find Arlene Dudas and possibly her lover. We can't divulge her whereabouts to Clem without her approval."

Bud, as usual, needed to point out that he was way ahead of Stan. He leaned forward and laid it on him. "That's why I called the Rev this morning and set up a meeting."

Stan gave him one of his *what-the-fuck* stares. "We talked to him yesterday."

Bud wagged a finger at him. "When that nutty dude took me to see his snake, he and I were growing some rapport. There's more going on, and we need to understand before we charge into some mean shit."

Stan looked annoyed, but obviously he was mulling it over.

Bud added, just to emphasize the point, "That guy's fishy, and it's not just the snaky stuff. Fishy enough to cut his wife into slivers and dump them into one of those country cesspools. I'm just agreeing with what you said before, partner."

"You called Dudas this morning without talking to me." Stan looked like he was still deciding how pissed he should be.

Bud saw Mel, on the other side of Stan, frowning. She always wanted to smooth things over between them.

"Like I said, I'm the guy who can get the most out of him."

Stan nodded slowly. "All right, buddy, if you say so."

Next, they went over the names Clem Dudas had provided, Clem's congregation, Elton's friends, Arlene's friends and family.

Mel chimed in with, "While you studs are out interviewing, I'll get on the net and check Arlene's background, her mother in West Virginia and her two brothers in Arkansas, any cousins I can find."

Like Bud, Mel knew exactly what to do. Stan was just one of the team, after all. (The one with his name on the door and signature on the checks.)

"Hey, Melanie," Stan said. "Arlene and Elton, they've got a couple of deadly rattlers with them. Those snakes could have harmed someone."

"Yeah," Bud said. "Maybe they brought the snakes into a coffee shop to get four burgers, and lost control. Is that your theory?"

Mel ignored Bud. She did that sometimes to get his goat. "I'll check on deaths by snake bite around Southern California, West Virginia near the mother's place, too. Find out if Arlene Dudas or Elton Snivel shows up in a hospital log back in her old hometown.

She touched the back of Bud's hand. "By the way, did you notice the mother's married name?" Bud gave her a blank look and Mel said, "Velma Buttz."

Bud smirked. "Yeah."

Stan looked up from his computer and said, "You notice something about these lists Dudas sent? The last names."

Mel chuckled. "Yeah. The ones Dudas wants us to talk to are all guys. The ones he says to avoid, same last names. Those are the wives."

Imagine that.

# CHAPTER 31

## MELANIE

Of course, I adore being with Stan, the man I cherish. Throw Bud into the mix and you have a new dynamic. They tease each other. Bud tortures Stan (a little), who doesn't quite know how to keep up. Bud laughs at Stan's confusion. Stan joins in, because he loves to see Bud happy.

This may be news to you, but women can see what men never do. A woman sees the boy a man once was. The adolescent Stan and Bud come out when they shriek in fake pain about some baseball player getting hit in the nuts with a line drive or make up gross stories to see me cringe. None of it would be funny, but when they dissolve in laughter, watching them is the real hoot.

I do my best to keep in the game. When Bud mentions *balls* that way, I'll maybe say, "Testicles."

Bud might come back with, "I love it when you talk dirty."

Stan could add, "Watch it, that's my fiancé."

When they tease each other, when I see one of them seeking the other's approval, Stan and Bud bring back childhood memories. I grew up at the edge of the San Fernando Valley, not in a hillside mini-mansion, or even a tract house, but a twenty-unit building in the flatlands, a block from Ventura Boulevard. We didn't own the place. My mom managed rentals for the owner. My dad taught elementary school for the Baptist congregation. Didn't pay well, but he told me God had placed him there to keep His little lambs respectful.

I strayed from Dad's teachings during his life, but never from his love.

We lived downstairs from another black family, this one with two boys, Alan and Alfred, *the two Als*. The older, Alan, was studious. Younger Al was the crack-up. The two Als, Sissy and I made friends with all the kids there, but Sissy and I shared a special bond with the Als. Maybe that was because we four were teased lots of times, *teased* being a gentle word for what some of those kids dished out to black kids. We stood up for each other.

When the two Als walked to elementary school, the older one, Alan, marched with purpose, carrying his lunch box and loose-leaf notebook. Alfred trailed behind, keeping an eye out for mischief; a girl with a ponytail to tug, a boy whose mom had made him wear a fancy shirt and who was therefore due a good-natured insult.

In high school, it was Alfred *borrowing* a neighbor's car for a joy ride; Alan trying to talk their parents out of grounding him for a month.

Seeing Stan and Bud together, I glimpse the boys they were, like the two Als. Their boyish smiles, their actions. Bud's the Alfred who looks for an angle to make Stan laugh or impress him, dying for Stan's appreciation.

Stan tries to entertain Bud too. At the same time, his antennas are up, ready to protect Bud from his self-destructive ways. (Bud could easily screw things up for himself or for our detective agency with some over-the-top nonsense, like juggling snakes with Clem and getting someone bitten. I wouldn't put it past him.)

AFTER STAN AND BUD went off to the mountains that day to interview Reverend Dudas's congregation, I called *my other boyfriend*, Dave, who worked in administration for the Highway Patrol.

No need to worry; Stan knew about our friendship and encouraged it. Calling Dave my *boyfriend* was our little joke. He was a good-looking gay guy. Occasionally he needed a female to hang with, maybe attend a cop party.

I know; it shouldn't have been that way in 2021. A gay fella should feel okay standing up for his identity. True, in a perfect world. The Highway Patrol celebrates Pride Day with a cake at the office each year, so why worry? The cake comes in a box, and no one has the nerve to cut the first slice. It sits untouched until the janitors come at night to gobble it down.

Dave was black, which was already one strike against him with some cops. They might mock a guy in ways that weren't half funny. They might shun him or "lose" the information he needed in his job. The majority were cool with a black dude, but homosexuality on top of black could be three strikes and you're out. Dave relied on those guys to cooperate in investigations. He needed management's support for promotions. He wanted respect, and, more important, comradery. He was a heck of a nice guy. Who was I to judge?

I gave Dave a description of Arlene's pickup, Elton Snivel's Blazer too, and the date they left town. "Call you back, sweetheart," he said.

"Thanks, honey."

I checked snakebite reports online at hospitals within fifty miles of the Dudas place. Only a couple of teenagers had come in for treatment. I followed up on Arlene's mother, Velma Buttz, in West Virginia. She'd divorced, remarried, and changed her last name all within the last six months. Arlene's brothers were the stable ones; both still married and living in Arkansas.

I tracked down Elton Snivel's birthplace, his high school, his mother and father's current location, all in Southern Oregon. His high school yearbook, 2004, informed me that Elton played sax in the school band and was a wizard at chess.

That's when Dave called back. He'd tracked down both of their license plate numbers and found a moving violation outside Oklahoma City—speeding. The truck was Arlene's; the driver, Elton Snivel, with one female passenger. Great info! They'd been heading east three days after leaving Clem in the snake-infested mountain dust of Southern California.

It made sense; Elton had gone with Arlene. Were they a couple now, friends, or just escaping together? If Elton and Arlene were in her truck, what about his Blazer? Were they bound for West Virginia so Arlene could introduce her chess-playing snake-lover to mom? Arkansas to visit a brother, perhaps? So many questions.

# CHAPTER 32

## STAN

Stan was behind the wheel of the Escape again, Bud riding shotgun.

Bud wore one of his tropical short-sleeved shirts, this one sporting green palm leaves and yellow canaries. Not very professional, but, hey; Bud would be Bud.

Stan's friend sipped from his Starbucks latte and set it back in the cup holder. "When you drop me off at Dudas's place, give me a good hour with the viper-loving dingbat, okay?"

"Sure."

Bud went silent then, not his usual mode. Stan glanced over and saw a smile on his friend's lips. Also, unusual.

"Thinking about your Russian honeybun?" Stan asked.

"How could you tell?"

Stan pulled into the driveway to the white two-story, and saw Dudas swinging on a two-person glider on the front porch. Bud got out, and Stan drove a half mile to the Hanson's place.

The Hansons were on the reverend's list—Harbin Hanson for them to interview, Cassandra Hanson to avoid. The dwelling was what Bud would have called a "cheese box house," rectangular and uninteresting, pale brown with yellow window frames. A woman answered Stan's knock, opening the inner door, and leaving the screen closed between them. She looked forty, blond, in a white tee shirt and blue jeans. She shot him a wary look.

"Mrs. Hanson? … I'm Stan Stein. Reverend Dudas asked me to investigate—" Cassandra Hanson's glare silenced him for a moment. "There was a theft a month ago, the night your preacher had an unfortunate incident with a rattlesnake."

"My husband isn't home."

"Could *you* talk to me?"

Her lip twitched just enough to register as a smile. "One snake, two snakes."

Did she mean what he thought? "Are you referring to two snakes going missing, or the reverend getting bitten twice?"

"No, I mean … *Forget it.* Come back and talk with Harbin. He's an electrician, working in Temecula today. He's buddies with the rev. He'll tell you what Clemmie wants you to hear."

Great luck to catch her alone. "I'd like your opinion if you're willing."

"The Rev is paying you. He may not want you to—"

"You may have useful information. Sometimes a fact that seems trivial will help solve a case." (At least that's what the cops said on TV.)

Stan backed up a step to seem less threatening. "When you said two snakes before, you weren't speaking of two actual serpents, were you?"

He looked up at the sun and wiped his brow. "Going to be hot today. The reverend, how should I say this? There might be more than one opinion about him?"

"Harbin thinks he's godly; that's all that matters in our house."

She was looking Stan over, deciding.

"I understand that a woman alone has to be careful. I could come back with my fiancé, or return when your husband's home, if you'd be more comfortable."

Mrs. Hanson took in a breath and inclined her head toward the back of the house. "Picnic table's out there. I'll bring iced tea."

The back yard might have been a nice lawn in the spring. Now it was dried-up grass, bordered by oaks.

Stan sat between spots of bird poop at the green picnic table.

Cassandra came out with only one glass of tea. She was shorter than he'd imagined. (She'd been a couple of steps above him back at the front door.) Skinnier too. She plopped the glass down and stepped back, watching him.

He took a drink and smiled. "Thank you. That hits the spot."

She waited.

"Apparently, Arlene took Reverend Dudas's two prize snakes when she left."

"One, two, three snakes." She looked pleased with herself.

"And she left with Elton Snivel. I guess you'll say, 'four snakes.'"

Cassandra smirked. "You said it for me."

"You have any idea where Arlene might take off to?"

Mrs. Hanson folded her arms across her middle. "No."

"No need to worry. My job is to get the snakes back, not mess with Arlene."

"Don't care about Arlene. She's not *my* friend."

"Oh—"

"Might say she's the opposite." Cassandra exhaled. "Now I'm going to tell you why I don't like the so-called reverend." She gestured at his glass. "After that, you'll finish and be on your way."

# CHAPTER 33

## BUD

B ud stepped onto Reverend Dudas's porch. The Rev smirked at him. "Hey, Budster. How's the Good Lord's world treating you today?" He patted the white glider he was sitting on and slid to one side.

Bud noticed white paint chips on the floor under the glider and a couple on the shoulder of Dudas's turquoise short sleeve shirt. He settled beside the Rev.

Dudas grabbed his thigh, chuckled, and let go. "You ever been snake-bit?"

The two of them made it fairly tight in the glider, but Bud angled himself a little, to look the Rev in the eye. "Can't say I've had that pleasure."

"Bud, you come to tell me you tracked them down so soon, Maynard, Dobie, and the others?"

*Snakes before people, just like the Good Lord intended*, Bud thought. "I'm here because there's more to the story of Clem Dudas, his bride, Arlene, and their friend Snivel. A detective needs details."

Dudas scratched his chin, as Bud pictured a swarm of ticks holed up in there, mountain ticks, the worst kind. "There's plenty to the story, more than you can shake a snake at."

"And there's more to Clem Dudas," Bud said. "Not just a country minister, acting more holy and less intelligent that he might truly be."

Dudas really looked at him then. "What you talkin' 'bout, young fella?"

"You saying I'm wrong?"

"Ain't sayin' nothing, friend. Not a goldarn'd thing."

This was one weird dude. Zany, hopefully not dangerous. Bud chuckled. "There you go with your Ozark. You told me the other day; you worked with lawyers and computers, trying to help Trump. You say 'congregation' one time and 'my home folks' another. You say 'goldarn'd.' What the fuck is that?"

The Rev broke out laughing and slapped Bud's knee.

"What are you doing for Trump?" Bud asked. "You asked me if I'd done anything for him. I haven't. Maybe I should."

Clem scrutinized Bud, his face close, a whiff of BO blowin' in the breeze. "That's secret, Bud. I cain't get into that 'less I know a fella real well."

"You know how to say *can't* and *unless*, don't you, Rev?"

"I do. And I believe you when you say you support Trump, but I can't tell you everything, day one."

A fly buzzed past Bud's ear, and he waved it off. "Fair enough. Tell me why Arlene took off, and why she was angry enough to snatch your favorite slither-dogs."

Dudas grimaced and stood up, making the swing wobble. "It's early, friend. Too early, but I'm opening two beers. We're going to drink together."

In Dudas's living room, with mounted animal heads looking down, the Rev took out a brown photo album. They sat on the sofa, drinking beer.

Dudas laid the book open, one side resting on each of their thighs and flipped pages. Bud saw the glint of a tear in Clem's eye and glanced down to see a wedding picture. Dudas looked young, clean shaven, in a black tux and bow tie. Arlene wore a long veil over the full wedding garb—pretty. Everything was black and white, including the white roses in her bouquet.

"She was my dream, Bud. Beautiful with that long black hair and curvaceous body. We'd only known each other a few weeks when we tied the knot. She was new to Californ-ee, loving the freedom here. Her lips, her nakedness, her vulnerable womanhood, she shared everything with me. She worshipped Jesus, and she believed in America. At first, she was scared, but with the Lord's help and my coaxing, she was able to touch the snakes and then hold them."

"What happened?"

Dudas flipped a few more pages to a photo of Arlene hugging a big brown poodle around its neck. He scowled and said, "We wanted to have kids, but the Lord didn't provide. She went in for tests. They didn't find nothin'. She told me to give them a sample of my … stuff. Made me mad, it did."

Bud felt a little sorry for Dudas. "How'd that turn out?"

"I argued, but she wouldn't back down. Damned if I was going to jerk off for some doctor. I brought a sample of snake venom to the test and squeezed that into their test tube."

Bud laughed. "Did they figure that out, or just decide you had a deficiency of swimmers?"

"Yeah, no swimmers. I think Arlene suspected what I'd done, but she said, 'Okay, Clem, we ain't gonna be having kids. You got your diamondbacks. I'll get myself a pooch.' That's what she damned well did."

Clem shook his head, flipped the album closed and gulped the rest of his beer. "She was never wanting kids; not as much as me."

Bud thought that most women were raised from a young age to desire a baby, one with two legs and sparse fur. Apparently not Arlene. With all those lethal snakes in the house, who could blame her?

"She got that ugly hound," Clem said. "Bought it every toy and contraption you can imagine. Doggie beds, chewy things, a pen to romp in, even a little house, Victorian style, with carved wooden thingies along the eves. She took to flirting with every man in my congregation." He took a deep breath and let it out with exaggerated patience. "I prayed to the Lord, and He helped me restrain myself after that. But now ..." Clem stood and flung the album toward the slate fireplace. "Now, all bets is off."

# CHAPTER 34

## BUD

Bud heard tires on gravel through the open windows—Stan pulling into the driveway in the blue Escape. He got up and took a step toward the door. "Time to head out."

"Sure, Mr. Budster. One thing first." Clem grabbed his forearm hard.

It didn't hurt but it pissed Bud off a little. He stood still.

"When you find Arlene, you goin' ta tell me where she's hanging. You ain't have ta splain to your partner."

He looked Clem in the eye. "You can let go now."

The Rev took his time releasing Bud, his eyes fierce. "Arlene's a hard-assed bitch. When you find her, don't let her play all helpless and hurt-like."

Bud opened the screen door, then turned around. "Maybe you're the hard-ass, Clem. That worries me."

"You ain't worried, Bud. You ain't gonna answer me, is you?"

Of course, he wouldn't, and he wouldn't deliver Arlene Dudas to this dickhead.

When Bud got in the car, Stan said, "You learn anything from the Rev?"

"Yeah, he's weird as a fucking mongoose, and proud of it. He was furious with Arlene, even before she took off with his serpents. *Serpents*; I really get off on the sound of that word."

"Think he'd harm her?"

"Shit, yeah. He'd stab her with a kitchen knife and call it holy retribution for depriving him of his dear Maynard. How about you? You get anything?"

"Mrs. Hanson says the Rev is the third snake in our story. He hit on her a few times, until she hauled off and punched him, gave him a black eye and shiny red balls."

Bud laughed. "She tell her husband?"

"No. Hubby thinks the Rev is one peach of a guy."

BUD AND STAN visited more households up on the mountain. The guys all spoke up for Clem. The women, aside from Cassandra, were stubbornly silent.

Last stop of the day; they drove down the hill to see a brunette named Bobbie and her husband, Art, who ran a realty office. Bobbie wore a navy pantsuit and a perky, fake smile. She flinched at the mention of Arlene. Her dapper husband, in a maroon sweater, sat at his computer, doing an obvious job of ignoring Stan and Bud.

Sitting across from Bobbie at her desk, Bud brought up Clem and Arlene and the snake dancing church events.

"You should try it," Bobbie said. "It brings you real close to God; to your mortality, you know."

That hung in the air for several seconds.

Stan asked, "Were you surprised when Arlene ran off with Elton?"

Bobbie glanced at her husband, still staring at his computer. "You sure they went together?" she asked.

"We are."

She sighed. "You know, when a relationship goes sour, when a man is mean ..."

Art, still typing, gave Bobbie a look.

Her smile vanished. "Things happen in life, that's all."

Bud avoided Stan's eyes as he asked, "You mean the Rev is screwing around?"

Bobbie blushed, her eyes darting toward Art. "I didn't say that. If you two are going to drag this into the mud—"

Stan frowned, apologetic. "We don't mean to intrude."

Stan's mealy-mouthed approach rankled Bud. "Hell, lady, we're trying to help the Rev."

"Everything's confidential," Stan said.

Bobbie got up, not glancing at her husband, and walked to the door. "Look. I can't talk about this."

She stepped outside with Bud pursuing, Stan just behind. "Arlene, then," Bud said. "Is she the wild one? Why do you say Clem's 'mean?'"

"Ask Harbin Hanson about wild—" Bobbie stopped short, looking back at the doorway.

Art stood there, red-faced. "Drop it, Bobbie. Harbin is a friend. Clem Dudas built our church with his own hands. His marriage is *his* business."

Bobbie looked like she wanted to say more. Art's glare warned her off.

The husband pointed at Stan. "Find Arlene, and bring her home, if that's what he wants. Don't invent some wickedness where none exists, or ..."

Stan held his ground. "You have any ideas where they could have gone?"

"Arlene's from back east," Art said. "Could have run back to her stinking family."

Bobbie looked down and muttered, "Bringing her back, not a good idea. If she wants to stay in one piece."

Back in the Escape, Bud said, "Good info, partner. Lots of nookie happening in snake-land."

Stan sat still, probably deciding if he should complain about Bud's direct style of questioning. He grinned. "Yeah, Bud. We're making progress."

On the way home, stuck in traffic on the 10, Bud read between the lines for his naïve friend; "Clem's mad as hell at his wife, so he's fucking all the pretty snake-jugglers."

Stan shook his head. "You have a way with words, pal."

"Arlene's doing her share too. Something sure-as-shit going on with Harbin Hanson. You talked with his wife. What d-ya think?"

"Maybe," Stan said. "Cassandra made a point of saying; she was *not* Arlene's friend."

# CHAPTER 35

## BUD

Mel had found a phone number for Arlene Dudas's mother, Velma, back in West Virginia.

Bud listened in with Mel, while Stan called her.

The woman sounded twitchy, which Bud immediately noticed. Stan's antennas weren't as fine-tuned, but maybe he caught it too.

Stan led off with a lie, which was totally the right thing. "I'm Stan Stein, a vice president at SimiBank here in California. Am I speaking with Arlene Dudas's mother?"

"… Yes, I'm Arlene's mother."

"Good," Stan said. "We're trying to get in touch with her. She doesn't seem to be at her California phone number. She left your name as a contact."

"That's strange," Velma said.

"No, Ma'am, its standard procedure. You see, we received a check drawn on Arlene's account for $3000, and we wanted to make sure—"

"Strange that Arlene put my name on her paper."

Stan was a crappy liar, but he'd insisted on making this call. Bud nodded and gave him a thumbs-up.

"I don't know about that, ma'am. We need to get in touch with Ms. Dudas. Has she been in touch lately?"

"… Well. She come by here with a fella. Surprised daylights outta me."

Now Stan looked like the twitchy one. He hated lying too damned much. "Can you tell me, is she still there in West Virginia, Ma'am? … We have a branch of our bank down there, and it would sure help if—"

"Arlene stayed a coupla days, and then … *Hold up* … Hey, are you really with the bank?"

"Yes … Sure … You can call our office and verify."

*Damn it, Stan*, Bud thought. *You've gotta speak like you know what you're doing.*

"You're some scam guy? You phishing me, honey? You think I'm going to make good on that $3000 check or somethin'?"

Stan was freezing up. Bud wanted to take over but couldn't.

"… Yeah, you son of a dog, mother scammer varmint." Velma snarled. "Get off the line, before I use the Lord's name in vain at ya." The phone went dead.

Mel winked at Stan. "Looks like someone gets an all-expense paid trip to glamorous West Virginia."

Stan still looked shaken up. "Yeah, if Dudas approves the cost."

"I'll ask him," Bud said. "That snake-man loves my ass."

DUDAS OKAYED THE TRIP. "Economy class, an' no fancy hotels," he said. "You're the guy taking the trip, Bud. I want my best man on the case."

"Stan might want to go himself," Bud said. "Either way, it's economy plus."

140

"Stan ain't no gun-totin' redneck," Dudas said. "No card-carrying Trumper like you and me. They'd eat his ass alive over in West Virgini-i."

"You're reverting to your twangy goof-ball lingo," Bud said. "But you have a point."

Mel arranged the tickets. That next Monday, Bud Ubered to the airport.

# CHAPTER 36

## BUD

Sveti and Bud had spoken several times in the week and a half since he'd returned to the States. He itched to go see her, even more for her to visit him in California. He pictured her that day at the picnic, lying on her blanket in dappled sunlight by the Neva River, smiling up at him. Every time he heard her voice on the phone, it made him smile.

So, here he was that Tuesday morning, calling Sveti from a cheap room at the Daisy Laze Motel, along a four-lane outside Little Hope, WVA.

After whispering a few sweetheart words to each other, Sveti said, "I just back from, take train to Moscow. At U S Embassy, I write all papers for tourist visa."

"Great, honey. I did the forms on my end, too. But they told me it could take months to approve."

"Oh, Bud, that very too long."

"It's all right," he said. "I've applied for another visa to go see you. I'll come next month."

Little did he know.

LATER THAT MORNING, Bud put on a dress shirt and tie and stopped in to see Velma Buttz. The house, up a long dirt driveway in the woods, had weathered bare-wood siding and faded green window frames coming apart at the corners.

Before he could knock, she confronted him on her porch, wrinkly old, pointy-faced and decrepit-looking, in a worn yellow house dress.

"Ms. Buttz, I'm Anthony Shorttower." He gave a winning smile. "You can call me 'Jake.'"

"My butt ain't Buttz no more. I got hitched." She looked pleased with herself.

He tried to look apologetic. "Sorry. I came about your daughter, Arlene."

"Don't tell me you're from that bank that called, cause I ain't buying that."

Not a good start. "I *am* from the bank—really. Please don't take me for a liar." How would an honest guy look? Offended? Apologetic? Bud held out his hands, palms up to god, giving her a few seconds of *sincerity*. "You told my associate your daughter came to visit with a man. Can you verify ..." He showed her a picture of Elton Snivel (that Mel had pulled from the internet). "We think he may be the cause of her difficulties." *Good line*, he thought.

Velma Buttz (or whatever) eyed it and spit on the floor. "Yeah. That's the son of a twitch that come with her. Livin' in sin they was. Fornicating like Satan's spawn in every town across the U.S.A. Big city Cal-i-fornicators. We don't do that 'round here."

Bud shook his head, eying the fresh spit on the porch floor, trying to look shocked. "I'm sorry to hear that, Ms. er Mrs. "

"Damned awful, her showin' up. I got a new husband. We worship the Lord Jesus Christ. Satan come into our midst; we crush him."

Bud could see how this woman had rendered Stan speechless the other day.

"Like I told your boss—is it? —Arlene left after two days. Ain't coming back. I told her; 'Stay away until you ditch that snick and find the Lord Almighty.'"

"You have any way to contact her? This man she's with; he's a known thief. There is also the matter of that check."

She gave Bud a hostile stare, like he might be a Cali-fornicator (which, okay, he was) too. "Tolt you all I know. Go on, now, get off."

He figured she was telling the truth, at least mostly. Her daughter probably bolted. After a few visits, who'd want to stay around that bitch? To verify, Bud stopped by a few motels, showing pictures of Arlene Dudas and Elton Snivel. At the third one, he found their den of wickedness. The kid at the desk identified them and verified Velma's story. She'd left after a three-night stay. A maid provided one interesting detail; Arlene had thrown two suitcases into the back of her pickup and peeled out. Alone! No sign of Elton Snivel.

Arlene could still be in the area. Maybe she moved to a different motel or a friend's place. She could have dropped Elton at a bus station, or they could have met back up. More sleuthing needed.

He called Stan, and they decided Bud would book two additional nights at the Daisy Laze Motel and do more recon.

That night he planted a surveillance camera, an imitation robin (hello CIA), in a tree outside Velma's place. Nice little birdy with a digital memory.

The next day, he rented a pole and went fishing at a state park. Caught three pike and threw them back. He downed a burger and fries, took a nap and watched some tube. After dark, he retrieved the camera, grabbed another burger, and munched it, watching the recording.

There was a man, big hunk of a guy, leaving Velma's house in the morning, in a red Jeep Cherokee. The guy wore a denim shirt with some kind of logo on the pocket. An exterminator maybe. A delivery guy toting five-gallon bottles of pure spring water? (No problem for this dude.)

Velma left that afternoon wearing a fancy hat. She drove off in an old Dodge and returned a half hour later. Not long enough to have a knock-down, drag-out with her fornicating daughter. More like a run to the Handi-Mart. A couple of cars stopped by her place after that. A black man got out of a RAV-4, carried a duffel bag to the door, and handed it to Velma. After he drove off, a woman arrived in a late-model Ford and delivered another bag looking more like groceries.

The big dude returned at sundown, charging into the house like a guy eager to see his wife. –Velma's new hubby, still basking in the glow of their union. (Hello, Betty.)

Sitting on his bed, Bud considered: He had only one vehicle tracking device, and two vehicles to consider. The new husband, if he was a real man, would drive whenever he and his bride rode together. On the other hand, the new bride would want to keep her prize husband far from her sinning Satan of a daughter. If Arlene was around somewhere, and Velma went to see her, she'd drive alone in the Dodge.

Bud snuck in before dawn and attached the tracker under the Dodge's fender. He stuck its camouflaged satellite transponder in a tree.

He filled Stan in by email, and Stan wrote back, *Want to call your pal, Clem, and fill him in?*

Bud called Dudas the next morning, as he drove to the airport. "Hey, man, I'm in West Virginia on your case."

"Bud," he said. "How much for the hotel?"

"Sixty-five a night, plus tax."

"Two nights?"

"Three. And don't forget this rental, a slick Mercedes limo."

"Friend, you're costing me an arm and a leg. I hope you got good info."

Bud filled him in.

"You're sayin' you got bupkis?"

"Don't give me that, Clem. We know about Arlene and Elton now for sure. They came to see her mother and left. They stayed together in one motel room. We just don't know yet where they went after that." Bud didn't mention the part about Arlene leaving the motel alone. It might mean something … or not.

"You told me nothin' about my serpents. Nothin'."

"Look, we'll be tracking Velma's car remotely. We are going to find Maynard and Dobie."

"It's disappointment you're hearin' in my voice, brother Bud. Disappointment, capital *D*."

"And this is the sound of an annoyed detective who's working hard for you, Clem."

"Well … yeah. Look, Bud, you know my work?"

"Which work is that?"

"I told you; advancing the Cause, *Make America Great.*"

"You didn't tell me shit about it."

"Top secret, Bud. Anyway, I'm runnin' over on that project. Gonna have a payday soon, but right (rai-at) now, you and your friend Stan gotta tighten your belts. Get it?"

"You're over-doing that Ozark talk, Clem."

"Sometimes I like to do that. I ever mention my degree from the U of Virginia?"

"No, Clem."

"You're a detective. Y'all can looky it up."

In the airport lounge, wearing a damn mask, Bud texted Mel, and she wrote back. *BA in Public Communication. Can you believe it? By the way, check out Clem's YouTube pages. Great snakes alive!*

An hour before his plane, Bud ran a couple of Clem's UTube posts on his cell—snake worshippers dancing in religious frenzy. Clem had 500,000 followers. Bud was willing to bet that the Rev made a few bucks off the snake bite treatment and growth hormone ads on there. He sure wasn't making it as a humble snake preacher.

After only one gin and tonic in Economy Plus, he landed in LA.

# CHAPTER 37

## BUD

That Thursday night, Bud found an envelope in his box. Return address: the Russian Consulate in Houston. That was fast!

He ripped it open as he walked up the sidewalk, whipped out the paper and saw a big red *REJECTED* stamped on it.

*Goddamn it.*

He went inside and sat on the couch.

*DEFECTS* were checked off on the second page:

*Provide original passport,*

*Provide new passport photos,*

*Provide documentation of Russian Sponsor for the visit.*

Besides that, a note said: *SPONSOR MUST BE A REAL PERSON!!!*

Some asshole had written at the bottom: *This is a new application, not a continuation of your previous one. You must provide complete documents.*

Bud popped a beer and sat back down. *A REAL PERSON, what the fuck?*

It had been so easy before, when *Russian Brides Unlimited* handled everything.

He verified on the internet: For a personal visit visa; he needed an invitation from a (real) person. He'd put Sveti down on the application. What was wrong with that?

Bud called her and told her how the lousy Russians had screwed him over.

"Russia like that," she said. "Little government men show they have power. Reject, Reject. Reject." She gave a snarky laugh. "Instead of penis, have rubber stamp that say 'Nyet.'"

"I'll have to submit everything again. I'll use your name as my sponsor, like I did last time, and—"

"No. No. No," she blurted.

"I need to get this application moving."

"Give them my name; you not ever get here."

"Why not? When they rejected me, they said I had to 'use a real person.'"

"Reasons there are, dear Bud. This I not talk on telephone about. When you come see me, I will tell. Darling, I want see you very soon."

Sveti, a woman of sweet mystery. The vulnerability in her voice made him even more eager to see her. "Then how can we—"

"I find someone who invite you, one my cousins."

They fantasized for a few minutes about his visit, and he told Sveti more about their case.

"Snakes, we have snakes in Russia (Roos ee a) also. When I little girl, my parents have dacha-house in country. We go two week in summer. Father pay me two ruble, every snake I kill. Three ruble for poison snake. Big spider, one ruble."

"Rattlesnakes?" Bud asked.

"What is rattle snake?"

"The kind that makes a noise like this to warn you before he strikes." He tried to make a rattle by clucking his tongue several times fast.

She laughed. "Snakes in Russia not warn you. Politicians same way. I can not say which politicians on telephone."

She didn't have to say. She hated Putin.

# CHAPTER 38

## BUD

Bud didn't know shit about Russian visas. Mel didn't need to. She was a whiz on computers, and she volunteered to help. She worked on the snake case and on Bud's case, all at once.

He called Sveti, next day, to fill her in. "Good morning, Sveti."

"Good afternoon, Mr. Bud. I been practicing English. I say *afternoon* right way?"

"Sure, honey. Just right. I have good news for you. You want to hear it?"

"Yes. You come soon. Yes?"

"You remember I told you about Melanie at my office? She checked things out. If someone invited me for a *personal visit visa,* it might not happen until spring."

"That horrible news, Bud!"

"Don't worry, honey; we have a better plan. If I book a tour to Russia, the visa will come right away. Melanie found a company, *Adventure Russia.* They'll arrange a flight to Moscow, a train trip and hotel stay at a *resort* near you." (The *resort* being the key ingredient to satisfy Moscow.)

"Wonderful, my Bud. You come soon, then."

"Once they get the visa moving. I'll let you know."

"You very resourceful man, Bud. That a word *resourceful*?"

"You bet."

They smooched over the phone and made lovey-dovey. Thrilling for him, but not something to write for public consumption.

# CHAPTER 39

## BUD

Bud and the gang still had that amazing case to solve.

Turns out they had an ace in the hole. Arlene had a credit card at SimiBank, the place where Stan and Mel used to work. Their ace was a gal named Dolores, who worked in the credit department there. It took Mel a week and a fancy lunch to convince Dolores to bend a few rules.

New discovery: Coming back from her mom's place in WV, Arlene had used that credit card to buy gas at stations in Indiana, Missouri, Oklahoma, New Mexico, and Arizona. Which meant she'd headed home to California several weeks back. With or without Elton Snivel? That was one question. With or without Maynard and Dobie? was another, the one that most interested Clem Dudas.

Arlene spent $9.52 at a Taco Bell in Barstow, CA. Then, damn her, Clem's wife stopped charging stuff on that card.

Stan and Bud went to see another couple from Clem's list, Tom and Millie Lovely.

They found Tom in the driveway of his yellow one-story, working under the hood of an old VW. As Bud and Stan pulled in, Tom's wife, Millie, popped out. Bud recognized them from the church roster booklet. Millie wore cut-off blue jeans and a pale green tee with silly drawings of pastel cats on it. Despite the felines, she was a hot number with long black hair and a gleam in her eye.

She walked up to them, as they climbed out of the Escape. "You those detectives Reverend Clem hired? I wondered when you'd come by."

Tom came over, wiping his hands on an oil rag. He was of medium height (a touch taller than Bud), handsome with brown hair and mustache. "Easy, hon. Give them a chance to get their feet on the ground."

"We both love Reverend Clem," Millie said. "In case you're going to ask."

Tom tossed his oily rag back toward the VW. "The Rev admires Millie specially."

She laughed. "Tom's jealous, because … well … Reverend Clem enjoys fondling me a bit from time to time."

Bud gave her back-side an obvious ogle, just for fun, which seemed to please her.

Tom chuckled. "You're giving them the wrong impression, hon. The Rev just enjoys the fine pieces of sculpture our Lord created."

Millie beamed and curtsied. "The Rev knows my limits, and he knows how Tom feels. Reverend Clem is cute as a mountain copper head."

"In a dirty old man sort of way?" Bud asked.

Millie wrapped her arm around Tom's waist. "The Rev might be dirty, but his cologne covers real well." She let Tom go, but stayed right beside him.

Bud couldn't help asking, "And the snakes; what's that crap about?"

Millie puffed out a breath and crossed her arms in front of her. "Religion. It's about God."

Stan made a face, which told Bud he was annoyed by this diversion, but serpents were the fascinating part of the case. "How do you figure that?"

Tom pitched in, "I grew up Episcopal, but their services didn't move me. When we first moved up the mountain, Millie and I forced ourselves to drive into the valley on Sundays for church. Then we met Clem."

"No fun with the Episcopalians," Millie said. "No titillating music, no euphoria, no deep-down surrender to the God within." She glanced up, presumably at heaven.

Tom looked really satisfied, as he said, "Love for God, but not so much passion for Him."

Millie swung her hips and spun around, raising her arms over her head. She looked at Stan and then at Bud as she moved to the music that lived in her head. She stopped and focused on one of her hands. "When I hold Melody, that's my copperhead, I see the predatory gleam in her eyes. Satan right there staring into me. We'll be singing holy songs, and I'll eyeball Melody. I can feel the Lord's spirit holding her back to save me."

Bud was getting off on this crazy shit and still admiring Millie's use of the word *titillating*, enjoying the idea that the names Melody and Melanie bore such a close resemblance, when Stan threw cold water on the event. "How well do you know Arlene?" he asked. "We're hoping you can give us ideas about her whereabouts."

*Damn it, partner.*

"We get along great with her," Tom said. "Her friends are up here on the mountain. If she's not staying with one of them, I don't know where to look."

"If she were nearby, we'd know," Millie chimed in. "And I don't think she got along with her family back east."

"Elton Snivel," Bud said. "How about him?"

Millie raised her hand in a helpless gesture. "He's pretty new here. Quiet. A mystery man."

Tom nodded in agreement.

Bud gave him a sideways glance. *Hiding something*, he thought. "Arlene ever make eyes at you, Tom?"

Tom shook his head and shifted his weight, looking at the ground.

*A definite yes.*

Millie stomped a foot in the dirt. "She better not."

"No way," Tom said, just a tad too slow. "Look, we have a great relationship with Clem and Arlene. There's no dirt here to dig. Right, Millie?"

Millie avoided Tom's eyes. "Since you're looking for gossip about Arlene, check with Harbin Hanson. He might shed some light on that." Millie smirked, letting her catty side shine.

BACK IN THE ESCAPE, Stan called Cassandra Hanson on speakerphone. When she answered, he said, "Mrs. Hanson, it's Stan Stein … you know, the detective. I really appreciated talking with you the other day. The iced tea was great."

"Well…"

"Do you have a minute?"

"…No. I don't need a loan for that."

Before she hung up, they heard a harsh man's voice. "Cass, who is it?" The line went dead.

Stan and Bud gave each other the eye.

"Harbin Hanson," Stan said.

"Sounds like a mean S O B." Bud observed. "Bet he'll know where to find Arlene."

"If he's involved with her, he won't admit it."

"We can put a tracker on his vehicle."

"Expensive." Stan laughed. "You think those things grow on trees? Anyway, it'd be hard to sneak up. They have spotlights and cameras all around; saw them when I visited her."

"The wife's the key," Bud said. "If Harbin's screwing Arlene, Cassandra's gotta be suspicious, pissed off, too."

# CHAPTER 40

## CLEM

Harry Duberry texted Clem that Tuesday to tell him the set was ready. Clem called his computer guy, Dusty. "Hey, friend," Clem said. "We need you down in Riverside."

"Super, man. I'm ready for you."

"You programmed the pieces we talked about?"

"Yeah, dude; like I said."

"You got those videos for the fake windows? You know, school busses, kiddies playing."

"I finished those last week. Been sitting on my ass, waiting for you," Dusty said.

*Little prick.* "Taking in 100 per day for that ass-sitting."

"Thanks for that. It's 100 per day, to keep me on tap plus sixty per hour for on-site work."

"Right."

"Plus, three-thou for the programming."

"I thought Artificial Intelligence did the programming."

"This isn't news to you, is it, Clem, my man? We discussed those fees ahead."

"Glad you reminded me, friend. Run over to the studio and get your wires hooked up this afternoon. Meet me there tomorrow morning."

"Roger Wilko."

*What the fuck?* "Call me this afternoon, when it's up and running."

"Ten-four. Don't forget the double time on weekends."

*Pain in the ass nerd.*

Dusty called him late that afternoon. Clem headed down in the morning.

# CHAPTER 41

## MELANIE

I'm sure you want the best for Stan, so you might wonder about the fact that I live with my mom.

She's a widow now with a serious illness. (Let's just say her breathing is more than difficult.) My sister and I are on call 24/7. *Sissy* and her husband live down the block. She's on duty three or four nights a week, which gives me three or four to be the best lover I can for Stan. The other nights I sleep upstairs from Mom.

I don't want to go overboard with this, but my mom is the best. She supported Sissy and me in whatever we wanted to do. She calmed my dad down when I stopped attending those Sunday Baptist services he so loved. (Mom loved them too, but I think mostly for the music.) She taught me life lessons and comforted me when kids were mean.

Mom and Dad came when I earned my AA from Santa Monica College. Mom hid a boat horn in her purse. When I stepped onto the stage for my diploma, she blasted it, loud as a dying elephant, which embarrassed and kind of thrilled me all at once. Just one example of the healthy mother I had before illness brought her down.

Stan's the best too. He's willing to move close to Mom, when we get married, so I can keep doing my share.

Enough of that. Time to continue the story.

Stan and Bud hadn't gotten back to the office by 5:30, so I headed out. I took the bus to Stan's neighborhood and grabbed moo goo gai pan, egg rolls, and fried rice from China House. Stan pulled in just as I unlocked the front door of his house.

I held up the bag of takeout. "Dinner."

Stan wrapped his arms around me. "My favorite."

We kissed.

Inside, I started spooning food onto plates.

Stan poured glasses of rosé. "I have an assignment that needs a woman's touch. Are you game?"

"Field work?"

He kissed me again. "You're going to be great at this."

I laughed. His smile was so adorable. "You giving me a Glock? I think I need one."

"Machine gun." He sipped his wine. "Only Bud carries a gun."

"Stan, you're kidding?"

"Bud *has* a gun. That part's true. Hell, he's probably in the NRA. He's agreed not to carry it at work."

I whisked fake perspiration off my forehead. "Phew."

Then Stan detailed the assignment.

*NOVEMBER 2021*

THAT NEXT MORNING, Bud beat Stan and me to the office. (A first.) He sat at the table with his laptop open and waved us over. "I'm tracking Velma Buttz's movements back in West Virginia. This is so damn cool."

Stan and I moved in to look over his shoulders. Standing there, I noticed the pink scalp where Bud was going bald.

"See, here, she's driving to the Handi-Mart. That was two days back." Bud clicked his mouse. "She's going again yesterday and then to the hardware store. She drove from there to the park where I went fishing."

I knew the answer, but I asked to make Bud happy, "This works with a bug attached to the car?"

"Yeah, and a transponder thing hidden in a tree by Velma's driveway."

"The transponder, one of those birds?" I asked just for fun.

Bud smiled up at me. "Looks like a dead branch, with little twiggy antennas. Every day when Velma comes home, the bug on the car sends info to the branch. The branch passes it to me over the internet."

"So, Velma was having a picnic by the lake," Stan said. "She bought a sandwich at the market, a cream soda, a bag of chips."

"Cream soda," I said. "What's that?"

Stan looked incredulous.

"She didn't go to the lake," Bud said. "She went to the far side of the park, way back; miles of hiking trails up there."

"She the athletic type?" I asked. "Gatorade, then, instead of soda."

Bud snorted. "She's pretty old, maybe sixty … Skinny. I don't know."

"Why follow her now?" Stan asked. "We know Arlene's back in California from her credit card receipts."

Bud looked stupefied. "Because it's fun. Because we can. Besides, you shelled out lots of dough for that tracking contraption. Let's make some use of it."

"I want you to work on one of the other cases today," Stan said. "Melanie's coming with me to see Cassandra Hanson."

Bud took in a breath and lowered his chin, wounded. "This is about treating that woman with kid gloves, right?"

"Right, Bud. We're setting up a woman-to-woman thing, here." Stan ran his hand up my spine and tickled my desire.

An hour later, Stan and I pulled up to a pale brown house with a wide lawn and a massive oak off to one side. We walked to the side door. Through the screen, I saw the living room fireplace and a black leather couch. Stan knocked. A blond woman appeared and glowered at Stan. "You keep showing up. You called. Why?"

Stan stepped aside. "I brought my fiancé this time."

Cassandra Hanson looked me over, wheels turning in her head, thinking, *What's this white fella doing with this black chick?* Or maybe the other way around. I wondered, *Coming up the mountain, how far back in time have we traveled? Pre-civil war? Jim Crow? George Wallace days?*

Stan said, "You remember, last time I came, I thought you might have been uncomfortable with a man alone?"

I smiled at her. "Stan, he's so intimidating."

"No, dear," Cassandra said. "Stan's your fiancé; he's pretty nice. Just a bit nosy."

Stan chuckled. "Of course, I was nice. You gave me iced tea on a hot day."

Mrs. Hanson looked me over through the screen, smiling. "Would you like some, Miss … Miss."

"Please, call me Melanie."

"Good. Then, I'm Cassidy; I prefer that. My husband calls me, 'Cass.' My least favorite."

I wondered if her husband realized, but figured he did from Cassidy's sour look. She said, "I'll give you tea *and* cookies." Without glancing at Stan, she opened the screen door, took me by the hand and led me inside. "I don't get to meet many new women, way up here on the hill."

The screen door clicked shut and I looked back to see Stan still on the front steps, staring; amazed, I was sure, by Cassidy's warmth.

"I could join you," he said. "Or leave and come back in an hour."

Cassidy nodded without looking his way. "That would be fine."

A couple of minutes later, I was on the leather couch in Mrs. Hanson's living room, sipping tea. She sat beside me, telling me she hated how the police had murdered George Floyd. "My husband, he didn't think a thing. He called Mr. Floyd a law-breaking N-word." Tears dribbled from her eyes. "I'm sorry. I shouldn't be saying that to you. My husband and I … We."

Not the first time I'd heard that story. I patted her hand. "That's all right, Cassidy. I understand. You're not like him, are you?"

"It's just … When I married him, I thought I knew Harbin, but …"

I let her cry for a minute. Then I said, "Stan heard some things about your husband."

She straightened, apprehensive. I gave her a moment.

"About … women?" she asked.

I nodded. "You ever suspect anything … maybe with Arlene?"

She stared. "I didn't know who, or even if." She pouched her lips, considering. "Never thought it would be her. It's just …" Cassidy got up and took a box of tissues from an end table. She wiped her tears, sat back next to me, and took my hand again.

I felt awful for her and took a moment to make sure I wouldn't tear up. "I'm sorry to suggest such a terrible thought. We can try to find out, but only if you want us to."

"Don't apologize, dear, for giving me a wake-up." Cassidy sighed. "I thought Harbin was over it. He used to come home late Tuesday nights. I bought his excuses about being out with the guys. Then, after Arlene took off—now that I think of it—he came home on time for a while. Now he's out late again. Now—screw him *and Arlene*—I'm putting the picture together. Bowling with his buddies on Tuesday. Sure …"

"We could find out for sure," I said. "We could put a device on his car and see where he goes."

Cassidy gave a teary half-smile. "No need, Melanie." She left the room and came back holding her cell phone. "I got an app," she said. "If someone has an iPhone, and you have one too, you can set it up to track him …" She blew her nose, looking almost happy. "I got hold of his cell one day when he just finished sending a text. He went out of the room, and I rigged it."

She touched the screen and showed me. "He's got a job today, over in Hemet. See … Harbin and his phone are at the hardware store."

On the screen I saw a red dot flashing on the map inside a little rectangle with the label, *Happy Hardware*.

Cassidy set her phone on the table. "Last Tuesday night, he wasn't at a bowling alley, like he said. He went to a bar in Temecula and then a hotel."

"Creep." I wanted to ring his neck for her. "Does he go to the same places every week?"

"Don't know." Cassidy said. "I just started this."

"You have plans for next Tuesday?"

Cassidy winked at me. "I'll give you and your fiancé a blow by blow of where my husband is. Then you all are going to tell me what that jerk is up to."

We got up, held hands for a moment and kissed each other on the cheeks.

I was almost out the door, when Cassidy said, "Be careful. Harbin is like the Rev and his snakes; easy mad. Easy to strike."

*The Rev and Harbin too.*

Stan was strict about not taking on marital disputes, but it looked like we were about to solve the case of Cassidy and Harbin Hanson as a side note to the missing snake escapade. I was beginning to see why Bud thought this was so much fun.

# CHAPTER 42

## CLEM

Clem arrived on the set that morning and looked things over. Pretty damn great (if you could overlook the chairs, too-large for seven-year-old butts). The enormous screens along the back wall, that were supposed to be windows, were in place, but dark, waiting for a little animation.

The contractor, Harry Duberry, showed up on time, eight sharp.

Clem pulled papers out of a folder and a pen from his pocket. "Got something for you to sign, Harry. Just a formality."

Harry gave him a blank look. "What?"

"Non-disclosure agreement. Something I need if you want to stay on the job."

As Harry signed, he asked, "You been talking to that lawyer of yours, eh?"

"Yeah. Guy's a stickler."

The computer nerd, Dusty, strolled in around half past, the prick part of this modern generation of lazy, slovenly, atheistic crud. Crud gifted with computer smarts.

"Welcome," Clem said, looking at his watch.

"Thanks."

Clem offered the agreement, and the nerd signed too.

Dusty set his laptop on a desk and punched some keys. A scene lit up across all three giant screens. Along the back wall, little kids played on a slide, tykes ran, hopped, skipped. A school bus waited for its passengers. Behind all three scenes lay a suburban neighborhood of attractive, middle-class homes. "This what you had in mind?

"Nice," Clem said. "Good work, Dusty."

"I got more," Dusty said. "You want to be in Georgia?" He typed on the laptop. Oak trees became magnolias. Most of the white kids turned black, still running and jumping. The bus driver stepped out of his vehicle, also black, friendly, smiling, like it was a pleasure to haul those little kids.

Dusty punched more keys. "Colorado." The bus vanished. The three windows showed kids playing. Most of them had turned white again. In the distance, behind the houses, hazy mountains appeared.

"Winter," the nerd said. Now the kids slid down a little hill on metal saucers, tossing snowballs at each other.

Clem grinned. "Damn, that's just the thing we need. How about inside the classroom? You do that kind of magic here, too?"

There was a TV on a stand, off to the side, part of the classroom set. Dusty switched it on. The empty chairs in the room appeared on screen. Dusty went back to the laptop and populated them with cute little seven-year-olds.

Holy Moses. Clem had hired the right guy! Sixty an hour; a bargain!

"Show me the teacher."

"White or black? Pilipino? Native American? Man or woman? How old? Straight or gay? It'll take a minute, but I can put up a gorgeous twenty-five-year-old transexual babe."

"How about a teaching team?" Clem laughed. "One black tranny and a white gal with blue hair." He laughed even harder, guffawing like a madman, until tears dripped down his chin. "Maybe bring in a Billy goat, sitting on the teacher's desk." He saw Dusty look over at Harry Duberry and shake his head.

*This is it*, Clem thought. *This is how I'll get myself rich as Midas.*

DUSTY AND CLEM worked until five. That's when Dusty looked at his Apple Watch and said, "Gotta go."

Clem was dog tired. His leg throbbed from standing so long by the TV screen, giving the nerd direction. "Okay. I'll work on the story for tomorrow. You're coming at 8, right?"

Dusty gave a mock salute. "You're the boss, Captain Dudas."

The nerd was almost out the door when Clem called, "Just to be sure."

Dusty halted but didn't turn around.

"You don't need a full script, just ideas, right?"

Looking back over his shoulder, Dusty said, "You got it, Señor Dudas. You're the captain. I'm the first mate. A. I. is the writer, the set designer, camera person and all the actors put together."

"Wonderful."

Clem's nerves were hopping. He felt both exhilarated and dead as a mummy. He flopped into the teacher's chair. On a piece of paper, he wrote:

STORY LINE 1
RECRUITMENT
FIFTEEN MINUTE SCENE
Teacher is black, students white, a few of them little
    blond girls.
Teacher tells students they get to choose.
Their sexes are like the clothes they wear.

169

Wait a minute. Clem crossed out black and made the teacher a Jew. He sat back in the chair, too tired to think any more. He ran his eyes around the classroom, loving this moment. No way he was going home tonight.

With his cell he found a place called *Ace Rent-A-Bed* and called to order a roll-a-bed.

"I have to charge you double for after-hours delivery."

"No problem."

"You want sheets? Pillows?"

Clem ordered the whole enchilada. Then he called in an order for pizza delivery. Once his bed and dinner arrived, he downed half the pizza, flopped onto the bed and fell fast asleep.

# CHAPTER 43

## BUD

B ud was proud of their little team. Stan's terrific fiancé had taken her friend Dolores from SimiBank out to lunch again, plying her with sufficient champagne and shrimp cocktail to get Dolores talking. As a bank security officer, she had more resources than they'd imagined.

Dolores uncovered Arlene's three credit cards from different banks and her activities at several stores and a gas station in San Bernardino. A bank account, too, holding seventy-five thousand, exclusively in her name. No Clem!

Arlene was definitely back. Elton Snivel not so much. Stan called Elton's mother and one of his sisters up in Oregon. (Bud was getting the idea that Stan didn't trust him to question members of the fairer sex.) Mother and sister were worried. Neither had heard from the gallivanting Snivel in two months.

EVERYTHING WAS SET with Cassidy Hanson. If her husband, Harbin, was meeting someone, Bud and Stan could find them. If that someone was Arlene, game over.

Late Tuesday afternoon, they took seats at a bar in Temecula, awaiting Cassidy's text. The bartender—chubby dude in a blue denim shirt—seemed like a nice guy. He didn't flinch when Stan ordered soda water.

After fifteen minutes, Bud was about to order his second gin and tonic. Stan shook his head. "Please don't."

Bud was toting his Smith and Wesson under his bomber jacket, which had to be part of Stan's reason for the wet blanket act. (After Cassidy Hanson's warning about her husband, Stan had given in to Bud about toting the weapon.)

"Not a problem," Bud raised his glass and nodded to the bartender. When his gin arrived, Stan grabbed it, reached across the bar, and dumped it into the sink.

"What the fuck?"

"No more," Stan said. "I don't like you having that in the first place." He nodded at Bud's armpit, where the pistol napped.

Yeah, technically, maybe he was right. Didn't mean Bud had to like it. "Okay, Mommy."

Stan received a text from Cassidy and showed it to him, *Harbin's at the Blue Swan in Murrieta.*

They followed Google's directions to the *Swan* and parked. It was seven-thirty and getting dark. They ambled to the back corner of the lot, and there, where you might expect a philandering female to park, sat Arlene's pickup.

"Bingo." They went to opposite sides of the pickup and tried the doors—both locked. "We gotta see what's in here," Bud said.

"Don't break anything."

"No problem. I come prepared." Bud reached into his jacket, the side with no gun.

"Don't shoot it, either."

He gave Stan his what-the-hell I-ain't-stupid face. "Of course not." With a flourish, he produced the car door jimmy and got ready to jam the bar in beside the window.

Stan, on the other side of the truck, looked like a scared chipmunk, eyes darting across the parking lot. "Someone's coming."

They ducked down and watched a couple get into a silver SUV and drive off.

Bud stood tall and prepared to jimmy the thing.

"Another one," Stan murmured. "I think it's ... Arlene."

"Is the guy with her?"

Stan moved away, along the fence-line of the lot. "Come on." He gave Bud a desperate wave. Bud followed, jamming the jimmy into his jacket. He pretended to zip up his pants as he walked—just an innocent bloke taking a piss in the bushes. Arlene—it was definitely her —eyed him, as she headed to her truck.

He caught up to Stan. "Let's confront her."

Stan pointed across the lot. "Harbin Hanson at two o'clock."

Bud saw the guy standing by his car, watching Arlene. He patted the S & W under his jacket. "We can take him."

Stan shook his head. "Let's get a crack at her truck first, see if there's any sign of our reptiles."

The two macho men hopped into the Escape. "They'll be shacking up after this. We'll have time to search her truck. Later, we'll catch her alone for a talk."

"You are one hell of a nervous dude, Stan."

"Cautious, my friend," Stan said.

Truthfully, Bud couldn't argue with his logic.

THEY HAD THE LUXURY of following Arlene without keeping an eye on her. Cassidy Hanson stood by to text her husband's new location. A half hour later, Stan parked the Escort behind the *Take a Chance Inn*. Not a bad name for their rendezvous. Sneaky Arlene again had parked in a dark corner of the lot.

Stan stood lookout by the driver's side, while Bud jimmied the passenger door. He reached across to unlock Stan's side.

Stan rummaged around. "Nothing under the front seat."

"Could have been a rattler down there," Bud said.

"Didn't think of that." Stan climbed behind the wheel and checked over the sun visor. "Anything lethal on your side?"

Bud popped the glove box and felt around. "No gun. Some papers and this." He brought out a lacquered wooden box that glistened in the dim light. Flicking on his cell phone's flashlight, he saw a painted red stripe meandering up the side and across the top of the box … not just any stripe. He almost dropped it. "Stan! It's a fucking red snake."

The driver's side door flew open. Bud saw Stan disappear from behind the steering wheel.

Bud's door popped open too. Arlene Dudas stood there grinning. She wasn't a bad-looking woman—black hair to her shoulders, dark eyes that glinted in the sparse light. Would have been an intriguing smile on someone who wasn't a surly bitch.

No gun in her hand. No knife. "You those two cock sucking detectives Clem sent after me? I heard about you."

He would have laughed then, but he heard grunts and thudding fists from the other side of the truck. He jumped out, pushed past Arlene, and bolted around the truck.

Stan lay sprawled on the ground, shielding his face with his hands. A guy kneeling over him took a quick look at Bud and turned back to wail on his partner.

The guy, Harbin, was built like a shot-putter. Bud figured he'd go for the gut really hard, try for some organ damage, and then back to Stan's face.

# CHAPTER 44

## BUD

Bud jerked his Smith and Wesson out, released the safety, and aimed it at Harbin. "Get off."

Harbin glared at Bud and held his punch. He rose slowly. "You break into my girlfriend's truck. What do you expect?"

Stan rolled toward Bud. He looked okay! But freaked out.

Bud wanted to hurt the bastard for beating Stan. "Fucker."

"Don't," Stan shouted. He held his hand toward Bud, pleading.

Bud took a breath. "Girlfriend, shit. You're Cassidy's husband." He pointed to Arlene. "She's married to the snake man." More breathing, taking himself down a notch. "We're not the bad guys here."

He heard Arlene coming up behind, across the gritty pavement, slow at first, then faster. He sidestepped, and her shoulder grazed his hip on her way down.

She landed hard on the asphalt. "Ohh. Owww! God damn it."

Bud was still worked up, but trying to stay in control.

"Nice try, honey," Harbin said.

Arlene sat up and rubbed one of her elbows. She looked from Bud to Harbin. "Don't worry Harby honey. They're just worthless private dicks."

Bud wondered, *How come my S & W isn't getting any respect?* He raised the gun to shoot it in the air, rejected the idea, and pointed it vaguely in Harbin's direction. Crap, maybe he *was* harmless.

Arlene dusted dirt off her shoulder. "My husband, Clem, *that piece of shit*, didn't like me to swear ... Piss on him. You're not taking me back there."

Harbin had seen Bud raise the gun but not shoot. He seemed to relax, even slouch a little. "You can swear with me anytime, honey. I like it just fine."

*God damn it, they're talking past me* and *my gun.*

Arlene raised one arm, then the other, rotated her shoulders, testing. "Clem had an entire repertoire of beat downs. Dick head. Ass fuck, that he is. You want me going back to him? Just shoot my ass."

Stan tested his chin with his fingertips. His nose was bleeding. "We don't want that. We don't do marital cases."

Arlene guffawed. "What the hell, then boys?"

"Snakes," Bud said. "Clem wants Maynard and Dobie back."

Laughing, she stood up. "That figures. The bitch-dog can have them. Come with me." She started toward the pickup.

"Hold it," Bud said. He nodded toward Harbin. "I'm not leaving him alone with Stan."

"Come on," Arlene waved for her boyfriend to follow. They walked to the truck's passenger side.

Bud stood back, keeping the gun ready. She took something from the truck and tossed it. It glinted as it flew, and he caught it in his free hand. The lacquered box.

"Open it." She snorted another laugh.

He slid the gun into his jacket, slipped the catch on the box, and raised the lid. "Oh, shit." The smell! "Oh, fuck." There was just enough light to make out the shapes inside the box: two matching snake heads, apparently putrefying. He dropped the box. The two heads popped out onto the asphalt.

Arlene howled. "Case solved, detective. Go ahead; give those boys to Clem with my compliments."

Still about to gag with the odor, Bud tried to figure out a good way to retrieve poor Maynard and Dobie and return them to their coffin.

Stan came up and touched his arm. "What's that horrible smell, pal?"

He pointed. "Our missing snake brothers."

Arlene turned serious. "One thing to think about, fellas. You help Clem find me after this…" She looked Bud straight in the eye, and her voice went shaky. "Tell him I didn't do this to his little besties. Tell him that, cause it's true. Don't let him come for me." She swallowed. "Clem's poisonous as any viper on God's green earth."

Stan reached toward her. "We don't know where you live, and we don't plan to follow you home."

Bud pointed at Harbin Hanson. "If you didn't hang out with this dip-weed, we'd never have found you."


THAT NEXT MORNING, the three amigos called Cassidy on speakerphone, Stan alternating between dabbing the cut on his forehead with a damp washcloth and telling Cassidy the story.

When he paused, Cassidy asked, "You got pictures of the two of them at the motel?"

"No way," Stan said. "Marital disputes aren't our business."

"But you were there. You had them."

"Don't complain," Bud said. "We're not charging you a cent."

Mel laid her hand on Bud's arm to shut him up. "I'm really sorry, Cassidy," she said. "You didn't deserve this."

Their case was all but over; that's what they thought, anyway. They only had to report their findings and deliver the goods to Clem. Naturally, Stan left that up to Bud.

# CHAPTER 45

## BUD

When Clem answered his call, Bud said, "Clem. It's me." Not much of a start.

"Hey, friend. You got some news for me? I have some for you."

"Clem, we found out what happened to Maynard and Dobie."

A pause, then, "What happened to them? … You got my snakes back, did you?"

"In a manner of speaking. Look, Clem, I better come up there and—"

"Something bad, ain't it?"

"You going to be home? If the traffic's okay, I can be there in an hour."

CLEM WAS WAITING for him on the swing. He stood, when Bud stepped onto the porch, holding the glossy box. "What you got in there?"

"Sit down, Clem."

"Not room in that little chest for any snakes." Clem dropped onto the swing, accusing Bud with miserable eyes.

Bud knelt by the edge of the porch, a few feet away from him. "You ready?" When Clem nodded, he flipped the lid open and backed away.

Clem shouted, "*Oh God ...*"

"I'm sorry."

"Give me that." Clem's nose wrinkled. He grimaced and started to get up but slunk back onto the swing. "That smell ... Is that? God damn it." He stood, jetting the swing backwards. It swung forward and caught him in the legs. "Ow." He staggered a little, his eyes bulging. "Where is she? Where's the bitch?"

Bud could see what Arlene meant about Clem's poisonous side. But the snake man had cause, didn't he?

"We caught up with her," Bud said. "But she's gone now. For what it's worth, she said she didn't kill them."

"Where is she? You gotta tell me."

"I don't know." Which was technically true. The next part was a lie: "We were lucky to find her. I doubt we can do it again, now that she knows we're after her." Of course, with the help of Mel's friend, Dolores at SimiBank, they could track Arlene anytime she used a credit card or wrote a check to her landlord.

Clem crouched by the box. Bud saw him choking back the puke that wanted out. Tears ran down his cheeks. "Maynard, Maynard, dear boy." He looked up at Bud, pitiful, and back into the box. "Dobie, good snake."

Bud gestured toward the side of the house. "Got a shovel in the shed?"

Clem nodded.

"I'll give you a few minutes."

When Bud returned with the shovel, Clem held the closed box in both hands. Bud wrapped his arm around Clem's shoulder for a moment. They walked together to a lilac bush at the edge of the lawn. Clem took the shovel and dug down a couple of feet. Bud set the box in the hole. Clem stood over it, lips moving, probably reciting one of those "Yea, though I walk (slither?) through the valley of the shadow of death …" incantations of his.

Clem shoved dirt into the hole with his foot. "I had something I wanted to show you, Bud. Can' t do it now." He pointed at Bud's Prius. "Go home or wherever."

Bud clasped his forearm and nodded.

"Come back to talk?" Clem asked. "Off the books. This ain't about the case."

How could a guy refuse a fellow human in such grief? "Sure, Clem."

# CHAPTER 46

## BUD

Their snaky case was a frolic for Bud. They had other jobs too; not half as interesting. Bud's major priority was fighting his way through Russian bureaucratic BS.

By the time Mel and Bud had the details of that *Adventure Russia* trip worked out, it was well into November. They scheduled the trip for early December.

With time on his hands, Bud called the Rev and drove up the mountain.

The two of them took up armchairs in the study.

"What you been up to, Budster?"

"Listening to members of your congregation saying you're out to screw all the women." (Bit of an overstatement there.)

Clem smirked and jiggled a finger at Bud. "Not true. I play with them, but my snake don't slither in their garden, if you get my meaning."

"So, it's all BS?"

"I'm a preacher, Bud." Clem paused, looking earnest. "The Lord commands we not covet, demands we stay true to our vows." He chuckled. "Commandments never said we cain't grab a little booby. You gotta believe me. I ain't never conjugated none of them."

*Wow, a triple negative.* "Actually, I do." Bud didn't believe any woman would consent to play that game. He let that lie for a moment and tried to sound casual. "Besides all my detecting, I'm going to Russia soon."

"Holy shamoley. Why you goin' to that hellhole?"

Again casual, "My girlfriend's there."

"Wow, Bud, a Commie babe? Congratulations. I bet she's pretty."

Bud was about to answer, when Clem laid a hand on his arm. "Enough about you, Budster. Wait till you see what I got."

Maynard and Dobie were apparently distant memories.

Clem picked up a remote and clicked on the TV. "You gotta promise to keep it secret."

"Sure."

On the screen, a classroom appeared; the teacher, a thin guy in his twenties wearing a yarmulke—Jewish school, then. The camera panned around the classroom full of little kids, seven or eight years old. Girls in blond pigtails, boys wearing white shirts and ties.

The camera returned to the teacher. He wrote on the greenboard; *You get to choose.*

What was that about?

The teacher stood by one girl in the front row. "Today's lesson is, 'You get to choose.' Doesn't that sound delightful?"

He touched the little girl's chin. She smiled up at him.

"You see, Stephanie?" He pointed to the girl next to her. "And you, Iris?" The teacher moved toward a little boy. "... You see, Sammy?"

"No, Mr. Schultz," Sammy said. "See what?"

"You get to choose," the teacher repeated. "Sammy, when you were very small, your mom and dad told you, didn't they? They said you're a boy?"

Sammy shrugged. "Well, yeah."

Mr. Schultz held a finger to his lips for silence. "It was like your mom and your dad; they'd decided you were a boy." The teacher looked at the girl in the middle. "And decided you were a girl, right, Iris, honey?"

Iris scowled at her teacher, then turned to Sammy.

"They never asked what you wanted to be, did they? But you don't have to be a girl, Iris ... or Stephanie. You don't have to be a boy, Sammy."

Clem clicked the remote and stopped the show. "You understand, Bud? This is happening all across America, and I can prove it. They're recruiting our blessed little ones!"

Fury knotted up Bud's stomach. So, it was true; all the talk about homosexuals and LGBTQ recruiting kids. "Shit, Clem. Holy, fucking shit."

"We gotta stop them," Clem said. "That's why I've been tracking this down, like a detective." He smirked at Bud. "Like you Bud. I got more of these films, too."

Bud's skeptical side wanted to deny it, but here was absolute sickening proof. "This is the *work* you talked about?"

Clem got up and aimed the remote at him. "Yeah, Bud. Making America great again. Keeping perves from taking our country down. We gotta fight back."

"And you have more? This isn't some one-time crazy thing?"

"You ask our man, Donald. He's been warning us; the Commies and the pervs are trying to destroy our great country. It's a conspiracy, and the government is in on it." Clem set the remote down and moved in front of the TV, the screen still lit behind him. "You want a film with a black teacher with ten-year-olds? I got it. We gotta stop them, Bud. It's God's work."

Bud stared at the Rev, seeing him with new appreciation. "You have a plan for that?"

Clem winked at him. "After I *uncovered* this, I got in touch with this representative guy in Florida. He contacted one of those Political Action Committee types, you know, patriots. I sent them this video last week." Clem stepped aside and eyed the TV, Mr. Schultz and little Iris still on the screen. "They paid some nice bucks. I'm going to make more films, and the world will find out. It'll be on Foxy News any day now. You know what I'm sayin'?"

Bud sat back in his chair, wanting to scream. Everything those right-wing politicians said, all of it, was true! Beyond his worst imaginings! Beyond evil! But he'd promised to keep it secret.

Clem grinned. "Pretty good flick, if I say so myself. I wanted your reaction."

"Hell no; it's horrible."

"I get what you're meaning; this teacher is damnable unto the Lord. But the video's first class, ain't it?"

"Yeah, for sure."

As he drove down the mountain, Bud was thinking; Clem's video was high quality. All those camera angles! How'd they do that? The only way was if the teacher agreed to the filming. Which meant ... someone shot this film as a training piece for other perverts who wanted to recruit innocent kids to their sick cult.

Why hadn't Clem mentioned that?

# CHAPTER 47

## BUD

*DECEMBER 2021*

B ud drank three shots of gin than evening, trying to forget that classroom and those innocent kids.

He'd seen with his own eyes, but he couldn't tell anyone, especially not Stan. This was so awful that, once Bud spoke up and Stan laughed it off as another conspiracy theory, Bud's anger could spiral (like their disputes over Trump in the past).

Bud felt better knowing that Clem was taking action, getting the video out. Clem and some Florida Political Action Committee. They'd take care of it. They had to.

He worked for the next few days to forget that damn scene and focus on his plans to see Sveti. The visa came with a week to spare. –All systems go for the trip on December 8.

On December 5, Clem called. "Hey, Budman, you still planning that trip to Russia?"

"Leaving in three days."

"What time you go to work tomorrow morning?"

"Nine-thirty. Why?"

"Okay, thanks." Clem hung up.

*What the hell?*

The next morning, Bud was brushing his teeth when the doorbell rang. He opened the door, his mouth full of paste and found Clem. The snake man wore a leather jacket, his hair and beard glossy, like he just came out of the shower or greased himself up somehow. "Got a gift for you and a favor to ask."

Clem marched in and looked around Bud's living room. "Pretty plain in here. You got no taxidermized critters on the wall?" He stepped into the kitchen. "How about American flags?"

Bud walked to the sink and spit out his toothpaste. "Great to see you too, Clem. What's the gift?"

"Just what you're lacking, son." Clem pulled a six-inch-wide American flag sticker out of his jacket pocket. "Where you want it?" Approaching the refrigerator, he pulled the backing off of the sticker.

Bud grabbed his arm. "Not there. The frig belongs to my landlord."

"The oven?" Clem darted toward it, obviously enjoying himself. "I get it," he said. "The microwave. That belongs to you." Clem slapped the sticker over the microwave's window.

"Gee, thanks, Clem."

"You're welcome, friend. Now you owe me that favor, but really, it's a second favor I'm doing you."

Bud stuck a coffee pod in his Keurig machine. "You want a cup, Clem?"

"Naw. I gotta get back to Herbert. You know how demanding pets can be. I'm just droppin' this off, so you can do yourself and me that favor." He slipped a manila envelope from inside his jacket and laid it on the table.

Bud hit the button on the coffee machine and gawked at the script on the envelope—indecipherable. "What's this? Cyrillic?"

Clem stroked his salt-and-pepper beard, still beaming. "Right, Bud. You said you'd like to help Donald Trump. Take this to Russia, and you'll be helpin' him."

*Contraband?* "What's in it?"

"You know that video I showed you, the classroom?"

"Sure."

"You'll be spreading the word. You just gotta mail this inside Russia."

He'd be glad to get the word out about those perverts. "Why Russia? I thought you had this handled."

"You're gonna do it, right?"

"Yeah, but—"

Clem grabbed a kitchen towel and wiped every inch of the envelope. "I got a few don'ts for you, friend. Don't ask questions. Don't get your finger prints all over it, and don't just take it to a post office over there. They got cameras. Be careful with this thing, all right?"

Clem patted Bud on the shoulder and headed for the door.

If Clem was wiping finger prints off it, this had to be more than a simple delivery. More like some serious shit. "Hold on a second," Bud said, but Clem was out and gone.

Just mailing a letter? Helping Trump? Sure, he could do that.

# CHAPTER 48

## BUD

The day before Bud's flight, screw it, he failed the friggin' Covid test at the pharmacy. He wasn't sick, just pissed off with a nothing cough.

Next morning, Bud threw the lab results in the trash, packed and went to the Aeroflot desk at LAX. He set his passport and visa on the counter.

A middle-aged man in a blue shirt with silly silver epaulettes looked them over.

Bud flashed a grin. "Ready to travel." He suppressed a cough.

The guy held out his hand. "Covid test."

"I mislaid the paperwork," Bud lied.

The guy gave him a look and aimed a finger toward the far end of the terminal. "Under the sign that says *health tests*."

"I just want to go to Russia to see my girlfriend. She's waiting."

The Aeroflot guy looked past him and waved the next passenger forward. "You have to test."

"Are you Russian?" Bud asked. "Your English is very good."

The guy was still looking at the people behind Bud. "I've worked here a while."

"If you're Russian, you understand love, right? And tragedy."

"What the heck, man. You got no tragedy. Just let them cram the stick up your sneezer."

"Did I mention how good your English is?"

No reaction.

Bud thought about mentioning that he liked Putin, but this dude was too much of a prick to care.

He took the test, just in case, and failed. He retreated to his apartment and called *Adventure Russia*. The woman who answered sounded Indian.

"Good afternoon," she said.

At least she knew what time zone he was in. "I was supposed to fly today. I went to the airport, but they rejected me for health issues."

"Mr. Randolph, you have the virus, I think. Yes?"

"Maybe."

"You try to get on a Russian plane, Aeroflot airplane, they test. Why even go to the airport?"

Good question. Shitburgers!

It was after midnight in Russia, but he called Sveti. "Hi, honey. Sorry to call so late."

It took her a moment to take that in. "Bud. Everything is okay? You at airport?"

"… I have to put off the trip."

Bud heard her take a breath. "I *really* want to come. I will come very soon. I got Covid."

"Oh. You sick, Bud, darling? You take medicine? You in hospital?"

"I'm okay, but they won't let me on a plane. I have to get tested in two weeks, then make new reservations."

"You sure, you all right? You still come? You not …"

He almost said it then, after all these weeks of quiet conversations and sweet goodnights. At that moment, when she needed reassurance, he almost said *I love you*. Instead, he said, "Dear Sveti, nothing can keep me away."

# CHAPTER 49

## MELANIE

I felt bad for Bud when he couldn't go to see his sweet Sveti. Ticked at him too. He's our happy, messed-up dufus. Stan and I love him, but he shouldn't have even considered taking a plane with Covid. He shouldn't have wanted to come in to the office or go out to investigate. Stan told him to stay away and paid him sick leave. He did stay away from us, but Lord knows who he contaminated during those two and a half weeks.

Back at work, Bud waited for Stan to leave the office one day and rolled his chair over. "I'm falling for Sveti."

I laughed. "Tell me something I don't know."

"She's devoted to her grandmother."

I wondered why he mentioned that. "Great."

Bud smiled a crooked smile. "Granny's been dead for years."

*What a sweet, devoted woman.* "Okay, Bud. This can bring you closer. Talk to her about granny. Have her tell you stories about the old gal."

"She's told me plenty of those, about her grandmother and great grandma, who's some kind of saint, about Russian tzars too." Bud walked to the window and back. He plopped down in his chair looking sheepish and uncertain—not his customary demeanor. "Sveti wants to bring her grandma's bones to the US if she moves here."

I whistled. "So, you're talking marriage? Bringing Sveti—and grandma—home to meet Stan and me?"

"Yeah, maybe. Pretty weird, huh? Dragging a carcass around the world? I'm a *toss my body in the oven and throw the ashes in the trash*, kind of guy."

I chuckled. "I'm with you on that, but I've attended some interesting funerals ...."

Bud beckoned with his hand for more info.

"When my mother's uncle Fred died, they had an open coffin at the funeral home. I was just a girl, and it freaked me out, especially when one of his female friends began screaming. 'Freddie's my lover. He's with the Lord now. Alleluia. Alleluia.' She reached in and patted Fred's face and then his shoulder and ran that hand down past his chest. She leaned halfway in. I thought she'd topple and land on old Fred. Another woman came up, elbowed this gal aside and did almost the same thing, wailing even louder."

If I'd had time to dwell on that funeral and the others I'd attended since, I might have gone from lighthearted to weepy, but Bud was listening and there was more to tell.

"Sounds like a great time."

"Mom and I went to lay flowers on Uncle Fred's grave, and one of those women—I don't actually know who she was—she was sitting back against the gravestone, reading a book to Fred. I don't get that, Bud. I think, when you're gone, you're gone, but hey, what do I know?"

I expected one of Bud's wisecracks, but he looked serious. "Did they try to dig Freddie up?"

"Don't think so."

"You see why this worries me?" Bud asked.

Of course, I did, but his worry came out of love, and the love brought Bud's tender side out from hiding. I got up from my chair and smiled down at him. "I do, Bud. But if you love her, if you think she's the sexiest woman alive, if that's the only thing that bothers you, seems to me you're one lucky dog."

He rotated his chair 360, twice around, and smiled at me. "Yeah. I am. You think Stan will let us keep granny's bones in his backyard?"

# CHAPTER 50

## BUD

*A*dventure Russia pissed Bud off. Their guy on the phone said, "Mr. Randolph, we arranged everything, but *you* changed the date." Bud felt like the guy was stifling a chuckle. "Difficulties can occur with Russian bureaucracy. *Adventure Russia* solves all problems." Naturally, there were fees for this *difficulty solving service*.

They made arrangements for Bud to fly into the teeth of a Russian February.

The news said Russia was doing military exercises on the Ukrainian border. Okay, normal stuff, Putin saber-rattling.

Bud was on his way, at an airport bar in Anchorage on a stopover. Tucked in his jacket pocket, he had his passport and visa, plus *Adventure Russia's* blue plastic folder of vouchers and tickets. He slid off the barstool, heading to the gate.

Biden showed up on TV—split screen with an aerial view of Russian military vehicles in a snowy field. Bud halted mid-step. Biden said the situation with Russia was "serious;" the US government was "monitoring the situation." Biden tried to look strong, but he just didn't have the moxie.

Nothing to worry over.

The flight was long. It was colder than a California guy could damned well imagine that day in Moscow! He took the train east and a taxi to the *resort AR* had arranged, a few miles from Sveti's town. A nice location with a sweeping lawn leading to a pine forest. The building was a blocky five-story, the lobby basic with a touch of wood paneling behind the reception desk. The painted walls needed a new coat. A dark-haired jowly man at the desk, looked up at Bud and went back to his computer.

Bud tapped his fingers on the counter and waited maybe five minutes.

"Mr. Randolph," the man said. A statement, not a question.

"Right. You know my name because you only have one new guest today?"

"We have several." The guy's English was easy to understand. He held out his hand. "Passport and credit card."

Bud handed them over.

He looked through the passport, every page of it, typed information into his computer. He took his time paging through it a second time.

Why waste time on blank pages? "You never see one of those?" Bud asked. "USA."

"I see many." The man scanned the information page and handed it back. "Many Americans who strike fingers on desk. Hope I move faster." He looked Bud in the eye. "Very impatient, Americans. Too important to wait."

*Fucker.*

The man handed over the key. "I put you in nice room, top floor." He smiled. "Elevator broken. Fix tomorrow."

Turned out the bathroom was down the hall. Shared bathroom at a *resort*! The hall was stifling hot, the room freezing. Bud messed with a knob on the clunky old radiator. No luck. After a shower, he lay under three blankets on his too-damned-soft bed and smiled. Sveti would arrive soon.

Three walls in that dump of a room were painted dirty taupe. Large windows on the other side made up for it. He looked out across a lawn with patches of snow, to that pine forest and far-off mountains. Thinking— *A couple of decals on the wall could fancy this up, maybe a photo of Putin reviewing the troops. What was that guy up to with Ukraine?*

The TV showed Putin talking at some kind of assembly. On another channel, shots of Russian troops marching, jets soaring, the announcer barking Russian gibberish.

Bud found his blue flannel shirt and put it on, added gray slacks. A little warmer. He paced the floor to stay warm and flicked to other TV channels; finally, an English channel. International CNN—*progressive* news. Crap!

A good-looking brunette came on with a map of Russia and Ukraine behind her. "At this hour, the US State Department reports that Russia has moved, and I quote, 'massive concentrations of troops to Ukraine's eastern and northern borders.' We have two reports for you."

The screen split into halves. A gray-haired guy with a Moscow scene, blabbed first. "Russian sources declare that 'Routine military exercises are underway. There is no cause for concern.'"

Next a blonde by an onion dome church, in Ukraine: "President Zelensky insists Russia will not attack. He wants the world to know that talk of war is causing undue alarm. Ukrainian citizens should stay calm and go on with their daily lives." Bud's skeptical side screamed, *bullshit!* The phony CNN news was making a heck of a deal out of *no cause for concern.*

The brunette returned. "Despite that rosy prediction, sources with the US State Department quote covert Russian sources, claiming that an attack is probable. President Biden has warned Vladimir Putin of 'serious consequences.'"

At 5 PM, Bud heard a knock at the door. He muted the TV and opened it. Sveti wore a white quilted coat, and she landed in Bud's arms in an instant. They made out like two horny teens, and he loved it.

She frowned, even prettier than he remembered. "Very cold in here."

Bud pointed to the radiator. "I tried to turn it up."

She went over and messed with it. "They want you must freeze?" She looked around. "You have telephone?" She went to the bedside table, dialed the phone and demanded something in Russian, not sounding a bit like his sweet Sveti.

A lanky guy showed up, wearing gray overalls with lots of pockets. Sveti glowered and pointed to the radiator. He pulled out a blue-handled wrench, knelt by the radiator and turned a bolt.

Sveti snapped a few words as the man retreated out the door. To Bud she said, "Sheety hotel too cheap to heat you room. I tell that man, you important American fellow. Not treat you like jail prisoner."

"Thanks, sweetheart. You really take care of me. Could you tell him to fix the elevator?"

She frowned. "I take elevator here. It perfect."

There was a little glass vase with a few daisies on the night table. Bud grabbed it and hurled it against the wall. He looked back and saw Sveti's eyes, wary.

He took a breath, as she watched him. "That clerk is a son of a bitch. He hates Americans."

Sveti didn't' move. Bud thought back to what she'd told him about living with her sister and her brother-in-law the angry drunk.

"I'm sorry, honey." He did his best to relax, hoping for her good mood to return.

She touched his arm. "Do not let him upset you. You want break lamp now, throw chair at mirror, break everything. Okay. I leave and you can do, or you act sensible. You and me have fun together."

"I'll go for the fun."

She smiled and flopped onto the bed. Bud jumped on and they made out. Thinking back to that day by the river, he unbuttoned her coat and wrapped his arms around her.

"Easy, big man, Bud. Still cold in here. We keep clothes on today, okay?"

"You still like me, don't you?" Even to himself, he sounded pathetic.

She laughed and gave him another glorious kiss. "I give you then, what you call in America? –a *come-on*? You remember touch my breast. You go back America and dream. Then you *come on* back see me."

*What an honest thing to say.* Sveti seemed young in some ways, and then mature … honest; just right for him. Anything she wanted, he wanted too. Going slow would be great. How un-Bud-like he felt with this woman.

Bud smoothed back her chestnut hair and saw her glance at the television. "What they say?" she asked.

"The US says Russia plans to attack Ukraine. Putin says no."

"You should not trust Putin." Her eyes went wide. She looked around the room and put a finger to her lips. "I not mean that. Putin not so bad. Some things he say, true. He say Ukraine full of Nazis."

"You believe him?"

She cupped her hand around Bud's ear and whispered. "I been to Ukraine. Putin is Nazi, not Zelensky. Putin is pooking liar."

Maybe he should stand up for Putin. Trump and he were two tough hombres making their countries—not Nazi, just powerful.

Her hair tickled Bud's ear. He kissed her cheek as she whispered. "Putin not kill people, but if man he hate be killed, he make killer good job in government."

Bud thought about the guy who wanted to run against Putin, who'd been poisoned with some nuclear cocktail.

After a moment, she looked at Bud with tears in her eyes and said out loud, "Bud, I tell you, my father from Ukraine. Russia invade, kill Ukrainians, that be worst. More than person can ..." She went quiet.

They snuggled for a while on the bed. Then Sveti stretched and said. "You want have dinner?"

"You bet."

"Then take walk."

Bud wasn't sure about going into that frozen night, but he wasn't about to argue. "First I have something for you."

Sveti watched as he pulled his carryon from under the bed. He removed the gift he'd brought for her and Clem's envelope with the crazy Russian address. He handed her the box.

Sveti smiled "Candy?"

"Really good chocolate, dark; that's the best," Bud confirmed.

"What is that?" She pointed to Clem's envelope.

Remembering the snake man's advice to keep things secret, even to avoid getting finger prints on it, Bud held up his finger for silence and handed it to her.

Sveti glanced at it, crammed it into her coat pocket, took a step back and said, "Thank you very much for gift. Now Sveta hungry for dinner." She moved in close and murmured into his ear. "We talk later."

They took the elevator down to the upscale dining room where they split a shrimp cocktail and a steak dinner, plus a few vodka martinis.

Bud carried a pint bottle of vodka from the bar in one hand and held Sveti's hand in the other, as they walked into the dark night, crunching through crusty snow.

In the middle of the lawn, she faced him. "We not inside, still speak quiet. What you do with this?" She pointed at the envelope in her coat pocket.

"It's important. A client asked me to mail it."

The hotel lights were faint but sufficient. He saw her narrow her eyes. "Address on envelope say *Agriculture Ministry*."

"I'll be damned. You look pretty when you're cold."

"Be serious, Bud. Bottom of envelope say *Swine Good Feeding*. I not know right word in English. *Good feeding*?"

"Nutrition maybe?" Bud offered.

Sveti took that in. "*Nutrition*, new word, thank you. What you should know, Bud, Agriculture Ministry in Russia not help farmers feed pigs. Agriculture Ministry secret place."

"It's okay," Bud said. "I'll just mail it, and—"

Sveti shook her head. "No. I take this, find out truth. You not speak about. Not admit you ever have this." He was about to argue, but she looked him in the eye and said, "I protect you, Bud. You not understand my country."

Bud saw Sveti's fear and decided. "As long as you bring it back tomorrow."

"Of course. It belong to you." Sveti took his hand and brightened. "We talk something different now. You want spend time with me, I think."

He kissed the side of her head. "Definitely."

"You, me be honest, yes?"

"Sure."

"Not talk about Ukraine. Talk USA. I think I would like your America, Mr. Bud, but I not sure. It amazing country they say?"

Her question reminded Bud of Clem's video, and other shit that had gone down back home. But he had faith; Trump would come back, clean house and make it right. No reason to down America to Sveti.

"Best country in the world," Bud nuzzled his cold cheek against hers. "If you come, you'll see."

She pulled back and frowned. "People say that before. Now, not so much. America say 'democracy, democracy, yes, yes, yes.' Putin say your election sheet."

Huh…. Bud's chest tensed up. He sipped from the bottle of vodka and passed it to her.

US elections had been crappy lately, but only Americans could say it. "And your elections; how are they working for you?"

"We know, ours are sheet. Everyone, always know, Russia not honest—*corrupt* (cor-oopt)—Is that word? But you, America, preach us, preach every country in world. Now your man, your Trump say election cheated, say is sheet also."

Stan said that Trump was ruining America's reputation by denouncing the election. Maybe it needed a downgrade. (Maybe … probably … maybe not? Who the hell knew?)

She puckered a cheek and eyed him. "What else is lie in US. If you want me to go there, you tell me."

Bud sighed. "Okay, the election was screwed up, but Trump's coming back to clean house."

Sveti shook her head. "I see news from Amerika and other place. I have internet and VPN. Trump is like Putin, but giant-big, loud, all orange."

Bud would have resented that from Stan, but Sveti was pretty and playful. She seemed to have the inside track on Putin. "Trump may be carroty, but he's not Putin. He's what we need in America. We have to get the illegals out and flush liberal BS down the toilet."

Bud felt his chest tighten. "Listen, Sveti, the big reason I like Trump is about jobs. The factory where I worked in Georgia closed down a few years ago. All those people out of work. None of the politicians gave a crap, but Trump did. He tried to keep factories open."

Tears ran down his face, which really surprised him. Sveti brushed them away. "You one of them, lose job?"

"I did. My friends too."

"Hurt you, made you sad." Looking into his eyes, she brought his hand up and kissed it. "I watch American news, learn English. Trump people, every minute angry. No good in world they say. All terrible. Your Biden blow nose, they complain wrong cloth he use. No way to live mad as hell like that."

She stroked Bud's cheek. "Sometimes I see you mad-face, Bud, not just about hotel clerk. What angry make you?"

He thought about that for a moment. "All kinds of things, Sveti. The election bugs me the most. Other stuff too, like when the cell phone company makes me go through crap to get help."

She grinned at him. "You lucky fellow, telephone company help you." She kissed his hand again. "You lose that job and everything go bad?"

"Maybe."

She kissed his cheek. "You much better when happy face. Sveta make your face happy?"

"Absolutely. But my cheeks are freezing out here."

After Sveti left, Bud poured a shot of vodka and sent a text to Mel, *What the heck is a VPN?*

Answer: *Virtual Public Network. It lets you be anonymous on the internet.*

All sorts of ideas buzzed through Bud's head that night. Sveti had made a good point. Why had it taken a woman, who watched American news from thousands of miles away, to point out how angry Trump people—like Bud—were? How scary that might be, especially to a woman, *Hey, buddy, pay attention and take it easy if you don't want her to run.*

# CHAPTER 51

## BUD

Sveti arrived the next morning. He pulled her into the room and wrapped his arms around her. She spoke into his chest. "I have my cousin car today."

"Great. What do want to do?"

"Ride in country. Fresh air, Mr. Bud."

He was dying to ask about Clem's envelope but couldn't until they got outside.

After breakfast they hopped into the small, yellow, boxy car. It was freezing in there. Sveti wore a lime-green knitted hat and matching gloves. Her brown hair streamed from under the hat down to the collar of her white coat. She smiled at him as she drove away from the hotel.

"Safe to talk in here?" he asked.

She pulled onto the road. "Yes, dear Bud. You want ask about Agriculture Ministry, Swine Nutrition, yes?"

He nodded.

"These top-secret swine—that right way to say, *top-secret*? I find out what they do, that swine office. Cyber deceivers. Send lies on internet. Propaganda for Putin."

Bud had convinced himself that he needed to mail Clem's envelope. But all last night, after what Sveti had said, he'd doubted. "How do you know?"

They were out in the country, white snow-covered fields and forest, Sveti intent on her driving and glancing frequently at the rear-view mirror. "I tell you; I have special computer. I go on black web. If you mail package, you help Putin propaganda."

Clem's video wasn't a lie. It uncovered a program promoting perversion in America. Something the world needed to know. Actually, just America needed to know, so they could fix it. Helping Putin discredit America; he didn't like that.

Sveti slowed and turned down a dirt road. "They watch everywhere, me for sure. Sveta on their list." She glanced at Bud. "Not worry, no one follow now."

They bounced along the dirt road past a red barn with peeling paint, heading toward another farm. "They find out you mail this, think you spy. They think me spy, too." She shot him a look. "I have plan for envelope." She patted her pocket.

She had a point. Mailing it could be dangerous, not just for him. Why did she say they watched her *for sure*?

She pulled to a stop near a barn with a pen of some sort, really stinky there. "We give to Swine Nutrition Program." Sveti got out.

Bud met her at the back of the car. She opened the trunk and pulled out a bucket of spoiling vegetable scraps. He spotted carrot tops and wilted lettuce swimming in brown liquid.

She nodded to him. "Trust me, Mr. Bud. I take care of it for you." She looked straight into his eyes.

Time to decide. He pictured crazy-ass Clem grinning. How had the snake guy decided to send this to a Swine Program? What the fuck was going on?

He trusted Sveti or he didn't.

She handed him the envelope.

He ripped it open. A flash drive dropped into his hand. He held it a second and let it fall into the bucket. He tore the envelope into pieces. The scraps landed in the stew.

Several pigs came close, fat and muddy. They snorted and snuffled their way through Sveti's slop. The flash drive disappeared.

"Now I take you skating," she said. "You know how?"

As they drove toward the rink, she said, "This client tell you to mail. Not trust him. Make danger you."

Later that day, he got a text from Clem: *While you're playing at that fancy resort, don't neglect your mission. You get the job done?*

Bud hadn't mentioned a resort or told Clem when he'd arrive. Not a chance Stan would have informed him. *How the hell does he know?*

Bud sent back: *Delivery complete.*

Clem's reply: *Proud of you, Budster. Kiss your commie babe for me.*

# CHAPTER 52

## BUD

For the next two weeks, whenever he was with Sveti, Bud hardly thought about Clem's nonsense. But, alone at night, he alternated between anger at Clem for exposing him to Russian intrigue and guilt over abandoning his mission (which somehow was supposed to help Trump).

He and Sveti skated and danced, necked in the back of a theater, and Bud's favorite, renting a private room at his resort with a hot tub, renting it four times! Sveti never took off everything, but she took off a lot. Bud, he was buff-naked by the third tub adventure. They truly got to know each other.

Without saying the word *marriage*, they talked about her coming to the US, about spending months together, maybe years, *maybe* ... They didn't define what that last *maybe* meant.

In the tub the last time, wearing her bathing suit, top and bottom, Sveti turned on the jets and moved in close. She looked too earnest for what Bud had in mind.

"Before have fun, I talk. No one hear but you." She kissed his cheek. "Russia not good place now. My country, I thought would become good place, be more free, be democracy. There was Yeltsin; he want free; he want democratic. Too drunk to make for president. I just girl; my grandma tell me. Putin come. People think he good manager man. Think he make all better. I think you like Putin, but each year we less free. He close newspaper, tell television what they can say; all good things for him. People believe lies Putin tell or they afraid to speak." She looked close to tears. "You have liars in America too."

It was good that Sveti was opening up to him, showing emotion, but this was lousy timing, with only an hour in the tub. "At least we get to hear the other side in America."

She stroked his thigh—a good sign. "I think about what you say other day. Your Trump, you think he lie?"

"He tells the truths that need to be said."

"You believe him, believe everything? And Trump friend, man with shoe polish on face? I see on internet. He say twenty ways election fake. Not possible, you think? Not make sense."

Bud had tried to sort that out before. Some of those theories were screwed up, but some had to be true. There was no way Biden had won. "Trump's lawyers went a little overboard with that stuff." Showing more certainty than he possessed, Bud added, "Trump definitely won."

She gave him a skeptical nod. "Russians believe what Putin say. He say Ukraine Nazi, people agree. Your Trump say election rig, and you buy it—that expression, *buy it*?"

This was not going the way he'd hoped.

"So if man have shoe polish on face, he lie. Man with orange face, he always speak true?" She looked into Bud's eyes and patted his face. "Sorry I not all the time agree you, but in Russia, Putin tell politician they not run, and they quit. Some he lock up, like best man, Alexei Navalny. I know this, because I try help Navalny. I know more, because special internet contact VPN, get information not censored. This not free country, Bud. This place go to hell." She took a deep breath. "Have to be careful who you believe, not only in Russia."

She touched his face again. "Sorry, I talk too much. Hope you not angry-mad."

She leaned back and pushed the button, shutting off the jets. "Now we kiss." She took off the top of her suit, and his disappointment vanished. His heart soared and his eyes feasted. He and Sveti caressed each other beyond distraction.

BUD LAY AWAKE for an hour that night weighing Sveti's words. He was a detective, a guy who followed clues and evidence. Clue: Biden shouldn't have won; he was dull as crud. Evidence: The stuff Trump's lawyers threw out pretty much fell apart. Clue: Trump said he'd won by a mile. Evidence: Really sparse in the details. If Trump was lying about the election, that made *him* the thief, and everything he'd said to put down American democracy ... reprehensible.

Not possible. America needed Trump. Bud buried his head under a pillow and dozed off.

ALL BUD WANTED was to share his days with Sveti, but things kept cropping up. Granny was one diversion. They went to the little chapel in the cemetery, where Sveti's ancestors hung out. Bud sat on one of the ice-cold benches, listening to his sweet woman talk with her great grandmother in the silver coffin, with her mother—briefly—and last her grandma, Polina, for half an hour.

Later she told Bud; she'd scolded her mother for making life so hard for her dad; so hard that he drank himself to death, his body sent back and buried in Ukraine. She praised granny Polina for blessing her childhood with love and kindness. Sveti's sweet tones with Polina warmed him to the old girl, whose carcass, apparently, they might take to America. (Funny, after thinking that over for the past few months, it seemed almost normal.)

The much more serious crap that invaded their good spirits was that Russian army lurking on Ukraine's doorstep. Though she tried to hide it from him most of the time, it obviously tore Sveti up. The CNN channel—not just CNN reports, but the whole channel—disappeared from the TV in Bud's room. His Wi-Fi at the hotel dropped Facebook and all of Bud's usual news sources.

She was in touch. Every day she brought outside news from that special internet setup she had. What Putin didn't want the Russians to know, Sveti found out.

They talked in the hot tub with jets roaring, or out on the snowy lawn behind his hotel.

One day they paced back and forth together, in that park near the cemetery.

"Pooking, pooking Putin! Your government, your Joe Biden, he say Russia go to invade. My father home country, Ukraine! My father gone. Many uncle, aunt, cousin. Still there!"

"Biden doesn't know what he's talking about," Bud told her. "Putin won't do it."

"Putin not care. Russia, *criminal state*." She stopped and heaved a sigh. "Alexei Navalny."

"You mentioned him in the tub. The guy who got poisoned."

She whisked tears away with the back of a hand. "The guy *Putin* poisoned. We all know." She nodded and kept nodding until Bud pressed his hand to her cheek.

"This criminal state," she said again, looking toward the cemetery. She heaved a sigh. "Not place for Grandma Polina."

She sat on a bench for a couple of minutes and then smiled into his eyes. "None of this your fault, dear man. You deserve good time with me."

She gave him a good time every day, because she was good, and bright; happy to be together, loving, whenever she wasn't obsessing over Ukraine.

Sveti's first put-downs of Putin had annoyed Bud. But being the open-minded guy he was, he listened. He hadn't really known that much about the guy, thinking he was okay, because Trump admired him. Now, seeing the news disappear from his TV and computer, hearing the things Sveti told him, Bud homed in on Putin's dark side.

In the hot tub or in his bed he held her tight, inhaling her adoration. He felt her suppress her fury, doing her best to stay upbeat for him.

Wasn't he doing the same; every time the hotel clerk gave him a mean look along with the key to his room. Every time a waiter said "Amerikan?" with a nasty inflection; papering over his feelings so he wouldn't upset her? Every time he considered the idea that America's election might not have been stolen, after all.

# CHAPTER 53

## STAN

Stan made coffee in the kitchen that Monday morning, getting ready to heat toaster waffles. Melanie was taking a shower. As he took butter and blueberry jam out of the frig, he wondered what Bud was up to with his Russian sweetie. Hoping things were going well in romance-land and that Russia wouldn't invade Ukraine.

The phone rang, and he picked it up.

"Mr. Stein, this is Emilia Clark."

"How'd you get my home number?" Stupid question for a detective; for anyone in 2022. "Skip that. What do you want, Ms. Clark?"

"I hope you're not still annoyed, Mr. Stein. I have another job for you. Similar, but—"

"I'm not interested. You weren't honest with me."

"But—"

"You didn't tell me about the federal involvement. You hung up on me when I wanted more info."

"I didn't lie. How was I to know about that? This is different, Mr. Stein. You did a good job. I value your work."

Stan felt foolishly pleased by the compliment.

"I'm willing to pay you up front, pay you double. Just conduct surveillance on a man in Redondo Beach. A man in his forties who's suspected of a financial crime overseas."

She gave the address, and he jotted it down.

Bud's absence would continue for another week, and Stan had had to reduce their worker's comp workload ... and revenue. He'd not only rented the expensive office and leased the Prius for Bud, but he'd also bumped Bud up to three weeks' paid vacation and reimbursed for the sick leave he'd taken for Covid.

"The same work as before," she said. "Photograph people coming and going. Let me know if the man leaves the house. You don't need to follow him; just report what car he drives."

"Do you really work for KatzBank?"

"You checked me out; I know you did."

"You won't allow me to call the Bank and ask for you?"

"I definitely work for them," she said. "I told you; some of our international portfolios are just too confidential.... I checked on you, too, or I wouldn't trust you with this sensitive assignment."

He'd done his due diligence; looked her up on the internet and verified her identity—a vice president of the bank—from her photos on the bank website. He'd met her just down the street from the Bank, the same woman from that website.

"I'm not saying yes, and I'm not saying no. Give me the address, and I'll look the place over." Although he wasn't sure what good that would do.

"I'll transfer $500 to your account to start you off."

Five hundred wouldn't hurt; more to follow. "No, you won't. I'm not taking the job until I say I am. I'll call you this afternoon."

"I have a new number. I'll call you." She hung up.

Melanie came in wearing a white robe, her hair in a turban. As the waffles toasted, he filled her in.

Her reaction, as they sat at the kitchen table: "Not a good idea, Stan. You can't trust her."

"I'll just park nearby and get the lay of the land."

She grabbed the waffles out of the toaster, plated them and spooned jam onto them. (No butter.) "Which means you plan to work for her again."

"No…. Well…. I'm thinking about it. The money would come in handy. If it's a different person we're watching, there's no reason to think the feds are involved."

Melanie frowned. "You don't have to. If our business is in trouble, we'll cut back."

"No. No. We're fine." Which was true. The business had enough in the bank, but Stan was a guy who planned for what-ifs. What if no new cases came in? What if they lost a workers' comp contract? What if Bud stayed in Russia? No. Not even a Bud-in-love was that crazy. *God, I'm such a worrying wimp.*

STAN PARKED DOWN the street from the place in Redondo, a handsome Craftsman with white pillars and a wide porch. He got out, strolled past the place and around the block, thinking that Emilia Clark could be a great contact. If she trusted him enough to hire him for the bank's most confidential assignments, there'd be more work.

He climbed back into his car and watched. A man came out and stooped to pick up the paper. A man in his forties. Okay, Emilia had told the truth about that much.

# CHAPTER 54

## MELANIE

Stan dropped me at the office and headed to Redondo Beach on Emilia Clark's job. Not a great idea, but, as you know, Stan's an innocent, sweet guy, who just naturally wants to help people.

Emilia had never come clean about those federal agents meeting the blond woman. (If she knew herself.) I toyed with the idea that the blonde was in witness protection. Was KatzBank involved in something shady?

I finished a case report for California Workers Comp, poured a cup of coffee and heard a knock on the office door. It swung open, and in came a tall brown-haired guy in a grey suit, and—a head shorter—a Latina wearing navy.

The man moved in fast, holding out an ID wallet. "Special agent, Everhart, FBI." He tilted his head toward his partner. "Agent Gonzalez."

The woman flashed her wallet.

My first impression was; *How could any guy make his face so grim?* My second thought, *Emilia Clark; damn her.*

"You must be the secretary," the man said. "Melanie ... something."

"Melanie Cranston," the partner supplied. "*Office manager.*"

The man tipped his head toward the table. "Sit with us." More than an invitation.

I complied, with butterflies flitting in my stomach. The agents took chairs across from me.

"Your boss, Stanley Stein, he's your boyfriend too?" the man asked.

I wanted to say *fiancé* but held up. If they were out to get Stan, no need to offer them anything … I ignored the question.

"Surveillance spotted your boyfriend's car on Maple Lane in Redondo Beach this morning."

I felt my heartbeat thrumming. "Is that a problem?"

The Latina agent gave her partner a look, and he seemed to relax. She said, "Ms. Cranston, we know it can be … intimidating when federal agents show up." She smiled, friendly. "We're not here to get anyone in trouble. Just looking for information."

"It's a new case. I really don't know …" What else could I say? "Look, I expect Stan back at lunchtime." Damn it. Nothing like throwing one's fiancé under the bus.

"In the meantime, I'm sure you can fill us in," the woman, Gonzalez, said. "Since you have a close relationship with your boss." She eyed Melanie's hand as if just noticing. "Is that an engagement ring? Congratulations, Ms. Cranston."

*Stan's just out on a case. He's done nothing wrong.*

The male, Everhart, leaned forward. "You are the office manager. I'm sure you can answer; is S. Stein Investigations registered to represent foreign interests?"

I jerked back in my chair. "What the hell?"

"What countries have you listed on the disclosure?" the man asked. He waited a beat and added, "We have found no registrations in Department of Justice files."

Gonzalez waved her hand in the general direction of her partner. "I checked on the internet on the way over here and didn't find any. Probably a clerical issue."

"We aren't foreign agents," I blurted. I needed to catch my breath and shut up.

Everhart clucked his tongue, giving Gonzalez an incredulous smirk. "Some clerical issue? Five-year jail sentences. Hefty fines …"

I knew what these S.O.B.s were doing, and it teed me off. I tried to chuckle, but it came out as a croak. "I don't know what you think we did, but you can cut the bad guy, good Chica act."

"She *is* a good Chica," Everhart said. "Right, Gonzalez?"

Gonzalez gave him the mean eyeball. I'd used it myself on a few pricks.

I stood. "I have nothing more to say. Okay if I get back to work?"

Everhart stood up too, looking surprised. "Sure. When your boyfriend returns, have him wait for us."

"*Fiancé*," Gonzalez said, and I thought she came close to winking at me.

# CHAPTER 55

## MELANIE

I f you're like me, you believe in Stan, in his wisdom and, most of all, in his heart, but you'll probably agree that pressure situations are not his forte

When Stan returned, the FBI twins were right behind him.

Everhart gestured to the table. "Care to join us, Ms. Cranberry?" Screw him. He knew my name was Cranston.

Stan and I sat on one side, Everhart and Gonzalez across. Gonzalez glanced at her partner and then lasered Stan with mean eyes. "We have several questions, Mr. Stein. For one, would you tell us what your partner, Andrew Randolph, is doing in Russia?"

*Damn. They've been digging pretty deep.*

I saw Stan swallow, choke up for a moment. He said, "He has a girlfriend there."

"What else is he doing? Has he been in touch with Russian authorities?"

Stan looked at Gonzalez for a second, then dropped his gaze. "No. I don't think … No reason he would."

I have to confess; at that moment, Stan even looked shifty to me.

"Political contacts?" Everhart asked.

Gonzalez pitched in; "Other foreign nationals? *Iranians?*"

"What the heck is this about?" Stan asked. "Bud went to Russia as part of a Russian bride's program." He pointed a finger at Everhart, his hand shaking a little. "You already know this, if you've done so much snooping."

Everhart gave a derisive little snort. "Mr. Stein, you've been following a foreign national, first on ..." Everhart pulled out his cell phone and scrolled. "—Raleigh Drive in Manhattan Beach. Am I correct?"

"I had a job there. Sure, but—"

"Then you tracked her from Manhattan Beach to Redondo Beach. We want to know how you did that. Who's the mastermind? Who's cooperating with you? We take informants in the federal government very seriously."

Stan glowered at Everhart. "What the heck are you talking about? In Manhattan Beach, I took pictures of a blond woman. In Redondo it was a ... guy ... a man, a different person. You mean ..."

Everhart nodded to Gonzalez, and she said, "Don't pretend, Mr. Stein. The U.S. Marshalls relocated the woman and re-identified her. You know who she is, and we know who she is, but none of us will say her name to anyone; you understand?"

Everhart pitched in; "You tracked her, you son of a bitch, and we want to know how. Is your informant in the US Marshalls? The FBI? State Department?"

Stan sat back and took a few breaths.

"Emilia Clark," I blurted. "She works at KatzBank. She's the one who—"

"Stop," Gonzalez said. "Don't bullshit us."

"She's telling the truth," Stan said.

"It's going to go hard if you don't cooperate," Gonzalez said. "Obstruction of justice; you heard that term? Aiding a foreign adversary …"

Everhart held out both hands, palms up. "How about this? We know you've been meeting with the right-wing agitator…" The FBI man consulted his phone again. "Clementine Dudas. You've visited him multiple times up near Hemet."

"The snake preacher?" Stan said. "A right-wing activist?"

I couldn't help myself from asking, "*Clementine?* That's his first name. Really?"

"Look," Everhart added. "Make this easy on yourselves. Prison's not a friendly place. You don't owe your foreign handlers any favors."

Gonzalez was staring at me. She reached toward her partner. "Hey, Everhart," she said. "Ms. Cranston, here … Melanie. You see how she's reacting. She's telling the truth. She doesn't know what this perp is up to." She gestured toward Stan, who seemed to shrink in his chair.

I wanted to point out that Stan was oblivious, too, but didn't want to insult my fiancé. The moment passed, as Everhart leaned across and shouted a series of threats at Stan.

The conversation went like that, circling back to the same questions for another hour. Foreign nationals, Iran, Russians, how Stan knew that the blond woman had been disguised as a man and moved to Redondo Beach.

They mostly left me out of it. I felt miserable and helpless. Useless, a total waste in the face of their attack, unable to help the man I loved. Exhausted.

In the end, Everhart gave a malignant sneer, stood and said, "Mr. Stein, since you refuse to cooperate, you're coming with us. Are you carrying a weapon?"

"I don't even own …"

Stan, in his short-sleeve shirt, pretty obviously wasn't carrying. Everhart came around the table and gave him a quick pat-down, anyway.

Stan touched my hand and gave me an imploring look that tore at my heart before they led him out.

I slumped in my chair. Leaning my elbows on the table, I laid my head in my hands. Who could I call to help him?

The phone rang. Caller ID: California Highway Patrol. I picked it up.

"It's Dave, sweetie. I've got some information about your case."

It took me a moment to get it; Dave, my *boyfriend* from the CHP, calling about our snake case.

"Not now, Dave." I choked up, as I said that.

There was a pause, and Dave said, "You all right, Melanie?"

"Hell no, Dave. The FBI just grabbed Stan."

It occurred to me that Dave might be heaven-sent right then. "Hey Dave, you're law enforcement. You know anyone with the feds?"

"A few, but we don't get along."

It took a few minutes, asking Dave questions, but I finally had to accept that he had no great friends with the FBI. He gave me the name of a manager in the federal attorney's office. "Better you don't mention my name with him," Dave said.

We hung up without discussing Arlene or Clem Dudas or even the word *snake*.

# CHAPTER 56

## BUD

As Sveti entered his room, she said, "Your Trump, he say Putin genius." She challenged Bud with furious eyes. "You think he genius?"

Bud didn't at that minute, and all he wanted to do was to ease her heartbreak.

That was the day Putin declared that two chunks in the eastern part of Ukraine were independent states.

Two days later, Sveti came again. He took one look at her face, tears streaming down, and he knew. "They invaded, didn't they?"

She wore blue jeans and a pale green shirt under her coat. She nodded and walked in past him. He closed the door, and Sveti pressed her forehead to his chest. He wrapped his arms around her, feeling her body shutter.

Her voice was muffled in his shirt. "I have to do something, Bud. I have to."

He pulled back and looked at her. "What can you do?"

"Protest. I can protest. I haven't told you before, but …" She went quiet then, looking around the room, shaking her head. She went over to the bed, piled two pillows at the top of it, and sat with crossed arms. Bud moved in beside her, gently pulling her against him.

After half an hour, they went outside and walked the grounds, where she could talk.

"What I not tell you; I go to rallies for Navalny two, three years back," she said. "Putin send thugs. They watch us. Times they bring clubs and crack heads." She grinned a little. "Not my head. I fast running."

"That's why I couldn't use your name for the visa?"

She frowned. "Okay, truth; one time they lock me up a little. They put me on list. Men come to clinic where I work. Say, I want keep job, I shut mouth; no more rally. Now, Russia invade my father's country. Not possible be silent. On internet, they call it flash mob, yes? –I see this on VPN. Flash mob in Sergach, Wednesday. Moscow later in week."

Locked her up *a little*? "No, Sveti. I need you with me."

"Today, you have me. Tomorrow I be nurse in clinic. Wednesday, I go Sergach and scream at Putin. Maybe television camera come. Someone see. That all we have." She reached out and touched Bud's arm. "After, I run back to you."

"No. You can't."

She laid her fingers across his lips. Her despairing look shut him down cold. "You no understand, Bud. I try to make fun for you, not let you see how horrible is this for me. This my country, I love … so bad country it was … so great country it was becoming … I hate what he does to it. I more than hate it. What stronger word?"

WEDNESDAY MORNING CAME, and Sveti showed up at the hotel. "I not go to rally in Sergach," she said.

Bud's heart felt a ton lighter. "Great, darling."

She shook her head, looking around his room. "We not talk here."

Bud picked up two wrapped breakfast sandwiches and a couple of coffees from the hotel dining room. They went out to sit on a bench. Pretty damn cold, but a place where they could talk. They unwrapped the sandwiches and set them on their laps.

She took a swallow of coffee and looked toward the forest. "You remember what I say about my grandma, Polina?"

He remembered—very well—but he didn't answer.

"I not want Polina live this damned country, no more. You know what I want?"

"I think so but tell me."

She turned to look him in the eye. "We take Polina away." She hit her forehead then. "Oh, Bud, I not saying I expect you marry me. Not unless you want. Not unless I agree. But Grandma Polina, she must to leave. I leave too. Go somewhere. We figure out together or I figure out myself."

Okay, he could deal with that. He grinned at her. "You're pretty feisty. Marrying you could be interesting."

She looked puzzled, probably about the word *feisty*. "If you asking me, not good time for asking. You should not propose because I want leave Russia. Tonight, I get my cousins. We go to chapel. We take Polina and hide her." She paused a moment and then asked, "You come with us?"

"Wouldn't miss it."

She took a breath, looking like she was about to cry. "I afraid to tell you this, but I still go to protest, one in Moscow."

His heart put on a ton of weight.

Her chin quivered, but she held that determined look. "We get Grandma Polina safe. We get you, my darling Bud, safe. I go protest in Moscow where television cameras see."

"They'll arrest you."

"Not if I run fast, yes?" She didn't quite manage to smile at her little joke.

"Don't. Sveti, please. We'll get you out. I'll get that fiancé visa from my country. Or—"

She shook her head and kept shaking it, tears dribbling down her cheeks. Bud kissed her on the forehead, as she trembled.

Goddamn it! She was going to do this no matter what he said.


BEFORE HE WENT with Sveti to the chapel that evening, a text came from Mel: *Please come home, Bud. They're cutting off flights from Russia. I can get you on a plane tomorrow.*

He wrote back: *I need to stay a few days. Sveti's really upset.*

Sveti and he arrived at the chapel just before midnight, bearing candles. They lit a few and set them around. Two of Sveti's cousins, sturdy guys in workers' overalls, showed up around midnight. The taller one carried a good-sized metal trunk, three feet long, blue with steel corners. He held it, dangling from one hand, like it was weightless.

"Best not use names," she said.

Bud nodded, and they shook hands.

While Sveti held a discussion with her great-grandmother in the silver case, the cousins and Bud removed the heavy stone lid from her grandmother Polina's crypt. One cousin produced a small crowbar and pried the wooden lid off the coffin inside.

Bud expected something foul, maybe not the stench of Clem's snake heads, but pretty bad. Instead, your run-of-the-mill must floated up from a layer of bones, some dried up skin and decaying cloth. The two cousins slipped everything into a plastic bag and the bag into the blue trunk.

The shorter cousin—Bud noticed he was balding in the center of his head—leaned close to him and murmured, "Little suitcase be better."

Surprised the heck out of Bud; he hadn't expected any English from these guys. Still, the fellow had a point; granny's remains didn't take up half of the trunk.

The cousins replaced the coffin cover, and Bud helped them hoist the stone slab on top.

# CHAPTER 57

## BUD

According to Sveti's special internet network, the US State Department was urging American citizens to leave Russia. Not a bad idea. Bud's visa would be up in a week, anyway. His hotel manager gave him the nasty eye and asked when he planned to depart. Even Mel was after him with another message.

Aeroflot sent a text adding to the harassment: *We regret to inform you that your flight scheduled for Tuesday has been canceled. Not our fault. Blame the belligerent Nazi American president, Biden.*

But Bud had Sveti here, Sveti and a sack of bones that he was thinking of as *granny*. Sveti needed him.

On Friday, she arrived at his door in a brick-red corduroy jumpsuit and long black coat, her brown hair trailing onto her shoulders.

"You're beautiful," he said. "But you look too damned serious." Then he noticed the small brown suitcase in her hand. Was granny in there?

She set the case on the floor. "We not speak here." They left the hotel and followed a path someone had trampled through the fresh snow. She kissed him hard. "We take small trip." They kissed

228

again. "Then you take big trip." Another kiss. "No airplanes leave Russia now; you hear?"

That message from Aeroflot was one thing, but what about other airlines? "*All* the planes are stopped?"

She nodded. "Your country punish Putin. Many *sanction*. Is that word?"

Suddenly the idea, *trapped in Russia*, felt pretty damned ominous. "What's this small trip, big trip stuff?" he asked.

"Like I tell you, big rally in Moscow tomorrow. Protest. TV camera show world; Russian people not want war."

Sounded like a shitty idea all around. "You want me to come?" Was he willing?

She touched his cheek. "You go with me today, but not to protest tomorrow, Bud. I not want you prisoner Siberia work camp."

"But you shouldn't—"

A tear trickled down her cheek. "I tell you before, darling. I must do."

"I'll go with you. I don't care."

"We be together again. I have plan. Not together at protest. You not be there. Far too not-safe. You be there, make me danger. You leave country right soon. I go later. That is way has to be for both of us be safe." She looked Bud over with misery and pity in her eyes. "I see you, sad man. I sad too. Trust me. Help me. I give you very important job now. I be *grateful* to you; that right word? Very *grateful* always."

*Together again*, sounded encouraging, but *grateful always* seemed pretty damned final. Still, Bud accepted that Sveti had to do this. He believed her when she said he couldn't be there with her. If they found her protesting against Putin with an American comrade, it would be bad news.

SO IT WAS that Sveti and Bud traveled on the train to Moscow. She was bound for the protest. He was on his way to St. Petersburg, and from there, to Helsinki Finland, bearing his suitcase and another, with Grandma Polina's bones.

Sveti had assured him that those bones could rest in peace in any free country, including Finland. It was a smallish brown case, so light, 20-25 pounds. Was all of her inside, or had the cousins kept a memento of the old girl?

Sveti and Bud sat in separate rows on the train. "A precaution," she'd said. After a few minutes, she joined him. "Okay, I sit with you now. No one follow."

"How do you know?"

"My cousins on train too. They keep eyes to watch."

Bud spotted the shorter cousin then, a few rows ahead, peeking out from behind a seat.

Sveti pulled his arm across her chest and pressed it close. She held his hand that way. "We be together again, Bud. Not you worry."

"Then why are you crying?"

"I want be together tonight. I want every night with you."

That really got to him. He felt tears coming. "That's what I want too, but—"

"Do not spoil moment by argue." She waited a few seconds and said, "We get to Moscow; we not get off train together. Not look like I know you ... to protect you."

They rode holding hands that way. "This is my love," she said, gazing at their hands. "I hold you; say I love you."

"I love you too, darling." Bud squeezed her hand, and they kissed, just simple kisses, a couple dozen of them.

"We in Moscow soon. I tell you very important. They watch everything. They see us together and I in protest, you in danger, and I in danger." She gave him that serious look.

"I understand."

"We leave train not together. You take suitcases on train St. Petersburg. Travel first class, make you happy." She smirked a tiny bit. "Keep grandma close to you. Protect my Polina. Her spirit protect you. My cousin on train to St. Petersburg too, not close but near. Be sure you okay." She took a few breaths. "After St. Petersburg, you train to Helsinki. Russia Border police ask about suitcases, you wish them happy day, give them bribe. US dollars seduce Russian border man, all good." She kissed Bud's cheek. "If police ask how you have remains of Polina, you show this."

She took an envelope from her bag and slid it into his coat pocket. "Letter my cousins write for you, letter make okay you have grandma's bones. Letter say Polina born in Finland—small lie. You taking her back her birth country." She gave Bud a hint of a grin. "Really take grandma Polina to USA, if you can. Russia angry at US, so letter say you take grandma Finland."

A few more minutes, kisses, hand holding. The train slowed. Sveti stood. "Moscow next. You stay few minute after." Reaching up, she retrieved granny in her suitcase, said something to her and set the case in his lap. She gave him a stern look then that would have made him laugh any other time. "Not follow me." She moved a few rows up and took a seat. When the train stopped, she headed toward the exit.

It hit Bud then: *I'll never see her again.* He turned in his seat, catching a glimpse, as she shot a quick peek over her shoulder and disappeared behind the bulkhead. *This is killing me. I love her so much.*

*Don't follow, damnit.* He moved to the window and tried to see her, as passengers streamed onto the platform. Someone with long brown hair ... not her.

He waited to be the last out of the car and left with the two suitcases, his and the medium-sized, brown granny pack.

# CHAPTER 58

## BUD

Bud spent most of that trip staring out the window into the dark Russian night. One time, his compartment door opened, and a conductor looked in. Bud pretended to snooze but watched the SOB like a hawk.

In the morning, he disembarked into a crowd at the St. Petersburg station. Heading toward the ticket window, he saw one of Sveti's cousins wearing a heavy brown coat. They exchanged subtle nods.

*Where are you now, Sveti? Please be careful.*

A middle-aged clerk at the ticket window wore a blond comb-over and an attitude. "Passport." Bud handed it over. The guy glanced at it and grimaced.

"First Class to Helsinki," Bud said, trying to remember the Russian for *please*. No way that was happening.

The clerk laid the passport on a flat screen and checked a computer monitor. "First class all full." He wrote on a pad and held it up to Bud; *4900 Rubles.* (Fifty or sixty bucks.)

Bud handed 5000 over. The guy examined each bill. He gave Bud the ticket. As change he offered a few words of surly Russian that included some version of the word *Amerikan.*

"Thanks for the service," Bud muttered.

On the platform, a soldier examined Bud's passport again. He wore a khaki green uniform, head to toe, with a red emblem on his hat. "Visa," (*viza*). His voice was crisp and harsh. Bud showed it to him, trying to keep his hands steady. It wasn't just that the soldier was a foot taller and built like a football lineman. He had Bud's fate in his hands … granny's too. After several long seconds, the guy jerked his head toward the train. Bud stepped up, letting out the breath he'd been holding.

The train car was crammed full. *Every damn Cossack in Russia wants to get the fuck out*, Bud thought. Too late to find a seat. Wait for another train? No way! He set his larger suitcase in the entry area and settled granny beside it. On the old girl's case, the cousins had tied a holder with a card inside. It read: *Andrew Randolph, USA, Handle with Care.*

*If that card can slide in there, so can a fifty-dollar bill*, Bud thought.

There were ten other people in that compartment between train cars. He leaned close to the wall and removed money from his wallet, stuck it in his pocket, prepared for his first international bribe. Then he perched his butt on his suitcase and did his best to get comfortable. After two hours, the train stopped. Three women boarded. They wore neat brown uniforms with tin badges. Women! Were they receptive to bribes, too? Bud slipped fifty dollars in by his name tag, letting it poke out just a touch.

He showed his passport to one of the customs women. "*Amerikan*," she said. – An accusation.

Bud was tempted to say, *Yes. And proud of it*, but that might be an unpopular sentiment.

"What in here?" She pointed to the suitcases. She was a couple of inches shorter than Sveti, clipped blond hair, with keen eyes, maybe intelligent, maybe not a bad person, doing her duty.

"Clothing." He opened his mouth and pointed at his teeth. "My toothbrush." He picked up the smaller case that held granny.

She stared at it and ran her hand across the top. The fifty disappeared. She said something in Russian to one of the other customs women, and they moved on.

It worked!!! *Thank you, Sveti. Please be safe.*

Two hours later, Bud arrived in Helsinki. Happy day!

Fun fact: in Finland, they x-ray the luggage of incoming Russian passengers.

Bud was near the front of a line of worn-out travelers fleeing Putin land. At the security checkpoint, a Finnish guard in blue stared at the screen as his luggage conveyed past.

The guard put on a *what-the-hell* smirk and waved another customs guy over. *Cheerful*, Bud figured. *Not up tight like the Russians.*

A minute later Bud was sitting in a ten-by-ten, block-walled room across a table from a customs guy, whose nametag read *Koskinen*. The guy's blue uniform cap matched his tunic. He had a neat, black mustache and gray eyebrows. Bud's passport sat on the table, his suitcases on the floor. "Mr. Randolph?" *Not cheerful.*

"Yes."

"You are bringing human remains from Russia into Finland?"

The guy spoke better English than Bud did. He nodded.

"And you are an American?"

"Right" *The country that's keeping Russia from invading your ass*, Bud thought.

"Are these archeological remains?"

Bud chuckled, not so intimidated now that he was in Finland. "No, but I can explain." He pulled out the letter from Sveti's cousins, and handed it to the guy. "I'm returning the remains of these men's grandmother." He pointed to the letter. "For re-burial in her homeland."

The customs guy looked the letter over—apparently fluent in Russian too—nodding. Good sign!

"Why is an American concerned about this matter?"

"Your English is excellent, Lieutenant Koskinen."

"Corporal." The man glowered and stood. He didn't look amused or particularly flattered. "This is not a normal situation, I think. Not *run of the mill*, as you Americans say."

The S O B was happy to show off his English, but his irritable stare warned Bud to forgo another compliment.

"No. I guess not."

"You have plans to stay in Helsinki?"

"Only until I can fly home."

"And the corpse; is there some relative in Finland to receive it?"

Hell of a good question. Bud didn't plan to leave Polina there, but he couldn't say so. Time to improvise. "Before I leave, I'll arrange for burial."

Koskinen slipped Bud's passport into his jacket pocket. "You will like Helsinki for a few days, Mr. Randolph. Enjoy the sights. Eat pickled herring and reindeer. Arrange for the burial of this body. I'll keep your passport and the body safe, while you accomplish this and until you verify for me the details of the internment."

"Better for me to take her now." Bud tried to look hopeful.

The corporal smirked. "Another American expression I know; 'My way or the highway.'"

*Shit-buckets!*

Corporal Koskinen was kind enough to give him a note, explaining why he couldn't present a passport when renting a room in town. Bud found a cheap hotel and settled in. Helsinki was cold, but near tropical compared to Russia.

# CHAPTER 59

## MELANIE

The FBI had Stan! I called the guy Dave suggested at the federal attorney's office. I called my congresswoman's and senator's offices. They all gave the same answer: "We cannot interfere. FBI investigations, by design, are independent of outside influence." The only person who offered a bit of sympathy was an aide to our congresswoman. He urged me not to worry; they couldn't hold Stan very long unless they filed charges.

Charges!!! Stan had done nothing wrong!

Meanwhile, there was Bud, heading out of Russia (about time!), on a train to Finland. I checked online. The Finnish border with Russia was open. Trains were running.

Bud's situation worried me, but it was hard to focus on his antics with my fiancé in FBI custody.

I took a pill to sleep; something I never did. Next morning, I went to the office and waited. Stan trudged in around 10AM, unshaven and rumpled in the same button-down gray shirt and jeans from the day before.

I ran over and hugged him. "You okay?"

"Yeah." He backed up a step and struck a boxing pose. "They didn't lay a glove on me."

I had to grin at this Stan-like attempt at humor. "So, they were cordial?"

"I wasn't too happy with the ten hours overnight on a mat in their holding cell."

I winced. "Crap heads."

"I spent the time dreaming of you."

That warmed my heart. "You know why they came after you?"

"Pretty much what we knew yesterday. Something international. Federal Marshalls were hiding this woman. They disguised her as a guy and moved her. With ten hours to think, I'm wondering if she's some kind of dissident and her country is after her. Somehow the people who had me follow her—Emilia Clark or whoever she is—found out where they hid the woman and then again, a second time." Stan gave me a hopeless smile. "I think I convinced them that I'm clueless."

Stan knows himself so well. "Good job, honey."

I heard a jingle and checked my cell. "A text from Bud."

"He's out of Russia?"

I glanced at the screen. "I'll read it to you. 'Hey Mel. I made it to Finland but I'm in trouble here. I'll call when I get to a hotel.'"

"He's in a free country. What can be wrong?" Stan asked.

A half hour later, he called.

"Hey guys," Bud said.

"What's going on pal." That was Stan.

"Did you know the Finns get uptight when you bring a carton of bones into their country?"

"WHAT?" – Stan and me in unison.

Then Stan said, "You mean human bones?"

"I'm just doing a favor for Sveti. You know; she's a sweet woman, having a hard time. She needed my help."

"Your girlfriend sent you to Finland with a sack of bones?" Stan asked.

"A suitcase, actually."

"Not enough bones in Helsinki?" I asked.

"They're from her grandma, Polina. Sveti didn't want the old babe's remains to rest in Russia, with the war and all. She's pretty pissed at Putin."

Stan laughed. "You know, buddy, you're cheering up my day. It wasn't going great until now."

"Something wrong?" Bud asked.

"Nothing to worry about."

"I made it out of Putinland, but the Finnish border guys X-rayed my stuff. They asked if I was authorized to bring a Russian carcass to their homeland."

Stan still looked pretty happy for a guy just out of the slammer. "Did you baffle them with BS?"

"I had a letter from Sveti's cousins saying granny was born in Finland, so her family asked me to bury her here."

"Is that what your honey wants?" I asked.

"She'd really like granny buried in the US. Because of the damn letter, the cops are holding my passport *and* granny's bones until I do the deed here."

"Sounds like a doozy of a problem." Stan looked like he was stifling a laugh. As you must know, Stan's laugh can be contagious. At least it is for me.

"I've gotta nick her bones and get them on a plane home. Moving her to the US would make Sveti happy."

"BUD! You holding out on us?" I asked.

"You're getting married, pal?" Stan said.

There was a pause on Bud's end, and then, "Honestly, I don't know if I'll ever see her again." His voice choked up. "She insisted

I leave the country while she demonstrates against the war. It's chaos there and a nutty idea. I couldn't talk her out of it." Bud took another breath. "She's been in trouble before. She supported that guy, Navalny; you heard of him?" Another pause. "If they catch her …"

"Oh, Bud. I'm sorry," I said. "Is there anything we can do?"

Bud took a moment. "I thought this over on the cab ride to my hotel. Somehow, I'm getting granny's bones to the US. For Sveti; it's the only thing I can do for her. Mel, could you check that out on the internet, using your wizard brain, bringing bodies to America?"

I worried for him and for his idealistic, slightly off-kilter girlfriend. I could see by the look on Stan's face that he did too. "Sure, Bud, anything," I said.

"Signing off now. I have an appointment with a triple gin and tonic."

# CHAPTER 60

## MELANIE

S tan went home to sleep.

I searched online about bringing human remains into the US. We definitely needed a death certificate and some sort of signed permission from the relatives. Maybe a new letter from Sveti's cousins would do the trick.

I called our congresswoman's office, a second time in two days. "This time I have an international relations problem," I told the receptionist. A half hour later, a fellow named Josh called. I told him that, as an American citizen, I was offended and incensed. Confiscating a passport for importing a few bones. Really!

Josh advised me to 'hang tight for a while.' Finland was a neutral country. We had excellent relations with them. –Familiar advice after the FBI debacle.

Josh seemed nice. He joked with me, wondering what kind of nutty guy went traipsing around Europe with a sack of old bones.

I laughed. "You gotta meet Bud," I told him. Then I said, "Can you lay your fingers on the scale for him? Bud's a reliable person." (Mostly true, wasn't it?) "Could you ask the State Department to put in a good word with the Finnish government?"

"I'll try," Josh said. "Meanwhile, take a deep breath and give Finland the benefit of the doubt."

STAN AND I RENDEZVOUSED at the China Sky for a late lunch with Mai-tais. Stan had a second drink and headed home. I gave him a huge hug and returned to the office.

There was a message from CHP Dave on voicemail. "Hey, Melanie, if things have settled down, I have info relative to your case."

I called. "Hey, Dave."

"Hi, Melanie. Has the FBI released Stan?"

"They have. The female agent, was kind enough to tell Stan that they almost believe him. Almost! The male prick demanded he not leave town." I was just then realizing how angry I was at those agents.

"Don't trust those scoundrels," Dave said. "They'll hang him by the balls, if they can. You got time to talk about your case?"

"Sure."

"Remember, I sent an APB to law enforcement about Elton Snivel and Arlene Dudas?"

"Right."

"I included an inquiry about snake bite victims around that town, Little Hope, West Virginia, where Arlene's mother lives."

"You got something back?"

"Maybe. A body was discovered near there. Someone who'd been camping in a state park with only a sleeping bag. Died of snakebites a few months ago. They just found the body last week."

"You think it ties in with our case?"

"It was a middle-aged male, snake bitten several times, venom from rattlesnakes. That's all the testing they needed to call it an accidental death. It's not the first hiker to die like that."

"Great work, Dave. Would you email me the information, coroner's case number and like that?"

Dave sent the info, and I checked the coroner's website.

I brought my laptop to Stan's place, ready for a glass of wine and smooching with my fiancé.

Better still, Stan lured me into the tub with him. While he was running a loofah over my back, he said, "Super. This will take Bud's thoughts off missing his sweetheart."

(I hope you don't think we spend all our time taking baths together. Stan does have a tempting big claw-footed tub, perfect for the two of us, and baths can ease a troubled mind when the FBI lurks in your bushes.)

We watched a movie till midnight, 9AM in Europe, and called our man in Helsinki.

"Hey Stan, is Mel with you?" Bud asked.

I leaned close to the phone. "You bet I am."

"Bud," Stan said. "I know you've got your own problems, but we have news about the case."

"Clem's case?"

"Yeah," Stan said. "Tell him, Melanie."

I filled Bud in—middle aged man, snake bites, state park, Little Hope, West Virginia.

Bud asked, "What state park?"

I gave him the name, and he said, "That's where I went fishing." His voice kicked into high gear. "The place Velma went when we tracked her car."

"We noticed that." Stan said.

I leaned in to say, "With our keen detective minds, we figured—"

Bud interrupted with, "It's Elton Snivel's body. Skewered by serpents."

"Pretty interesting, huh?" I asked.

"Holy crapoli," Bud said. "I gotta get home, but I'm kinda tied up and ..."

"Stan is too," I said. "The FBI told him not to leave town."

That led to us explaining the whole weird FBI story to our overseas pal.

"Here's what I'm thinking," Stan said. "We have to get Elton Snivel's DNA. Compare it with the body in West Virginia. Make them re-open the case."

"Goddamned yeah," Bud said. "Something's dirty as shit here. So, where're you getting Elton's DNA?"

"We talked about that too," Stan said. "Since he disappeared, they cleaned and rented out his apartment, no evidence there."

Bud still sounded jazzed, as he said, "Swab Elton's mother's proboscis. Familial DNA."

I saw Stan nodding, so I said, "You're a genius, Bud."

"We can't just call Elton's mom and say her son's dead," Stan said. "We need a human touch. In person, up in Oregon. Clem won't pay for that trip." I heard the reluctance enter his voice. "Then more travel to West Virginia. If no one's footing the bill ... I'm sorry. This just isn't our case, guys."

Bud blurted, "Come on. We got snake heads. We have a murder. Stan, buddy, we gotta follow the evidence."

"Elton's mom needs closure," I said. "I just ... "

Stan was shaking his head.

It came to me then. "Elton's mother will pay. She has to be worried to death about her missing boy."

Stan stared out the darkened window for a second, thoughtful. "She might not agree."

Stan's our good man, wanting to help but feeling responsible for his business.

"We can front the money for the trip to Oregon, on spec," I said. "If she goes along with us, it'll be great for the bottom line."

Bud's voice crackled from the phone. "Come on, Stan. You know you want to."

Stan mulled it for a bit. Then he waved a hand toward me. "You're the only one who isn't on a short leash, Melanie. Are you as good at sales as you are on the computer?"

"My turn to travel. Yay!"

I was going to ask Bud about Sveti, but he dropped off the line.

# CHAPTER 61

## MELANIE

Stan called Daisy Snivel, giving her very little information, except that we needed to talk with her in person. I was proud of the way he handled it, so very caring.

I flew up to Bend, OR, toting a sampling kit with a long-handled cotton swab and a contract for detective services.

On the way, I obsessed over the next steps. If Mrs. Snivel okayed our plan, I'd have to convince the coroner and then the sheriff, in rural West Virginia, to look at our case. The sheriff!

I was a black, female, not-quite-private-detective, from California. Each of those attributes could lead to a condescending rejection. (My California-ness could be the most damning in conservative West Virginia.)

Mrs. Snivel turned out to be a petite, very sweet, sixty-year-old grandmother type. She gave me a quick once-over and welcomed me. We sat, sipping coffee, in her bright yellow kitchen; everything, from the table to the wall color to the curtains and potholders. We talked about her son's "snake worship peculiarity," as she called it. It surprised me that she knew about it.

Mrs. Snivel took a deep breath. "Dear, I'm watching your face. You look like a nice woman with bad news to tell. Better to just lay it out."

I swallowed and made myself look her in the eye. "We're not sure of this, but it's possible ... Elton may have passed."

She nodded, grim, but not shocked.

"The authorities found a body in West Virginia. They haven't identified it yet."

That surprised her. "All the way over there. How ..."

"Is it all right if I touch you?" Daisy nodded, and I reached for her hand. "We didn't mention when we called you before, Mrs. Snivel. We knew your son had traveled there with a friend."

She sat back in her chair, still holding my hand, her nostrils flaring with indignation. "Friend? Who was that?"

"Another one of the snake ... congregation."

"Oh. A woman?"

"Yes."

I followed, as Daisy Snivel got up and walked out onto her front porch. We stood, looking toward the houses across the suburban street. It was dusk, and the lights in the windows came on, one by one. "Women always liked Elton," she said. "Some boys back in school called him 'geek' and 'four-eyes.' It hurt my Elton. He was more serious, more intelligent, too. The girls, though ... I don't know what it was. They ..." She broke into tears, and I hugged her.

Back at her kitchen table, we talked for another hour. She gave me a DNA sample. I secured the swab in the sample vial and explained, "We'll get the results in a week. Then I'll take them to the coroner in West Virginia."

I waited while she dabbed her tears with a tissue. "Here's the thing, Daisy. Identifying Elton is one thing. The coroner will agree to that. But we think your son may … actually … have been murdered."

She stared and swallowed. "I see."

"They ruled this case accidental. It may be difficult to convince the sheriff to investigate."

Her eyes still brimming with tears, Mrs. Snivel reached across the table and took my hand again. "Dear Melanie, it's simple. You get the laboratory to do their work. When it's time to go, I'll join you in West Virginia. No coroner and no sheriff—man or woman—will refuse a grieving mother, searching for answers about her only son."

On the plane home, I was haunted by Daisy Snivel's look as she swallowed her pain and resolved to move forward. Next, I thought of Sveti, somewhere in Russia. In danger. Captive? And Bud, who hadn't brought it up on the phone; he had to be worried sick about her. I did my best to focus on coming home to Stan for a movie and a snuggle.

# CHAPTER 62

## BUD

Bud hadn't heard from Sveti in two days. He tried calling but got no answer. Lots of thoughts ran through his head, scary, catastrophic premonitions. *Stop it! Distract yourself.*

Sveti would accept the idea of her grandma resting forever in Finland, but she really wanted the USA.

Because Sveti desired this; because she couldn't do it for herself; because he might never see her again; because he wanted to please her, Bud got to work on his plan to free his passport and Sveti's grandma from Finnish captivity.

The plan had shortcomings. Not uncommon in Bud's world.

First, he visited one of Helsinki's Orthodox churches with his letter from Sveti's cousins. Along with the letter, he offered $1000 to their children's charity. A guy in the church's business office assured Bud that a cemetery plot would be available shortly.

At a local mortuary, he purchased a plain pine box, which they stored on a table in a back room for him.

A letter came from the church, issued by the Bishop himself; a plot was waiting for granny. With the letter Bud convinced the customs agents to release the old girl's remains—but not his passport—to him. Damn them.

The bone-laden suitcase sat on the floor of his hotel room.

Now what? Bury granny there, so Finland would release the passport; then loot the cemetery and sneak her to America?

*Shortcomings.*

Then, a new idea. He texted Mel, and she called from her hotel up in Oregon.

"You got the DNA sample from Elton's mom?" Bud asked.

"I sure did, Bud. That, along with authorization for up to $5000 of our detective work.

"You're the best, Mel."

"And get this," Mel said. "Mrs. Snivel will go to West Virginia with me to help convince the coroner."

"Fantastic, Mel."

"Now tell me what's going on with Sveti."

His stomach knotted. If he started on that, he'd choke up on the phone. "I haven't heard from her, Mel. It's worrying the piss out of me."

"Oh, Bud, is there any way I can help? Maybe I could check about her online."

"No, Mel. Russia has tentacles everywhere. If they think an American is meddling it could screw things up for her. Let's talk about something else. Really, okay?"

"Sure, Bud."

"...Say, Mel, I've got a small project when you have time."

Mel agreed, and three days later Bud received the shipment she'd arranged at his hotel in Helsinki. The plain cardboard box divulged no secrets. It contained an inner carton with a ghoulish picture and the words: *Realistic Human Skeleton, Female.* Sitting on his bed with the *skeleton* staring at him from the open box and granny's real bones close beside, Bud visualized a deep conversation between cadavers. They had to be confused, but all would become clear if Bud's crazy-crap idea succeeded.

# CHAPTER 63

## MELANIE

With expedited service, Mrs. Snivel's DNA results arrived on a thumb drive a few days later.

She and I met at the Charleston, West Virginia airport. We hugged like old friends, which touched my heart. I drove her in a rental car to Little Hope, West Virginia, where we took rooms at the Daisy Laze Motel (Bud's old digs).

"Funny," Mrs. Snivel said. "That's my first name, Daisy." (Of course, I already knew that.)

The next morning, at a state office in Charleston, we met the coroner's assistant, a nervous man with dyed black hair and wire-rimmed glasses. Daisy Snivel laid her DNA results on the counter and told him in a choking voice, "I need to know if my son died here in those lonely woods." Who could resist that line?

A lab in Charleston ran a computer program and confirmed a familial match a couple of hours later.

We sat in our rented Toyota, while Daisy Snivel composed herself. "What now?" she asked.

Daisy looked frazzled. She'd had enough for one day.

"Tomorrow, I tell the Kanawha County Sheriff that we have evidence of murder." I saw her struggle to stay calm. "I'm sorry, Daisy. This is terrible for you."

Stan called that night. The FBI had set him free (and my heart with him). He joined us the next day.

# CHAPTER 64

## BUD

Sveti was, who knew where? Bud had stopped calling when he realized what a mistake that might be. He couldn't return to Russia. The border was closed to US citizens and attempting it could only endanger her. He'd been tempted to bare his soul to Mel about it on the phone, but what good would that do?

Stan and Mel would be in West Virginia, at the Daisy Laze Motel. Bud's motel! His snake case! (His comrade, Clem!) He had to get his ass there.

Before dawn that next day, Bud picked his way past the locked door at that Helsinki mortuary. In the back room, he opened the pine box he'd bought. He removed the *Realistic Human Skeleton - Female* from his duffel and draped it in the dress he'd found in a second-hand store—fake bones and dress, he'd artistically scuffed in ashes. Bud laid her out in the coffin and set the lid on top.

Later that morning, Bud returned. He found the friendly mortician who'd sold him the coffin. "Time to proceed with the burial," Bud said.

The mortician, a tall thin fellow with combed-back, gray hair, looked confused, like maybe he wondered where the body was. He followed Bud to the storage room, peeked into the box and went wide-eyed. He chewed his lip for a minute but didn't ask how granny had appeared, Houdini-style, inside. They sealed the coffin and buried it that same day. The burial certificate was the last step, as far as Corporal Koskinen was concerned. He released Bud's passport, with the snide comment, "We heard from the US State Department. Someone there thinks highly of you, Mr. Randolph."

Bud still had to get granny on a plane or even a slow boat to the US but now was not the time.

Worry about Sveti and an obsession over his snake case in West Virginia, USA competed his head. Going there would be the best distraction.

# CHAPTER 65

## STAN

Stan was really proud of Melanie. She'd brought Daisy Snivel onboard and together they'd convinced the WVA coroner to run the DNA match. Now he was free to pursue the case with them.

Stan, Melanie, and Mrs. Snivel presented themselves at the Arthur WVA Sheriff's substation that afternoon.

The sergeant, around 45 with a pudgy face and receding black hair, gave them one of those *What the hell do you want?* Looks.

Stan handed over the letter from the coroner's office stating that Mrs. Daisy Snivel was related to—possibly the mother of—the deceased snake-bite victim.

Melanie retreated with Daisy to a bench near the wall, handing her a handkerchief.

Stan said quietly, "We believe her son was murdered, and we need to speak to a detective."

The sergeant angled his chin toward the letter. "Says here the death was accidental."

Stan reached across the counter and pointed. "It says there was insufficient information to rule this anything but an accident. We have that information." Stan glanced at Mrs. Snivel, dabbing her eyes with the handkerchief. "The grieving mother deserves the truth."

The sergeant made a call, mumbling into the phone. When he finished, he said, "Leave your number. My captain *may* decide to call you."

May! "Did you inform him the deceased man's mother is waiting in your lobby?"

"Yeah. Have a little faith, will ya?"

They got the call that evening. Stan was watching a sitcom on television, Melanie in the bathroom. He muted the TV.

"Mr. Stein?"

"Yes."

"Captain Smith, Arthur West Virginia Sheriff. You have an appointment with me and detective Monroe tomorrow at Two PM."

"Thank you, I –"

"I understand you convinced an Oregon woman that her son was murdered in the park. If you've deceived her, if you're wasting our time, you'll regret the hell out of this boondoggle."

"We wouldn't—" Stan raised his hands in a helpless gesture, as the captain cut him off.

"Two PM, not two-oh-one. Bring the mother with you." The line clicked dead.


AROUND 11 THAT NIGHT Bud called. Stan laid the phone on the pillow between Melanie and him. "Hi, pal. What time is it in Helsinki?"

"Five AM."

"Yow. What gets you up so early?"

"I made reservations. I'm joining the fun in West Virginia."

Melanie smiled. "Bringing granny with you?"

"Naw. She's staying here, waiting for more instructions."

"What about Sveti?" she asked.

"Nothing new. Gonna hang up now." Bud was off.

Stan laid back on the bed. Melanie rested her head on his shoulder and cuddled in. She didn't say anything, but Stan knew, she was just as worried about Bud and Sveti as he was.

# CHAPTER 66

## STAN

Bud hadn't shown up. No time to worry about that.

Stan, Melanie, and Mrs. Snivel met Captain Smith that afternoon in a gray-washed conference room. Smith was about Bud's height, which is to say, not very tall. Early thirties, straight nosed, crew cut, and humorless; his beige uniform, also starched rigid. Smith gave Melanie a quick double-take and barely glanced at Stan. He took Mrs. Snivel's arm and led her to a seat at a metal table. Stan and Melanie settled beside Daisy Snivel. Smith spoke to Daisy, ignoring them. "I understand your son is missing."

She nodded, dabbing her cheeks with one of Melanie's handkerchiefs. "Yes, he is."

"And these people." Smith aimed a hand at Stan. "These people claim that someone murdered him."

Daisy Snivel sat straight in her chair. She dropped her hand with the handkerchief to her lap. "There's no need to use that tone, Captain Smith. Stan and Melanie are good folks." She smiled at them.

"I don't mean to offend, but there are unscrupulous types who'd take advantage of your situation."

Mrs. Snivel was about to say something, but Smith locked his eyes on Stan. "I see you have her convinced. What have you got, Mr. Stein?"

Stan kept his voice low and even. "You said we'd meet a detective, Monroe."

"First, interest me in your story," Smith said. "Let's have it."

Stan and Melanie had prepped for this (hoping that Bud would arrive in time to fill in the gaps). They'd also prepared Daisy Snivel for what they were about to reveal. They'd even called Clem Dudas that morning to get his help.

Stan kicked it off. "You've seen the coroner's letter stating that there's a familial match between Mrs. Snivel and the deceased from the state park." Smith nodded. Stan pulled out his cell phone and keyed the recording. A scratchy, deep voice said, "My name is Clem Dudas. I live up in the hills of Californ-ee-i-a. I'm one of those snaky preachers, if you know what I mean. My wife, Arlene, is from Lost Hope W V A. She and a smarmy weasel named Elton Snivel ran off on me back in September."

Stan worried about Daisy Snivel sitting there beside him. She didn't flinch.

The recording kept on. "Fornicators! I never thought my wife would…" Clem let out a loud breath. "They took … they stole …" Clem's voice cracked. "Stole the two best diamond backs in the world, my Maynard, and Dobie. They kilt my snakes and put their heads in a box, the dirty—"

Stan hit *stop* before the words *shit heads* played out. "So, Captain, you had two fugitives with rattlesnakes. One of those fugitives fits the description of your snake bite victim."

On cue, Melanie slid a letter across the table. "This is from a commander of the California Highway Patrol." (Melanie's friend, Dave). "It verifies that Elton Snivel was the driver of a car pulled over for speeding in Oklahoma back in September, three days after they disappeared with Mr. Dudas's snakes. The vehicle belonged to Arlene Dudas. If the two of them were heading to West Virginia, Oklahoma would be on the way."

"Okay, hold on." Smith stood and moved toward the door.

Stan felt his gut tense, but Smith didn't seem angry.

As the cop got to the door, it swung open. Bud appeared wearing a rumpled khaki shirt, wheeling a suitcase.

The captain blocked the doorway.

Bud said, "I'm with them."

"This is Bud," Melanie said. "He's got some great info for you."

Smith sidestepped past Bud and out the door.

Bud sat beside Melanie. "Sorry, they lost my damned luggage and it took a while." He looked toward the door. "Where's he going?"

"Needs reinforcements, now that you're here," Stan said.

Smith returned with a big, red-faced man in a white short-sleeve and loosened green tie.

*Good detective look*, Stan thought.

Melanie gave one of her winning smiles. "Detective Monroe, I presume."

They introduced themselves. Monroe listened to Clem's recording and read the note from Dave at the CHP.

Smith gave Stan a look. "Get on with it."

"I called Arlene Dudas's mother, Velma Buttz, here in Lost Hope. She verified that her daughter—Clem Dudas's wife, Arlene—came with a man."

Detective Monroe leaned forward over the table, chewing on his thick lower lip. "Pretty circumstantial, as far as I can see."

Stan knew Bud hated the word *circumstantial*. To him, everything was clear, even if it was nuts. If a bunch of crazies said the government was run by child molesters, that was all the proof he needed. Stan touched Bud's arm. *He's baiting us, Bud. Take it easy.* To Monroe he said, "Bud is about to fill in the blanks."

Bud pushed his chair back, pointing at Monroe. "I've got more *circumstantials* for you, detective. I flew here a coupla months ago and met Velma Buttz. I showed her a picture of Elton Snivel and she identified him. Her daughter brought that son of a bitch, like a prize catch to show off."

The two cops focused in as Bud laid it on them. "You know what?" he said. "Velma, salt-of-the-earth Buttz used the same word that Clem did on that recording: 'Fornicators.' She was damned unhappy with her daughter and her daughter's randy friend."

Stan wanted Bud to rev it down a notch, not only for the cops, but for their client, Mrs. Snivel.

Bud got up and walked to one of those white boards on the wall. He picked up a black marker and wrote *Velma Buttz* on the top left. Beneath it he wrote, *Maid at Crappy Motel*. He eyed the two officers. "Here's another piece of circumstance; Arlene Dudas's mother said Arlene and Elton Snivel didn't stay at her house and only remained in the area a couple of days." He pointed at the second line he'd written on the board. "I found the crappy motel where the fornicators shacked up. The kid at the desk there said they'd stayed three nights. That syncs with Mrs. Buttz's statement. I found a motel maid who swears that Arlene left without Elton Snivel."

"You know the name of that maid?" Monroe asked.

"I can get that for you. Just gotta go back and find the motel." Bud looked pretty happy. "I see you're interested, and we can help." He turned his back to the cops and drew stick figures of a house and a tree. He outlined a driveway and a car. He sketched a small cluster of branches in the tree and drew an X on the car's back bumper.

The room was silent, the detective enthralled. Great!

"I went back to California," Bud said. "But we tracked Velma Buttz's car after that."

Captain Smith shifted in his chair.

Stan interjected, "We aren't police. We don't need a warrant."

"I'm listening," Smith said. "There could be an issue with trespass, though."

Hearing the word *trespass*, Stan thought Bud should cut it off there, but that wasn't Bud's way.

Bud pointed at the X on the car. "You know how this works? A magnetic thing goes under the bumper." He flicked a finger at the tree branch. "A receiver up here in the tree. Once a day, the receiver sends stuff to the internet." Bud waved at Melanie. "Mel and I track Velma's car. Guess where she went."

The cops didn't respond, so Bud gave it to them: "You know that state park, where you found the body? Velma Buttz drove there a couple of months after Elton Snivel disappeared."

"Lots of people go there," Smith said. "Everybody in the county. Lake's a great place to hang out."

"Yeah, good fishing," Bud said. "Velma didn't bother with that. She went far back on the wilderness side, disappeared there for over an hour. I bet that's where you found Elton's body."

Detective Monroe stood and clapped. He actually clapped! He walked to the front of the room and shook Bud's hand. "Good work, fellas."

Captain Smith gestured at the whiteboard. "You going to erase that crap?"

"Naw," Monroe said. "Leave it. We'll use it as training for the new deputies—how not to draw a diagram." He looked like he wanted to slap Bud on the back, but refrained.

"There's a little more," Stan said. "… a suggestion."

Monroe gave the captain a look. "We're listening."

"Melanie." Stan nodded to her.

"The coroner's report," she said. "Before they decided the death was accidental, they described black fibers on the deceased man's clothing."

"We'll test them," the detective said. "You think Velma or Arlene dumped the body, or maybe that husband, Clem?"

"Clem was laid up back then," Stan said. "Bit by a snake himself."

Bud pointed toward Monroe. "Velma has an old Dodge. Her husband has a Cherokee. Both would have carpet inside. Black fibers, gentlemen."

"Not Arlene's vehicle," Stan offered. "She has a pickup. She was only here for three days. We tracked her route back to California."

Smith smirked. "You want to tell me how you *tracked her*?"

"Not a chance," Stan said.

DAISY SNIVEL RETREATED to her room for bed.

The three amigos sat on an armchair and the sofa in Stan and Melanie's motel room, drinking Lemon Schnapps and vodka.

"Holy shit," Bud said. "If Maynard and Dobie did the dirty deed on Elton Snivel …" He stopped. Stan figured he was waiting to see if they'd catch up with his logic.

Melanie pitched in with, "We could use snaky DNA, right?"

Bud grinned. "Yeah, Mel. Love the way you think."

Stan was feeling a schnapps-induced glow of affection for the two of them. "Can you even do that?"

"Don't know," Melanie said. "But the internet does."

"I know where the evidence lies," Bud said. "In the ground by Clem's lilac bush."

He turned to Melanie. "I know what you're going to ask." He took a slug of his drink. "I haven't heard from Sveti, and it's making me nuts. End of story. Full stop." He set the glass down and stood.

Melanie jumped up and went to block the door. "You may not be ready to talk about it, but you're not getting out of here without a hug."

Bud stepped into her arms. They embraced for half a minute, then Bud rushed out.

# CHAPTER 67

## BUD

When Bud was a kid, he decided that joking around was the way to get through a shitty situation. Not that his dad was tough; not at all. But Bud was a pain in the ass lots of times. Making Dad laugh had a big payoff and helped keep Mom at bay.

So now, with Stan and Mel, he joked his way through. He probably seemed happy. He could even *be* a little happy being with them. But he never stopped worrying about Sveti. He hadn't heard from her during that week in Helsinki or here in the US these last couple of days.

Mel saw right through him. She didn't ask again, but she gave Bud a sympathetic glance once in a while.

Had they arrested Sveti? How long would they hold her? —a woman who'd been *trouble* before, a person who Putin might call *traitor*.

*Please, Sveti, call.*

Bud only drank one gin that night after getting home from West Virginia. He popped a Xanax and lay down, letting the tears flow onto his pillow.

*Distract yourself; that's the best plan.* Falling asleep, Bud tried to picture Sveti's smile. Which somehow brought him to her words about Trump and Putin. Next Clem slithered into Bud's head. Weird. Clem the bizarro; Clem the die-hard Trumper. Clem who'd been willing to offer Bud's scalp to the Russian authorities.

What had the snake man done with his video of that pervert teacher?

Next morning, Bud called him. "Hey Reverend, you want me to come up to the mountains and fill you in on the latest?"

Clem took a moment to answer. "I made that recording for you guys, right?"

"Sure, Clem. Thanks."

"About Elton the Snivel and Arlene and my dear serpents." Clem spoke distinctly for once.

"We used it with the West Virginia cops. Worked great."

"What you workin' on now is about that skunk Elton, right?"

"Yes, Clem." Bud knew where Clem was going, but he waited.

"So, you ain't chargin' me for your time today?"

"Nope."

"Come on up, friend. I'll put on a pot of coffee."

"It'll take me an hour. Don't stick the pot on the stove yet."

Bud called Stan and told him, "I'm going up the mountain to swab those snake noggins for serpent DNA."

Stan laughed. "If you really want to stick your nose in there, have at it."

THERE WAS NO WAY Clem could know what Bud had done with that flash drive in Russia. (Except somehow, he'd figured out just when Bud arrived at the so-called resort.) Still, Bud felt a shiver of guilt, as he knocked on the snake man's front door.

Clem greeted him wearing denim overalls. He held out a blue metal mug of coffee. —Stale; Bud knew by the smell before he sipped.

"Come in. Got a treat for you."

Bud followed him through the kitchen, glancing at the American flag decals and tossing half of the coffee into the sink. The light was brighter in the den that day, giving him a good look at Herbert in his cage, sleek diamond skin, curled in overlapping loops.

Clem pulled a dead white rat from a paper bag and dangled it by the tail. "Fresh and warm." He held it out. "Feel it."

Bud poked the rat with a finger.

"Wrap your hand around."

Bud did. "It *is* warm." He pretended to sip from the mug and smiled. "You just strangle it?"

"Already deceased when I bought it. Thirty seconds in the micro-thingie. Herbert's not interested 'less it's warm."

"Gourmet snake," Bud said.

Clem laughed and held the rat close to the cage. Herbert gave a rattle and struck the metal bars, his gaping pink mouth, those nasty fangs, recoiling in an instant. Clem opened the flap in the cage's top and tossed the morsel in. It took several seconds for the snake to sense his nice, warm prey. He struck and wolfed it quicker than Bud's eye could follow. Soon Herbie sported a rat-sized bulge a couple of inches behind his head.

"That was a treat," Bud said.

"Like I told ya."

They settled on the couch, with a view of the snake domicile. Clem turned toward Bud, leaning his back against the arm of the couch. "How's that Russian chickadee of yours, friend?"

"She's trying to get out of there. Somehow, we're going to get her to California." (*Somehow* being the key unknown.) No way Bud was going to say more on that subject.

"Putin and his gang after her? … By the way, I appreciate you bringing my video to the commies."

Bud pictured the pig scarfing the flash drive. "No problem, Clem. Did you know the envelope was addressed to the Agriculture Ministry?"

Clem took a moment to answer. "Really? Your girlfriend translated for you, eh?"

"Yeah. It went to some Pig Nutrition Program." Bud chuckled. What was the deal with Clem and the Russians? "How'd you come up with that address, Clem?"

"Trade secret."

Bud had other questions for the snake-man, but Sveti and the situation in Ukraine were top of the list. "You know, I thought Vladimir was a good guy until he invaded Ukraine. Trump liked him, and—"

"Hold on, now, Budster. Just because Donald kissy faced with that heathen doesn't mean he and the Commie prick are buddies." Clem glanced over at the cage, like he was consulting the serpent. "Even Herbert here could see Donald was messing with Vladimir's head."

That actually made Bud feel better in some inscrutable way. Still, so much about Trump didn't sit easy with him now. "Clem, since you're so well informed, what are the odds that Biden really won that election?"

Clem gave him an incredulous stare. "You really don't understand, do ya?"

Ridiculous, but Bud felt embarrassed under the snake man's scrutiny. "About what?"

Clem snorted a chuckle. "Any true patriot knows; it ain't who got the votes. It's who belongs in that big white mansion in D.C."

Bud let that sink in; to Clem, being patriotic meant flushing democracy down the crapper. "Wow, Clem. That's … Wow."

"Damn tootin', Bud. Get your head around that, and you'll be a better American."

"I don't think I can, Clem."

"You can, Budster, because you believe in a higher power."

That power, apparently being Donald Trump. Wow.

Normally when a guy was spectacularly wrong Bud would get in his face, but Clem Dudas possessed some sinister power to deflate Bud's cojones. Not a good feeling.

Bud took a breath and said, "Changing the subject, we're still trying to figure out what happened to Elton Snivel."

Clem shook a finger at him. "I ain't payin' for this."

"No problem, Clem. Elton's mom is covering."

"I shelled out plenty to find Arlene. Where is she, Bud?"

"You paid for the snakes, Clem, and we delivered them. That's what you agreed with Stan."

Clem grimaced, reached over, and dug his fingers into Bud's thigh. "You and I had a side dealie, friend."

"Let go, friend." Bud glared into Clem's eyes until he complied. "Someone murdered that bastard, Elton. You want to hear about it, or you want to play who's the meaner hombre?"

Clem slapped his knee, grinning. "Hot damn, Bud. Why didn't you tell me?"

"You know any reason Arlene would kill him?"

"Arlene, murder a fella?" Clem looked thoughtful. "She could be spiteful; like when she got that dog and treated it nicer than me."

*Because you were shooting blanks*, Bud thought. *Because you treated* her *like a dog.*

Clem poked his beard with a forefinger and looked Bud in the eye. "How'd they do it, Samurai sword? Bullet through the ear? You going to turn her over to the po-lice? Better, just give her to me." Clem's eyes bulged. He grinned with anticipation.

"Snake bites. Looks like, after the snake bit him, someone laid Elton on a sleeping bag out in the woods to die." (The new coroner's report, just in.)

Clem frowned. "You think Maynard or Dobie? ... I mean, that'd make me real proud of them."

"We can find out, but we'd have to get a sample."

Clem's eyes went wide. "Dig them up?" He shook his head. "... You talking snake DNA? ... Hmmm." Finally, he began nodding. "Okay. But you got to do it. I'd never cut on my friends."

They took turns digging. Bud removed the little box, all caked in dirt, pried the clasp apart and opened it. The snake heads weren't as pungent now. Bud cut out small samples with his jackknife, putting them in zip bags. By then, even Clem couldn't tell which head came from Maynard and which from Dobie. Bud labeled the bags *snake 1* and *snake 2*. They reburied the serpents with due solemnity.

THE TWO OF THEM settled on the porch swing, Clem staring off into space. Bud let him have a minute before asking, "Now that your boys are back in the ground, how about filling me in on your video project?"

Clem shook his head, frowning. "It's the damnedest thing, Bud. My guy in Florida showed it at a few of those donor parties in Florida and Texas, joints where millionaires spend fifty thou to hob nob with fancy-pants politicians."

"Sounds like a good start." Bud was feeling dry after spilling the rest of his coffee on a bush. "You got beer, Clem?"

Clem hustled inside, letting the screen door slam, and came back with two bottles. He handed one to Bud and plopped back down on the swing.

"How'd that go?" Bud asked. "Those rich dudes toss in tons of cash?"

"Heck yes. I got a nice bonus too." Clem's grin was short-lived. "Then my guy put it up on the net; you know that outfit with the Birdie and the TickTocky."

Clem had a friggin' computer guy on retainer; why not just say *Twitter* and *TikTok*? "Good idea. Get the word out. I haven't seen the news lately. Your video must have been prime time news."

Clem got up, causing the swing to rock with Bud riding the wave. Clem walked to the porch railing and turned back, clenching his fists into claws, like he wanted to squeeze the life out of something. "Here's the thing, Bud. They pulled the video off of the Birdie and the Tocky real fast. Said it was fake!!!"

"Son of a bitch. How could they?"

"I don't know, friend. Those videos were perfect. That recruiting business is real. Those LGBTQ suckers are corrupting our great land! God bless us."

Bud took a breath, kicked in his nerve and asked, straight-faced, "Anything come of that copy I dropped off in Russia?" (Hoping the Russian pig that swallowed that flash drive had suffered no more than indigestion.)

"Not yet, but those Russ-kies will find a way."

"Shit, Clem. What are you going to do now?"

"Make more video. Make them better. Make the punk-asses listen." He sat back down beside Bud. "What we gotta do is get the lefty communists out of that Birdie place. Get them to quit censoring what good patriots put up."

Clem had a point. But how the hell was that going to happen?

# CHAPTER 68

## SVETA

Sveta had been on the run for how long? A week?

That first day in Moscow, she and one of her cousins taped Ukrainian flags on twenty shop windows in a neighborhood several blocks from Red Square. They hid for a while and then attended the protest that evening, carrying signs prepared by their fellow activists.

Brown-shirted police chased them, wielding batons, rounding up several protesters.

Sveta and her cousin abandoned their signs and escaped. They sat in a park, freezing cold and nervous. "I'm going home," her cousin said.

*Probably a good idea*, she thought. *If I want to see Bud again.* But escape had been easy an hour ago; she could do it again. "I'm staying," she said.

Her cousin took off. Sveta saw a splinter group of forty or fifty protesters marching by the park entrance. She joined in. A man handed her a sign, *Peace for Ukraine*. They followed the street for a couple of hundred meters. The leaders halted. "Brown shirts," someone shouted. "Up ahead." Sveta spotted them blocking the street, and then off to the side, she saw a line of gray trucks waiting for prisoners.

Men in blue uniforms appeared on the other side. Others, with plain dark coats, aimed cameras at them. Journalists? No, reporters wouldn't all dress the same. Sveta froze, as one of them snapped her picture, and snapped again. He was close enough for her to hear the clicks.

Protesters ahead of her turned and pushed past. She ran too, hearing the thumps of truncheons and people screaming, as she ran, thinking, *Oh God; this is serious. Bud. Bud, what have I done?*

Others fled beside her, frantic, turning any direction where they didn't see those horrible uniforms. The men in black had seen her, photographed her. The Secret Police knew her from her days with Navalny.

*What was I thinking?*

One of the blue shirts swung a baton at her head. She ducked and glanced back as she ran. The blue shirt tackled a man running behind her. She tripped on a curb but caught herself.

A side street ahead. A small grocery store with its lights on. She darted through the store to a back room with a mop bucket, shelves of supplies, boxes, a ladder … and a door!

Into a back alley. *Go left, away from the protest. Keep running.* Suddenly quiet except for her foot falls. *Go right, further, further away.* Her lungs burned.

She slowed in a residential area with three story apartments. The street was still. No; someone was moving—a woman, wearing dark glasses even at night, a scarf on her head. Sveta had seen her at the protest.

"Sveta?" she said. She stepped closer and raised the glasses, so Sveta could see.

A woman from the Navalny movement. "Brudia!"

A man emerged from behind a bush. "It's all right," Brudia said. "Come quick."

Brudia and her companion led Sveta a few blocks to an old Lada sedan, parked near a closed bakery. Sveta jumped in behind the man. Brudia drove slowly with the lights off at first, still wearing her dark glasses and scarf. She sped up as they left the center, the car sliding on icy patches.

Out in the country, Brudia rolled down her window. Frozen air swirled inside the car. "You have a cell phone, Sveta?" she yelled over the sound of the wind. Without waiting to hear the answer, Brudia tossed her sunglasses out. She slipped the scarf off her head and let it flutter away.

Sveta pulled her cell out of her coat pocket, rolled down her window and flung it into the bushes beyond the road. And with it her chance to call Bud.

Brudia rolled up her window. "I'd invite you to my apartment, but they photographed us at the rally."

"I understand. The police know us from the Navalny days. If they find us together, we're two cooked rabbits."

Brudia laughed.

"I have other *friends* from the movement," Sveta told her. "*Friends* not known to the Federal Security Service."

Sveta had left out much when she'd told Bud about her support for Alexei Navalny. Back in 2017, her sister thought she was working late at the clinic. Actually, she'd helped organize Navalny's campaign in their region. They arrested her at a rally and jailed her for a week. When freed, she went back to covert work disseminating Navalny's message.

The movement went underground when Navalny was banned from running against Putin, when he faced harassment, poisoning, and imprisonment. Sveta wondered how much the Russian authorities knew of her continued involvement. It couldn't have been much or they would have sent her to a labor camp. Still, men in black coats came to her workplace and threatened her. She stepped back and lost hope.

One benefit of her efforts; she held in her head the identities of many fellow collaborators, *friends* of Navalny.

BRUDIA DROPPED HER in a village where one of those *friends* lived. Sveta made her way cautiously to the man's home.

Some of Navalny's supporters she'd met in 2017, but not all. Old *friends* and new *friends* who would help. Loyalty was all they had left.

Each night a new *friend* in a different village. Sometimes she slept in their homes, sometimes in a shed or barn. She lay in those beds or atop hay bales, picturing Bud smiling at her, imagining a life with him in America.

Sveti saw Bud as a handsome man. Not so much his nose or his ears, or the way all his features fit together, but his smile was the best. She loved the way his eyes narrowed and little furrows formed beside them when he laughed with her.

Her friends at the clinic might shake their heads at this. Young women hadn't lived through many disappointments. They didn't really see a man.

Bud mentioned a couple of times; "You deserve a better-looking fella" He made fun of his ruddy complexion; "the Irish in me." He hadn't spoken of his shorter stature, but she could tell by some woman's intuition that it bothered him. She'd told him, as they hugged; he was the perfect height for her—true. Sometimes he looked at her with such affection and lust, it took her breath away. She saw the mischievous boy in him, that devilish spirit he hadn't lost, the way others had. Bud didn't smoke or drink himself senseless, but he could succumb to anger. He'd been controlling that for her those last few days. If only those days became the true man, he might make a wonderful husband.

EACH MORNING AT SUNRISE, she traveled to another town on her list. Moving east with the *friends'* life-saving help.

Finally, she made it to Anya's home, Anya with a VPN system for her computer. She called Bud.

# CHAPTER 69

## BUD

Bud was coming back from Clem's, westbound on the 10 Freeway. The Prius Stan leased for him had a nice touchscreen on the dash, which synced with Bud's phone. A call came in, 213 area code. *Junk.* He hit accept and barked, "Yeah."

"Bud. It's Sveta."

He cut off a semi-truck and skidded to a stop on the shoulder, thinking, *213, that's right here.* "Oh my God, Sveti. Where are you?"

"In Russia (Roo-si-a), silly man. Where are you?"

His heart was pounding, brain blowing up. "I can't believe it. You're safe? You're okay?"

"Yes safe, but hiding, Bud. They went my sister's house, try to find me. I throw my cell phone away, so they not track me. Could not get new phone. —They watching every place."

"The phone says you're calling from here in California."

She laughed. "I tell you before about VPN on computer. I calling on friend's laptop. Make call look like come from Brazil if you like."

"I've been so worried. I couldn't reach you." What Bud also couldn't do just then was speak. He laid his face on the steering wheel and let out a few sobs.

Sveti must have heard him crying; she waited a minute before saying, "I had to be *on the run*—that what you call it? —*on the run*? I hide. Move careful. I get to my friend's house. She have sympathy with Ukraine, hate Putin too. Have private computer, so I can call you. So good hear your voice."

Bud leaned back in his seat, able to breathe again. Two semi-trucks barreled by, shaking the Prius. "Darling, I'm so glad ... but they're after you? The police?"

"Federal Security Police, very serious, bad guys."

That sent a chill down his spine. "What are –"

"I have to leave Russia. But listen, dear Bud. This important. I want you forgive me, please." He heard Sveti take a heavy breath. "When I walk out of train, leave you in Moscow, my heart tell me what I do is wrong. Heart say, *stay with Bud, not do stupid thing; not make trouble for self. Not leave this man I love.*" Another pause. "I say again; this man I *love.*"

"I love you too." Bud had such a happy-sad mixture of feelings. Tenderness! Relief! Not enough relief! Fear! "You're going to leave Russia. How?"

"I can no tell you. Can no tell you who help me; no say where I am. This computer safe. Your cell phone not."

Even though Sveti said her friend's computer was safe, she cut the call short, saying she was going to move again, promising to contact him when she could. "Not worry, Bud, darling. I be careful."

It took Bud several minutes to get back moving—the first few to let his nerves calm down, several more to enter that crazy afternoon freeway rush.

# CHAPTER 70

## MELANIE

Stan and I were thrilled for Bud ... scared, too. He'd finally heard from Sveti. The scary part was the possibility that she might get locked away for the next ten years. Which seemed pretty likely.

I hadn't mentioned it to Stan, but I had to wonder; *Is this woman together?* She charged in to protest Russia's war. I admired her bravery, but Russia's a nightmare. Recklessness is not the best characteristic for a future wife. (You'll notice that I picked safe, sensible Stan.) Then there was the fact that she almost got Bud locked up in Finland for transporting her grandmother's bones across national borders. Bones, for Pete's sake! Had to ask myself; *Is Sveti stable enough for our friend?* Okay, that seems like a zany question, given Bud's mental processes. Would it have been better for him to find a calming influence? Yeah, maybe, but if Sveti would make a true and lasting companion, I couldn't argue with it.

WHILE THE FORENSICS lab in West Virginia analyzed the carpet fibers and snake DNA, Dolores, my friend at SimiBank, helped me track down Arlene Dudas. She lived in an apartment in San

Bernardino. Stan and I took Bud along *for muscle* (without his pistol) to visit Arlene.

She lived on the third floor. We three climbed the stairs. Stan and Bud stood on either side of her door. I knocked and gave her my friendliest smile through the peephole. Arlene opened the door half-way, and I saw her for the first time; a pretty woman in a yellow tank top and black tights. She had long dark hair with a hot blue streak running through it. "If you're selling something—" She saw Stan then and shoved the door.

Bud stuck his foot in at the last second. "Ow. Damn it!"

"That hurt?" Arlene asked. She pulled the door back and tried to whack his foot again, but Bud blocked it with his hand.

I winced when Bud did. Stan chuckled. "This doesn't have to be painful, Mrs. Dudas. We just have a few questions." (I thought that line was pretty good, considering Bud's tortured grimace.)

"Screw you," she said. "You think you can bust your way in? I'll scream bloody murder. My badass neighbors will beat shit out of you."

Stan smiled at her. "Do your neighbors know you're involved in a murder? How you poisoned your lover with snakebites and left him in the woods to die; you think they'll be sympathetic?"

My fiancé has a way with words, don't you think?

Arlene deflated a bit. "I did none of that. I only found out he was dead when the damned sheriff called me from West Virginia." She eased her grip on the door. "He called me thanks to you dip-weeds. Didn't he?"

"That's a bitch," Bud said. "Let us in, will-ya, Arlene?"

Arlene stood aside. The three of us headed for her icky-green couch. She paced the room from its little fake fireplace to the picture of the Golden Gate on the far wall.

"Elton and I went to see my momma in West Virginia. You tracked us there, right?" She looked like she wanted to spit. – Bud was the closest target.

Her face turned on a dime. With a dreamy smile, she said, "Ellie and I were lovers, thrilled with each other. I figured Momma would like Elton better than Clem. She didn't even know how Clem beat me, but she hated him. Clem attacked me with Dobie one time and gave me this." Arlene rolled up her sleeve and showed two small scars, one next to the other, from a snakebite. Creepy.

"Guess Momma saw before I did what a shit-hole Clem was. I showed up with Elton, all happy, but my momma screamed, called me a 'whore,' called Elton a 'homewrecker.' Threw us out with the nastiest look on her face. But she came out to the truck before I drove off. I rolled down the window, and Momma said, 'Come on back tomorrow, both of y'all.'"

From my end of the couch, I observed my men; Stan with his revulsion at the snakebite and his sympathy for Arlene; Bud's ready-for-mischief intensity. It didn't surprise me when Bud stood and stretched. "Your mom's a crazy old bitch, isn't she?"

Arlene cracked up. "Yeah, guess that's where I get it from." She came over and stood in front of Bud, trying to face him down. He held his ground. *Go get her, Bud*, I thought.

Arlene wrinkled her nose and stepped back. "That next day, we returned. My momma came out all sweet and nice. I didn't know what to think."

She reached for a framed picture on the end table and showed us, Arlene and Elton, by a waterfall, smiling at the camera. "Momma told me to go have breakfast at the diner. Said to stay out for a couple of hours. 'I want to get to know this handsome fella of yours,' she told me."

"That seem strange?" Stan asked.

Arlene kept suspicious eyes on Bud as he took a few steps toward the hallway. He held his hands down near his crotch, like a guy who needed to go. – Our funny, zany partner, preparing for action. I sure get a kick out of our man Bud (when he isn't annoying the piss out of Stan or me).

"Momma's always been strange," Arlene said. "If she wanted to flirt with Ellie, so what? Anyway, Momma's car was out in the driveway. Her husband's Jeep Cherokee was too. Momma had this new husband. Don't know where he was right then. Don't even remember his name. Momma gave me the keys to that Jeep and told me to take it and leave my pickup in the driveway."

"Why'd she do that?" Stan asked.

Arlene took her eyes off Bud to answer. "You want me to tell this story, or you want to show off with all your questions?"

She looked back, and Bud was gone. "Where the fuck did you go?" she yelled.

Bud's voice from the back; "Taking a leak." I heard a door close.

No way Bud was relieving himself; he was poking around. I waved my hand toward the hallway. "He has an issue with his bladder. Pretty serious too."

Arlene stared down the hall for a few seconds. I thought she'd go after Bud, but she glanced at the picture in her hand and said, "Like I was saying, Momma was in such a good mood, I did what she asked. Elton looked really nervous, but he agreed. I was proud of my Elton and happy. He was standing up to Momma for me."

Arlene set the picture down and looked at Stan and me, suddenly teary-eyed. "I never saw Ellie again. When I came back, Momma said that she'd told Elton all about me and he decided he *didn't want me no more.* – Momma talks like that, all double negatives, like a dumb mountain chicken. She said she dropped him at the bus station."

We sat for a couple of minutes, letting that sink in. I wasn't buying Arlene's crocodile tears, but Stan seemed to lap them up.

A toilet flushed in the back. Bud came in, winked at me and plunked down next to Stan.

Arlene set her hands on her hips. "You three ever getting out of here?"

"Snakes," Bud said.

Arlene eyed him.

"When we got them from you, they were just heads."

Stan added, "You said you didn't kill them."

"Oh, yeah." Arlene sighed. "I yelled at Momma for a few. About how she'd driven my man off. She grinned and said a few things, like, 'Personally, dear, I think he was happy to git away from you;' and 'You'll be thankin' me, hon.' I cried all the way back to the motel, really mad and hurt."

Arlene looked thoughtful for a moment. "I'd taken the snakes with us to see Momma; couldn't leave them at the motel. I went to get them out of the back of my pickup. That's when I noticed the boxes were still there, but the snakes were gone."

So many fascinating questions. "Who cut them up if it wasn't you?" I asked.

"Momma. She mailed me those heads in that nice shiny box, the one I gave you."

The three of us stood and looked at each other. Stan walked to the door. Bud scratched his head and said, "Were you pissed at Elton when he disappeared like that?"

Arlene snorted. "Hell yes. I thought the yellow belly had given in to Momma. Figured he'd call me to make up. Tell me he still loved me but just couldn't handle the stress or something." Arlene teared up again. "No news for months. Then I hear from the sheriff in Momma's town; Elton's dead." Arlene's tears were streaming down. "Snake bit."

Outside, Stan climbed into the Escape's driver's seat. I sat in front with Bud behind. Bud said, "Drive a few blocks and pull over. I took a picture I want to show you."

# CHAPTER 71

## BUD

B ack at the office, Stan set up a Zoom meeting on his laptop. Bud and Mel sat on either side of him at the table, just out of view.

West Virginia Detective Monroe appeared on screen, leaning back behind his desk. Probably the same white shirt and loose green tie they'd seen on him a week before. "Hello, Stan. Is Bud there with you?"

"Hell, yeah." Bud moved his chair close beside Stan and pushed the computer back for a better angle.

Mel slid her chair in on Stan's other side. "What am I, chopped liver?"

Monroe whistled. "You have the enticing Melanie there too; must be important."

Stan led off. "We want to fill you in on our interview with Arlene Dudas."

Monroe scowled. "Stop right there. This is a police case. You'd better not muck it up."

"Easy, friend," Bud said. "You'd just have a carcass with fang holes if it wasn't for us."

Monroe looked less pissed off, maybe a little amused. The guy obviously liked Bud, which made no sense for a cop. And—really hard to understand—Bud was enjoying this, too.

Stan chimed in with, "We have firsthand info. We spoke with her in person, not on a phone call from across country."

"You know," Bud added. "With eyes on a potential suspect, we clever sleuths can detect if they're lying their asses off."

Monroe chuckled, shaking his head. "You able to do that? You all trained at the FBI truth-detecting academy, or something?"

"We have some good shit for you, Monroe," Bud said. "Maybe you'd like to tell us what you've got." He waited a second and added, "And don't give us that cop BS about not divulging stuff from an ongoing case."

Stan gave Bud his warning look. Mel smirked and flipped him a thumbs up. All of which Monroe saw.

Monroe sighed and raised his hands in surrender. "You guys want to be colleagues, which you ain't. Still, I admit you gave me some good stuff before."

Bud figured Monroe was dying to brag about what he'd found out and needed an excuse.

The detective hunkered over a notebook on his desk. "Here goes: The DNA from one of the snake samples you sent—snake number one—matches the snake DNA in Elton Snivel's remains. The carpet fibers on the body are consistent with the carpets used in Dodges the same model year as Velma Buttz's vehicle." He loomed closer to the camera, ruddy face filling the screen. "Those two facts and what you gave me allowed us to get a warrant."

"Super," Stan said. "You searched her trunk yet?"

"We did, as a matter of fact."

Mel jumped in. "Any of Elton Snivel's DNA in there?"

"Don't have those results yet, *but* you'll like this, Bud."

"I'm waiting."

"We found a few dabs of dried snake venom stuck in the carpet. We're testing them too."

"Hot shit, Monroe."

"Your turn," Monroe said. "You spoke to Arlene and …"

Stan went into detail about their meeting with Arlene Dudas—so much detail!

When he wrapped it up, Monroe said, "Okay. Thanks. Velma Buttz matches that story in one respect; she says Arlene and Elton came by her place twice. She claims she ran them off both times. According to her, Arlene drove away with Elton and the reptiles in her pickup, bound for California the next day. What do you think of that?"

"Of course, she'd say that," Stan said. "It boils down to credibility. These two—" Stan nodded at Bud and Mel on either side of him. "—They disagree, but I found Arlene believable. She loved Elton Snivel. She left him with her mother. When she returned, Elton was gone. She was heart-broken, then shocked and grief-stricken to find out he was murdered."

Monroe observed them on his screen. "You think that's baloney, right Bud? Do you and Stan always argue?"

"Pretty much. I don't believe that beautiful bitch, Arlene, for a second; not after what I found in her closet."

Monroe chewed his lip for a moment. "And how about the marvelous Melanie? Your opinion is …?"

"Arlene is full of it; pretty good acting, though."

"Woman's intuition?" Monroe asked.

Mel gave Stan a fond smile. "Her sweet, sexy damsel bit might dazzle a man. I focused on her shifty eyes and fidgety behavior."

"*Hold on.*" Mel rolled her chair back from the table. "I just thought of something. You guys keep talking. I'll be right back." She wheeled to her desk and started typing on her laptop.

"Hope she has something good," Monroe said. "So, Bud, what'd you find in Arlene's closet?"

"You'll dig this, Monroe." Bud grabbed the photo he'd made and held it up to the computer camera. "Look and tell me what you see."

Monroe had that bemused look again. "I'm sure she opened her closet and pointed this out to you. Looks like one of those gaucho hats. So …?"

"Come on, Detective; check out the band."

Monroe's face came even closer to the screen. "Okay. Yeah. Snakeskin. She's some kind of nutty snake worshipper. They might just get hats like that made for their friends and all."

Bud wanted to jump out of his chair and shake a triumphant fist, "You remember I told you we videoed Velma Buttz for a couple of days back in November, how she got into her Dodge and drove off?"

"Yeah."

"She wore a hat identical to this one back then. If you find her hat, it will have the same serpentine skin attached. They're in this together, mother and daughter."

Monroe shook his head. "Your picture isn't legal surveillance, … but I might be able to work with this."

Bud was in his element, needling this hick WVA cop. "This is where your sterling detective skills kick in, Monroe. Go to Velma's and find her chapeau. Track down the dude in crazy-assed Appalachia who makes hats like that. Put Velma under a bright light and sweat her."

Monroe made a face. "Yeah. Yeah. You guys done, now?"

"Not yet," Mel called out. She rolled her chair over, with her laptop resting on her thighs. "Detective, remember we told you we tracked Velma Buttz driving to the wilderness at that state park in November?"

Monroe leaned back again, nodding. "Sure, Melanie. I've got a mind like a steel trap."

"It so happens that Arlene Dudas was in West Virginia that day."

That was news to Bud.

"What?" Stan gawked at Mel. "Arlene said she hasn't left California since …"

"Liar, liar," Mel said. "If you check Arlene's Visa card, detective, you might find she purchased a round trip to Charleston WVA arriving the day before her mother's journey to the state park."

Monroe laughed. "Over two months after Elton went missing. Of course, you won't tell me how you know that."

Bud nudged Stan aside to get closer to the computer. "See how great it is having us on the case?"

"Hanging up now, Monroe. I hope this helps." Stan reached past Bud and closed his computer.

Now that the call was over, Bud just had to say it: "Mel, you're a friggin' genius."

"Thanks, Bud. You're not bad yourself."

Stan wrapped his arms around both of their shoulders. "My team, we *are* so clever!"

# CHAPTER 72

## MELANIE

Three days after that first call from Sveti, Bud almost danced into the office.

"She called again this morning." Bud flashed his crookedest smile, the one that cracks me up every time.

Stan and I got up and charged towards him.

I reached him first and wrapped my arms around him. "She told you how much she loves you, didn't she?"

"Hell, yeah; a dozen times."

I let Bud go, and Stan gave him a quick embrace. "Great, buddy."

Bud took a breath, still grinning. "She has a long way to go, but she thinks she has a way out of Russia. I'll be able to visit her wherever she ends up."

I pasted a smile on my lips, but I worried. Sveti was one lone woman sought by the mighty Russian state. If they captured her, they'd crush our friend's hopes and dreams. Of course, Bud knew that too. He was covering his fear the best he could.

Stan and Bud went out to do fieldwork. After I finished the workers' comp report I was filing, I called Josh at the congresswoman's office. "Hey Josh."

"You just calling to say hello, or is that guy, Bud, in trouble again—let me guess—in Norway now?"

"You have a minute, Josh? I've got a love story for you."

"Sure, Melanie. Should I call you *Mel* since we're getting to know each other?"

"Bud calls me that. Not my favorite."

"Oof. How about Melania? Sounds Russian, don't you think?"

Josh flirting was not a bad thing, if it inspired him to help us. "Nyet, Josh. Stick with Melanie, if you want me to like you. Now, about that love story …"

I told Josh about Bud's adventure in Russia, falling for Sveti and transporting grandma's bones into Finland. Of course, he already knew part of that story.

"How'd that turn out?" he asked.

"Bud's home in the US. The bones are still over there."

"He got them buried in that Russian Orthodox cemetery, right?"

*Really in a storage locker.* "Yeah … well … that's another saga. Right now, let's deal with Sveti."

I told Josh what I had in mind.

"That's a tough one," he said. "Can't promise you anything, but I'll look into it."

"Thanks. I appreciate it."

"Ur … Ah … Melanie, I looked up S. Stein Investigations online; a delightful picture of you on the webpage."

Still flirting? Or about to go weird?

Josh continued with, "Since we're getting friendly, I was wondering … Are you married or anything?"

I took a breath. "I will be after May. His name's Stan."

"Okay then." His voice dropped an octave. "I'll get to work on your question."

"Thanks, Josh. You're one heck of a guy." After I hung up, I thought, *"One heck of a guy?" What a geeky thing to say.*

# CHAPTER 73

## SVETA

B ypassing the checkpoints between Russia and Kazakhstan turned out to be easy, if one had a friend who knew where to cross and had boots and warm clothing for the freezing night. Sveta had the coat. Her last *friend* in Russia provided boots and the location of a sympathetic Kazakh woman on the other side.

Sveta arrived before dawn in a rural Kazakh town near the Caspian Sea. She moved cautiously from building to building, following her directions. Light crept into the sky, and she was able to read a street sign. She found the neighborhood and identified the three-story residence from her *friend's* description. The town was waking up, a few men going to work. Sveta waited for an opening, then darted across to the house. She reached the door and knocked. A tall woman opened it, took one look and pulled her in. She wore a black sweater with a high neck and loose gray pants with a string belt. Sveta guessed she was around sixty, and striking, with a tanned face, weathered in all those years of sunny days and cold, dry air. She had gray hair tightly tied back behind her head. "I am Nalinka."

Nalinka spoke fluent Russian, of course. Kazakhstan was once a part of the Soviet Union. She explained that she'd been to a meeting supporting Ukraine the day before. "We had 200 people in the square outside the main mosque. Most of them I recognize from our town. Four strange men lurked in the back, all wearing the same gray coats."

A shiver ran through Sveta.

Nalinka looked her over. "Don't worry. It is safe in Kazakhstan, if you are careful. They haven't interfered for months."

"Interfered?"

"Taken anyone back."

"Where would they take a person? Who—"

"No one speaks of it in public. We who stand for peace are sure the gray men are from Moscow." Still watching Sveta, she said, "You wonder why our government allows them here. To look at Ukraine is to understand. We do not want to be next." She paused and said, "Four gray men at our meeting; more than usual."

Sveta's confidence poured out like wine from a broken bottle. Still, she said, "I need to contact my sweetheart in America. Is there a safe way?"

"I have a friend, Ivan," Nalinka said. "A man with an extraordinary computer."

Late that night, Sveta snuck out. Jittery. Gray-suited men could lurk behind any tree. Sveta was hiding behind one too, losing her nerve. She pictured Bud. His hopeful smile kept her strong. From a doorway, near Ivan's home, she watched for twenty minutes, before making her way to the apartment door. Ivan introduced her to his VPN equipped computer.

# CHAPTER 74

## BUD

Bud was parked in the Prius, watching a woman's house, waiting to see if she'd come out for her mail without the walker she claimed to need. She came now, a redhead wearing cut-off jeans and a tank top, good looking from this distance, pushing a walker ahead of her, like a useless prop. He picked up his camera, set it to take bursts of photos, and started shooting. Rat-a-tat-a-tat-a-tat-a-tat.

The phone rang. He saw a "+" sign with a strange country code on the dashboard screen. *Junk.* But there was a chance. He hit *Accept.* "Hello."

"Bud, darling. I sneak out. I am in Kazakhstan." Bud dropped the camera into the passenger seat and started shaking. He had no idea where that was, but it didn't matter; it wasn't Russia. They both cried on the phone, as he assured her, he'd work on a visa to visit her. They freely and without reservation exchanged the word "love." Sveti promised to call again in a couple of days. He wanted to ask, "Why not tomorrow?" but he knew, didn't he? Sveti hadn't mentioned danger, but he felt the quiver in her voice. He ended the call with, "Be very careful, dear."

When he looked up, the redhead was gone.

# CHAPTER 75

## MELANIE

I called Josh, nervous about how he'd greet me after I'd shot him down. "Great news," I said. "Sveti escaped to Kazakhstan."

Josh let out a loud sigh. "Shoot, Melanie. She couldn't have gone to Finland, like Bud?"

"Too risky. That's what Bud told me. Like I explained, the Russian secret police are after her. You still want to help, right?"

"Okay, I'm on it." He took down a few details and hung up. I wondered if he was really still interested.

For a few days, I heard nothing,

Bud was putting a good face on things. Stan might have bought his act, but I could see him plunging from great expectations to utter gloom whenever the phone rang and it wasn't her, whenever his pessimism kicked in. No point in building him up only to let him down. I told Stan about Josh's efforts, but left Bud out of the loop.

# CHAPTER 76

## BUD

The three amigos were at their desks around 9:30 AM.

Bud heard Mel's cell ring and he stopped typing. "Hello, Josh," she said.

Bud perked up his ears just in case.

"Is it good news?" Mel asked.

Bud glanced at her and saw her waving her cell in his direction. He and Stan both jumped up and came over.

"Hey guys," she said. "This is Josh from the congresswoman's office. Before you say anything, Josh, Bud doesn't know what we're working on, so be gentle with him." Mel gave Bud her 3000-watt smile.

A male voice said, "Hey, Bud, Melanie's keeping you in the dark?"

"Dark about what?"

"A surprise," Mel said.

The guy on the phone said, "Melanie asked me if there's a mechanism for a Russian to gain entry to the US."

Mel reached up and took Bud's hand. "Sveti's a refugee now. I asked Josh if she could seek asylum."

Bud felt his knees go weak.

Mel slipped out of her chair. As Bud dropped into it, he heard Josh say, "I checked with the State Department, and they verified—don't ask me how; some secret channel—Svetlana *is* being sought by Russian authorities. She's considered a dissident with a capital *D*."

"I figured that," Bud said.

From the phone — "To their government, speaking out is a crime. Even calling the Ukraine war *a war* lands you in prison."

Stan stood a foot away, grinning at him. Mel still held his hand. "She can seek asylum, Bud. Russia is a hostile state at war. They persecute people."

Bud's heart was dancing in his chest. Stan moved closer, his hand slipping onto Bud's shoulder. Bud picked up the phone and spoke into it. "You're saying she can come here?"

"Slow down," Josh said. "We have a few rivers to cross before we get there. What's important at this stage is the State Department acknowledges that Svetlana is a *target of oppression*. Melanie asked, and I did a little checking. Congress approved a limited number of asylum-seeking immigrants from Russia, specifically those whose freedom is threatened. Does Svetlana have technical skills? If she's a computer genius or a nuclear scientist, she'll hop to the top of the list."

The words, "slow down" from Josh struck home. Bud stifled his naïve hope as he told Josh everything he knew about Sveti. She was a lab technician and nurse (almost). She'd gotten in trouble for supporting Navalny and now with the Ukraine thing. Russian agents questioned her sister and her boss at the clinic, trying to find her. Her father had been Ukrainian. If she needed a sponsor in the United States, Bud was their man. If a fiancé visa would work better, that sounded great.

"It's a sympathetic story," Mel said. "Bud traveled to Russia to find a sweetheart, and he found her. Now his beloved is stranded in that hostile place."

"I hear violins playing," Josh said.

Stan was nodding. "That would make a super piece. You could get it on TV or –"

"Good publicity for your boss, the congresswoman," Mel added.

Stan and Mel were cheering for him, he knew, but they hadn't been in Russia the way Bud had. He felt the stare of that soldier scrutinizing his passport at the St. Petersburg train station. He remembered Sveti's fear and determination as she left him on that train and her edginess on the phone whenever she called. "*No. Make a big deal out of this, and you put her in danger.*"

"Crap," Josh said. "Bud's right. Sveta's a *dissident*. Kazakhstan is a friend of the US, but also Russia's close neighbor, probably crawling with Russian agents."

The three stared at the phone as Josh said, "Okay, here's what we'll do. Sveta needs to apply. Have her go to the US Embassy in Astana. Bud, I'm sending you a form to fill out. You'll write a letter of attestation too. Explain how you'll sponsor her in the US and the danger for her overseas. I'll do my best for you. I swear. We have a good chance of pulling this off."

*A good chance, right. The government is so good at getting stuff done.*

# CHAPTER 77

## SVETA

When Sveta called Bud from Ivan's computer one night—
the third time that week—he filled her with hope. "You
need to get to Astana," he said. "To the US Embassy. They'll help
you." She was so impressed by her lovely man; all wonders he
achieved for her!

On the way back to her refuge, she heard something; metal
scraping metal. She darted behind a bush, her heart racing.

A man emerged from a shed, carrying a toolbox. She waited
for her heartbeat to slow and the man to enter a building.

What if it had been one of the gray men? Did they suspect
she was here in this town? If they did, and if they lurked in
the shadows somewhere along these streets, silent, persistent,
patient … She tried not to think of what they might do to her.

Back at her refuge, Nalinka gaped at her. "You want to go to
Astana? That is 2000 kilometers away."

Sveta stared at her, deflating. "But I …"

Nalinka shook her head. "No one will drive you. I told you,
Sveta; Russia has so much influence. Strange men stop cars and
demand papers. No one dares stop them. You must stay here and
contact the US Embassy on Ivan's computer."

Which is what Sveta did.

# CHAPTER 78

## BUD

Sveti was out of Russia! Bud woke with that thought every day. (Followed by a cacophony of questions and doubts.)

He filled out Josh's forms and emailed them. Mel was working on Bud's visa for Kazakhstan. One way or the other, he'd see Sveti soon.

His cellphone rang at 5:30 AM.

The congresswoman's name showed up on caller ID. Bud hit *Answer* and held his breath.

"Am I calling too early?"

"Hey, Josh. That's a joke, right?"

"It's 8:30 in Washington. I didn't think you'd want to wait. Bud, I have great news."

"Tell me." Bud held his breath.

"Sveta didn't go to the embassy in Kazakhstan, but she submitted her forms online. I've forwarded your documents to the State Department."

There had to be more for Josh to wake a guy up at 5:30. Bud waited.

"My contact at State says there are slots available. She's in line for an emergency visa."

"Super, when can—"

"No guarantees, Bud, but I'm hopeful. Could be a week. Could be a month. She could still get bumped off the list, but we're moving forward."

*Bumped off the list* registered in his head, but he dismissed the thought. This had to work.

He hopped out of bed and looked out the window, waiting for Josh to say more. Outside, he saw a few high school-age kids ambling down the street. *Little bastards. Out this early, they're looking for trouble.*

"Not yet a done deal," Josh said. "There's Kazakh bureaucracy to deal with. It helps to have the congressperson on your side."

*But what if that isn't enough?*

"Kazakhstan," Josh said. "They're a bit of an unknown. The Russians have influence there. International transfers get into all kinds of issues."

*Like bones in your baggage.* "Tell me you're going to make this work," Bud said.

"With the Ukraine situation, refugees are flooding countries around Russia. I'm betting Kazakhstan would be happy to move one out."

One of the kids outside leaned over, looking into Bud's Prius, which was parked on the street. He would have opened the window and yelled at the little prick, but this phone call was so much more important than his shiny new car.

Questions rattled through his head. Instead of asking, Bud said, "Josh, I want to kiss you." Embarrassing.

Josh laughed. "Don't think we're out of the woods, but I'm working ahead of the game. If this pans out, your fiancé will have to make it to a US Embassy. They'll transport her to our Army base in Wiesbaden, where they'll clear the final paperwork."

"Should I go to Kazakhstan or Germany?"

"Hold on, Mr. Randolph." Josh laughed. "Stay put. Germany's premature and going to Kazakhstan could threaten our diplomatic efforts."

Bud felt *fidgety* after he got off the phone; was there any other word for it? Nervous … thrilled … worried. Would this really happen or would bureaucratic nonsense screw it up?

He made himself work that morning, following a worker's comp scammer who claimed a disabling back injury, as the guy visited an amusement park. Bud photographed him wielding a sledgehammer, trying to ring the bell at the top of a pole at the *High Striker Strongman* game. (The dude failed, but probably did better than Bud could have.) Workers comp scammers; gotta love 'em.

Bud took the afternoon off and walked the beach in Venice, watching the spicy, tattooed women in blue or pink hair, half of them on roller skates. Weird chicks.

Day dreaming of his rendezvous with his sensible, traditionally brunette, tattoo-free Sveti.

# CHAPTER 79

## BUD

Bud had nothing to do but wait, wait and hope. At the office, he typed his report and uploaded photos of the guy pounding the ring-the-bell machine. Mel would get a kick out of that, while she was pasting the info into a form for the State of California.

"That's all I can do today," he told Stan.

"You just going to hang around the beach again?" Mel asked.

A long walk sounded good. Feeling the ocean's surge was the one thing that might ease his damned nerves. "Yeah, maybe."

Bud walked from the office ten blocks to the Santa Monica Pier, then out past the Ferris wheel and game booths to pier's end. Looking down the coast, he saw dozens of people stretched out on the beach, a couple of crazies swimming. It was a chilly March day, and it would be cold as heck in the water. But a frigid swim might be just the thing to distract him. Driving home to get his bathing trunks, he imaged Sveti in her green two-piece riding beside him. If she was there, he'd run a hand along her luscious thigh and say, "You look great, honey." Sveti might pick up his hand, kiss it and say, "I plain girl. You are good looking one."

Bud was in his bedroom shedding his pants, about to change into his suit, while questioning the idea of diving into freezing water. If Sveti was here, she'd smirk and say, "Swim sound very fun. In Russia, this warm summer day."

The phone rang. *Clem* Dudas on the caller ID. Interrupting Bud's fantasy. "What do you want, Clem?"

"Is that any way to speak to a fellow patriot?" Clem waited, maybe for an apology and then said, "You in some cranky mood, I can fix that. Got a gift for you that'll impress the bejesus out of your Commie girlfriend if she ever sees you again. Haw. Haw."

Not a cold dip, but a visit with Clem would distract him.

*She is going to see me again, you shithead,* Bud thought, as he drove to Clem's place.

The snake preacher brought him into his den, where Herbert lurked in his cage. "Your gift is in here. I'll show you."

Glancing at Herbert, thinking of those side-by-side scars on Arlene's arm, Bud shivered. If the snake man went to open that cage, Bud would take him down.

"What's the gift? You got another rat to feed him?" Bud asked.

"Naw, he's still digesting on that last one." Clem took the remote control off his end table and waved toward the couch.

Bud sat.

Clem landed beside him. "Other day, you was talkin' nonsense about the election and all. I made this up to steady you out some." He clicked the remote a couple of times. The flat screen TV on the wall lit up.

*Another video of kids being brainwashed?*

Bud saw the crowd at the capitol back on January 6. The camera started far back, zooming in over a sea of red caps, blue posters, Trump banners. Bud had been in that crowd with his nutty friend Sarah.

President Trump's voice reverberated out of Clem's dual speakers beside the fireplace, as the camera showed their president from a distance, all the flags and the white house behind him.

Trump was saying, "And if you don't fight like hell, you're not going to have a country anymore." Yeah!

Thinking back to that day now; nostalgic, reliving those emotions; energized and also pissed off about the stolen election (or was it?). Bud didn't hear most of the words as the camera panned in.

In the back of his mind, he sensed something off in the recording. "And I say this despite all that's happened. The best is yet to come." Trump's voice wasn't right; maybe because the camera was still a way back.

Trump gestured. "So, we're going to, we're going to walk down Pennsylvania Avenue. We're going to the Capitol ..."

Closer in now. The voice was familiar, and definitely off. Trump's face looked different. Not his hair. No way. "The Democrats are hopeless," he said.

*Oh my god; that's my voice, and shit ....* It was Trump's body, but ... it was ... Bud's face, his lips saying, "We're going to try and give them the kind of pride and boldness that they need to take back our country."

Bud stared at his own face perfectly lip-syncing Donald Trump, the president, wearing his suit and overcoat. "So, let's walk down Pennsylvania Avenue."

The Bud/Trump got ready to exit the podium, but he stopped and said, "I want to thank you all ..." Bud was in Trump's clothing, a big, tall version of him, waving to the crowd.

He stared at the snake man, who wore a humungous smirking grin. "What the hell, Clem?"

"I knew it would tickle you, Bud. I took a few videos of you when you was here last. Hope you don't mind. My computer guy, Dusty, he mixed this up. Figured it might stiffen your spine."

Bud was thinking about that classroom with the little kids, the Jewish teacher telling them, "You get to choose." Clem said Twitter had called the video *fake*. Yeah, *fake*. Phony but convincing; fooled the piss out of Bud.

Clem, still puffed up and proud, said, "It's what they call, Artific-i-al Intell-ee-gee-ence."

"That video of the teacher, it *was* full of shit—"

Clem got up and stretched. "Not at all, Bud. Not at all. Those Lesbi-Homo-Bilaterals are trying to line up new perverts; we all know it."

Bud's gut boiled. The bastard had made a fool out of him with that crappy video. He felt like sticking Clem's head in that cage, letting Herbert take a piece out of it. Thinking, *Democrats are cheaters. Fakers! What if they forge videos like this? Or China? Put words in Trump's mouth that he didn't say.*

Bud jumped up, and glared eye-to-eye with Clem, who looked surprised and kind of disappointed.

"You made all of it up, you friggin' liar."

Clem gave him a disbelieving smirk. "We're in a war, Bud. Didn't ya know?"

*We're better than this. We're the good guys.* "This is some dangerous shit, Clem. Really fucking scary, you asshole. I'm out of here."

# CHAPTER 80

## BUD

Bud drove out of Clem's driveway, headed for CA Route 74, fuming. *Dumbass crap-head, Clem.* The snake man's intensity reminded him of people in the crowd back on January 6, all pissed off and righteous (actually just the way Bud had been). If they believed like Clem that votes weren't relevant, that only what you wanted mattered ... and ... *What if Donald Trump believed that too?*

His phone rang. Caller ID—*Official Police Business.* Right. "Yeah."

"You answer all your calls like a hostile dick?" –A familiar voice.

"Who is this?"

"Monroe. I'm in California."

"Appalachia too boring?"

"You free for a drink, Bud? I went to see Arlene. She's changing her story."

A drink sounded good, maybe a dozen.

Turned out, Detective Monroe was staying at a Best Western near the Ontario Airport. Bud and Monroe met at a bar near there and took a table off to the side. There was a stage in the center of the room with two poles. Babes would dance there later on. Guys would sit by the stage, getting a chance to reach up and personally tip the dancers.

Good thing the poles weren't in use. Funny, Bud loved women's bodies, and he used to go to places like this with his pals. He wouldn't tell those old friends this, but random women's butts in G-strings had never appealed.

The waitress, whose name-badge said *Scarlet,* came over wearing a low-cut black tee. She served up sexy smiles with their drinks.

"You have fun with Arlene?" Bud asked Monroe.

"Absolutely." Monroe reclined against the red banquette, cupping his Scotch in both hands. "She's scared of cops, which is a plus. She also doesn't know what *accessory after the fact* means, or she would have blown me off."

Bud noticed Scarlet—good looking in a top-heavy kind of way, but not half as pretty as Sveti—delivering beer to a couple at another table; the only other customers in the joint.

"You threatened her. Great plan, Monroe."

"Like this." Monroe leaned in and banged his glass on the table. "'You lied to me, Arlene.'" The couple at the other table looked over. "'You said you didn't know Elton Snivel was dead. You told me you hadn't been back to West Virginia since you came in September. *I know* you were there in November.'"

"Nice," Bud said. "Arlene tell you why she went to see her snarky momma?"

"Yeah. Velma called Arlene, spouting confessions and apologies. She claimed her husband was behind the dirty deed. A month after they offed Elton, hubby ran off with his podiatrist. Velma had killed a man to keep her man, all for nothing. She felt deserted and betrayed. Repented her sins and needed to confess."

"Christianity will do that to you," Bud said. "But confessing to Arlene was nuts."

"I told Arlene I knew about the matching snakeskin hat bands too. Her mouth flopped open." Monroe raised his voice an octave and mimicked, "'How in God's name did you know that, detective?'"

"In God's name, really?" Bud set his empty glass down, regretting that he had to drive back to Santa Monica. "Maynard and Dobie became the hat trimmings, right?"

"You got it, Bud. Don't know if we can test snake DNA on hatbands, but we'll try."

"Why kill Elton in the first place?"

Monroe chuckled and drained his Scotch. "Arlene's screwed up mother claims she did it for love."

"Because she loved her daughter so much?"

Monroe gave a crooked grin. "No, the husband. He's so born again; he has crosses tattooed on his nuts. When he learned Velma's daughter was fornicating like a warthog, he expected Velma to be just as irate as he was. Velma was mad, desperate, but not murderous. She decided; better to kill her daughter's sex toy than to disappoint hubby. Velma convinced Arlene to go have lunch. She drugged Elton Snivel. Her husband and she threw Snivel in the car trunk and dumped those snakes in with him."

*Crosses on his nuts*—no wonder Bud liked this cop. He waved to Scarlet for more drinks. "In November, when Arlene returned, Mama showed her the body in the park, right?"

"More like a scatter of bones. Arlene claims that's the first she knew of Elton's death, that day her mother took her out in that forest."

"You believe her?" Bud asked.

"Fuck no, but don't see how we can prove otherwise. As long as Arlene's willing to testify against her momma, we won't push it."

Scarlet landed two drinks on the table. Monroe leered. "You part of the show tonight?"

She put a finger to her lips and winked. "Can't ruin the suspense, hon."

She took off and Bud asked, "You know more about those stylish serpentine hats?"

"Absolutely. The guy who made them identified Velma. She brought in two headless rattlers. He did the rest."

Scarlet swung by, struck a pose and said, "I have to change for the show. You want another drink real quick?" She gave Bud's untouched G and T a disapproving pout.

Monroe downed half of his Scotch. "Sure, babe."

Bud laid two 20s on her tray. "Not for me."

She patted Monroe's shoulder. "You'll have another waitress, when I'm performing, but don't forget who gave you this great service."

A few couples and a half dozen studs came in. The music picked up, something country and western. Scarlet came out of the back in a short red robe.

Monroe stood. "Let's grab seats close up before they're all gone."

Bud followed the detective but didn't sit. "I'm going to take off."

Monroe was already sitting by the stage. He eyed the G and T in Bud's hand. "You going to drink that?"

"You want it? I gotta drive."

"Have that for the road. Hell, have a third."

"You have Mothers Against Drunk Driving in the backwoods where *you* live?"

The cop frowned. "Yeah, we got them mothers. Drink it. I have a second bed in my room, courtesy of West Virginia's taxpayers."

Bud saw Scarlet onstage, still in that skimpy red robe. She stretched, like she was loosening up and did a squat that gave them a hot peek up her thighs. "I'll pass on that, but I have a favor to ask."

Monroe took his eyes off Scarlet to look at him.

"What time's your flight tomorrow?" Bud asked.

"Noon."

"How about you call Stan at the office around nine thirty? Don't say you saw me today, okay? Fill him in on Arlene's new story."

Monroe shook his head. "I thought *you'd* like to tell him, you know, impress the boss."

Bud thought it over for a second. "He needs to be in charge more than he needs me to be his smart-ass sidekick. Stan will fill me in, and I'll say, 'Great work, boss; you really must have impressed that hillbilly, Monroe, for him to tell you all that."

Monroe got up and shook his hand, laughing. "Whatever you say, Bud. If you're ever back in West Virginia, give me a hoot."

"Sure, Monroe. And if you get stuck on a case and need some real detecting, give me a holler." Bud left his drink and walked out.

BUD GOT UP TO TAKE a leak around 3 AM. He was doing that more these days.

Back in bed, he rolled onto one side, a few minutes later, to the other side. Memories came; standing in that crowd on Jan

6; a recollection that didn't feel so awesome anymore. Dozing. He saw Trump delivering that speech, all those flags, the White House. Strange; the president sported a salt and pepper beard. Clem Dudas's voice bellowed from his mouth: "If you was a true patriot, you'd know; it ain't who got the votes. It's who belongs in that big white mansion in D.C." Bud woke, sweating.

# CHAPTER 81

## SVETA

Sveta was asleep in Nalinka's attic bedroom. A sound woke her—it took little these days. It was so dark, no moon, just the light of one streetlamp halfway down the block. She sat up.

Quiet footsteps on the stairs outside. Her breath caught. Only she came up here at night.

Like always, she'd gone to bed dressed. The window wasn't large, but big enough for her. There was a small roof below it. Sveta had leaned out one day and scoped out a path, from that roof to another and from there to a tree. She'd been an excellent climber as a girl.

She slid out of bed and moved to the window. The door burst open. A light glared, blinding her. Sveta unlatched the window. Bulky men seized her from both sides. "Quiet now," one said in Russian. Wearing one of those dark coats? She couldn't tell. Sveta screamed. She jerked her arms but failed to free them. A hand clamped over her mouth and nose.

A smell. Chloroform.

SHE WOKE——HALF-WOKE, lying on her back in the street, dark, but she could make out three-story buildings along either side.

There was fighting. Dark shadows colliding, fists pounding. She tried to sit up. A powerful hand shoved her back, pressed a cloth to her face.

That smell again.

# CHAPTER 82

## BUD

Sveti had called Bud every other day for the past week. She said it wasn't safe to give him a number to call back, so he waited. Then one Sunday there was no call. Monday either.

On Tuesday, Josh called. "Bud, what's going on?"

He felt his heart climb into his throat. "What do you mean?"

"Sveta was supposed to be in touch with the embassy this morning. She didn't call."

"I don't know," was all he could say. Then after a minute, "I haven't heard from her since Friday."

No word the next day, either. No way to reach her.

# CHAPTER 83

## SVETA

She woke to the sound of an engine revving. Dark, but she could see windows. She was inside the cabin of a small boat. She felt her arms; sore from where the men had grabbed her, but not bound.

The boat started moving. She saw a light slide past the window.

If it was still near the docks, if she could get out now, maybe …

She rolled out of the bunk, tried to stand and fell to her knees, so dizzy. *Have to get up!*

"Easy dear one. You're just waking." A woman's voice. – Nalinka … *Traitor!*

"You're safe," Nalinka said.

What a God damned lie!

Sveta managed to stand. Nalinka came over and wrapped her arms around her.

Nalinka was taller. Her arms surprisingly strong; Sveta weak and woozy. "Why, Nalinka? They're evil. I thought you were on our side."

"I am, my girl, and I told the truth. You *are* safe."

As the boat gained speed, Sveta slumped onto her bed and Nalinka explained it all.

Men in gray coats came for her during the night. Nalinka heard the floor creak as they sneaked past her bedroom. She went to two of her neighbors, who gathered several more. Some of them had old army pistols. There had been a scuffle, but, with Kazakh pistols trained on them, the gray men backed away.

"Of course, you can't stay in my town anymore." Nalinka let out a caustic laugh. "Maybe I shouldn't either."

"Where are we going?"

"A place where you'll be pleased to be."

# CHAPTER 84

## BUD

Bud's cell phone jangled, with caller ID from the congresswoman's office.

"Hi Josh. You have news?"

"Damned right, Bud. I have someone on the line who wants to talk with you."

"Bud, Bud, it is you?" Sveti's voice, excited.

"Oh my god, yes. Where are you, honey."

"I'm at Embassy, United States of America. That is where." She laughed. "I'm in Azerbaijan, Bud, darling. Baku, capital city is right on water. My friends bring me in boat."

# CHAPTER 85

## MELANIE

I woke early in my mom's house that next morning, still savoring Bud's amazing news. Energized.

I took an early bus to Santa Monica and stayed on an extra stop, so I could walk the promenade looking out at Santa Monica Bay. The sky was cloudy, but who needed sunshine? I was glowing. My wedding to Stan was less than two months off. And Bud—in my heart I knew that Sveti would make it to the US. She'd be the woman of his dreams.

I walked for an hour, then turned east along a street of shops and offices, heading for work. First Starbucks. I ordered two cappuccinos from a tall fella in black-rimmed glasses. I was about to swipe my Visa when someone tapped me on the shoulder. "I'll pay for those, if you share." A woman's voice.

I turned and there was FBI agent Gonzalez behind me. She was a couple of inches shorter than me with chin-length black hair, and pretty, now that she was smiling.

I thought about asking, *You're the bitch who locked my fiancé up, and now you want his coffee?* But I remembered the female comradery we shared when her male partner talked down to me.

"I can update you on our case," she said, as she slipped past me and hovered a credit card over the machine.

I stood stunned for a second. "That's a ballsy move," I said. But, truthfully, her jumping in like that to pay amused me.

She looked back over her shoulder at me. "My name's Rita, by the way."

As we waited for the drinks I asked, "Are you stalking me, or what?"

She laughed. "No way. My sister moved to an apartment over on Fourth. I spent the night babysitting for her twins, got them off to school this morning, and *really* needed caffeine." We watched the staff in their green aprons making drinks for a moment. "Okay if I call you Melanie?"

"Sure, Rita."

We took our cappuccinos (one of them Stan's) to a table in an outside courtyard. FBI Rita sat across from me, removed the lid from her cup (Stan's, actually) and took a careful sip. "I have to go to work, but I can take a minute to let you know what's up."

"You mean to apologize because Stan did nothing wrong."

Her gaze was sympathetic for an FBI agent. "The Agency isn't into mea culpas, Melanie. We move to the next witness and don't look back." She watched me for a second. "I bet you'd like a little closure. Former suspects rarely get that."

I hadn't expected to like Rita, but I was starting to think of her as a person, one who babysat for her sister's twins. I let out a breath and relaxed. "Okay, Rita. I forgive you."

"Good." She reached across and touched my hand for an instant. She looked at her watch and drank some coffee. (You know who's.) "You've got a good man there. We ruffled him a little, but he held up."

"He's my Stan; soft on the outside, strong core."

"Is that going well, him being your boss and your lover? I can't imagine …" Rita raised her cup to her lips.

"Absolutely. Agent Everhart's your boss, right? You could do worse than …" I couldn't help smirking.

Rita spit her coffee back into her cup. "Ever since you accused Everhart and me of playing *bad guy good Chica*, he hasn't stopped calling me that."

"Sorry," I said, but I wasn't.

Rita finished her drink. "Here it is in a nutshell: Your fiancé's totally off the hook. His information about the woman calling herself Emilia Clark helped us resolve our case. You can tell him we're grateful." Music to my ears (and, I imagine, to yours too).

"Going to give him a plaque then? Name a wing of the FBI building for him?"

She had a nice smile, her brown eyes sparkling. "Not likely."

A couple arrived at another table. The man pulled back his chair with a screech. Ouch. "You going to tell me what the case was about?" I asked. "That blonde Stan was tracking?"

Rita began shaking her head halfway through my question and didn't stop until I finished it. "Heck no, but I have a fun fact for you. You know that man, Clementine Dudas? He's one of your clients, right?"

I chuckled. "Clem Dudas is *so* not a client anymore."

"Good. US Fish and Wildlife is investigating Dudas. Just maybe he ordered an endangered yellow Botswana tree python from an illegal dealer. A minor infraction that carries a fine up to fifty K and prison time."

Rita winked at me, and I almost fell off my chair, laughing.

So, NOW YOU KNOW all about the snakes and the Russians, all about me too. I hope to have your blessing, marrying Stan. Can't wait to see you at the wedding. (You're definitely invited.)

# EPILOGUE

## BUD

Bud leaned back in the folding chair, taking in the view, inhaling the sea air and thinking, *This might be the happiest day of my life.* The ocean was incredibly blue. The top of Catalina Island poked through a low haze, way out at sea.

Fifty folding chairs spread on the grounds of a Victorian bed-and-breakfast, on a bluff over the Pacific. At the cliff's edge, a small patio, under a trellis of red roses, sheltered Bud's amazing friend. Stan wore a white dinner jacket and bow tie; looked great on him.

These things; the ocean, the roses, and Stan in his fancy duds, even the chairs filling up now with guests; all things beautiful and happy, Bud savored these days.

So much was going right. Stan's business for one; new cases coming in, the FBI butting out. Clem Dudas had vanished from Bud's life. Funny to think, but Clem had been a gift, freeing Bud of his fury over the stolen election. If people—Clem and maybe Trump—decided that actual vote counts didn't matter; if they proclaimed victory with no evidence ... How could a guy be irate over an election that wasn't actually stolen? Less anger and more love; who could argue with that?

Even the fact that Arlene Dudas was preparing to testify against Velma and her husband made Bud smile.

Beside Stan under the trellis stood Mel's friend Dave (Yeah, the guy from the CHP) in his navy suit, ready to officiate.

Stan put on that look he gave Bud sometimes, the *come-on-Bud-get-a-move-on*, patient-but-impatient gaze. He gestured and mouthed the words, "Get up here."

Bud squeezed his sweetheart's hand. He stood and smiled into her eyes. Sveti was the most beautiful he'd seen her yet with white flowers in her wavy brown hair and that pale blue dress revealing her collar bones.

Bud went up to stand by his friend.

A woman from the bed-and-breakfast played *Here Comes the Bride* on a piano. Mel's sister strode in on the arm of one of Bud and Stan's old army buddies. Then came one of Mel's friends with Stan's high school bestie.

Mel glided down the steps from the Victorian and across the lawn, holding the arm of her uncle, a dude Bud had just met at dinner the night before.

With every step closer, Mel became more stunning, her lovely dark skin contrasting beautifully with her pale-yellow gown, the white veil adding a touch of feminine mystery.

Mel stopped by her mother, sitting in her wheelchair in the front. They held hands and Mel bent to kiss her cheek before stepping up to join Stan. She pushed back her veil and winked at Bud. It warmed his heart.

He looked back at Sveti, sitting in the crowd. She mouthed something to him. He mouthed back, "WHAT?"

Sveti said it again.

Bud glanced at Mel for help, and she translated; "She said, '*YES,*' you big dufus."

❧❧❧

Nonsensical in a Nutshell

Preacher speaks with snakes
Missing lives, Russian brides, AI lies,
Ukraine explodes

# ACKNOWLEDGMENTS

Eric Myers is my editor for Russian Nonsensical. Eric went the extra mile for me, correcting my deficient punctuation, providing an amazing variety of ideas for plot and character development, and offering assistance above and beyond the manuscript itself. Eric is unstoppable. I appreciate his help and encouragement.

Kristin Bryant has again provided an intriguing, fun, artful cover. She enjoys her work, and that's contagious. Thanks, Kristin.

Jose Ramirez, at Pedernales Publishing, does a great job transforming my manuscripts into finished books and arranging all the publication details.

As always, my wife, Marguerite, supports and advises me, as my books evolve. She's wonderful at knowing what to discard and convincing me that I've gone a little too far now and again. Her ideas serve as springboards for character insights or plot twists. Her love sustains me.

# About the Author

E dward D. Webster's wide-ranging interests have led him to diverse careers; from teaching high school math to Navajo students in NM; to helping create an energy conservation program for a California county; to working to establish a center for abused, neglected and abandoned children.

Photo by: Patsy Wright

He is the author of an eclectic collection of books as well as articles appearing in publications as diverse as *The Boston Globe* and *Your Cat* magazine. His writing has been honored by groups ranging from the Colorado Independent Publishers Association and Midwest Book Review to the Boomer Times.

Ed admits to a fascination with unique, quirky, and bizarre human behavior. His acclaimed memoir, *A Year of Sundays (Taking the Plunge and our Cat to Explore Europe)* shares the eccentric tale of his months-long adventure in Europe with his spirited, blind wife and headstrong, deaf, geriatric cat.

In his historical novel, *Soul of Toledo*, about Spain in the 1440s, the diabolical nature of mankind stands out as madmen take over the city of Toledo and torture suspected Jews, thirty years before the Spanish Inquisition. (Based on a history by Benjamin Netanyahu's father.)

Webster also likes to mix unique characters to see what they'll do with/to each other. In his novel, *The Gentle Bomber's Melody*, a nutty woman, bearing a stolen baby, lands on the doorstep of a fugitive (but gentle) bomber hiding from the FBI. The result: irresistible insanity.

In his third novel, *Carlos Crosses the Line*, Webster cast his eye in other directions: the 1960s, the immigration quagmire, the validity of borders between people and countries—and most essentially, the question of what to believe if you don't accept your culture's traditional values.

*American Nonsensical* crossed new lines, with a pair of charlatan preachers, multiple missing persons, a body (dead or alive?) in an old mining pit and two detectives seeking to solve the cases while arguing over Donald Trump and conspiracy theories. Here, Webster delves into the nature of truth, religion and sanity in an America churning with unprecedented tension.

Now, with *Russian Nonsensical*, he brings snakes, Artificial Intelligence and Russian nonsense to the table for another slightly insane, sometimes poignant, and definitely fun adventure. Nonsense, of course, spans the globe, which provides the potential for endless adventures. Next time, something in southern hemisphere?

Webster lives in Southern California with his divine wife and two amazing cats.

E. D. Webster's Website: www.edwardwebster.com

Made in the USA
Middletown, DE
21 September 2024